AND STILL WE STOOD

Stephen McCaskill

AND STILL WE STOOD

A Nation Shattered

First published in the United States of America by

And Still We Stood Press, 2025

This is a work of fiction. Names, characters, places, and incidents are products of the author's imagination or are used fictitiously. Any resemblance to actual persons, living or dead, events, or locales is entirely coincidental.

Library of Congress Control Number: 2025920827

ISBN 978-1-969854-01-9

First Edition

Printed in the United States of America

To my wife of 28 years, who likely wondered when I would finally sit
long enough to write this—

and to our children, who make me so proud.

"For I know the plans I have for you," declares the Lord, "plans to
prosper you and not to harm you, plans to give you a future and a
hope."

Jeremiah 29:11 (ESV)

"If a political party does not have its foundation in the determination to advance a cause that is right and that is moral, then it is not a political party; it is merely a conspiracy to seize power."

Dwight D. Eisenhower

PREFACE

This story began over twenty years ago, with a dream that struck me so hard I wrote it down as a short story. I never shared it. But I never forgot it, either.

Every few years, I'd go back and reread it—make a note, rewrite a line, wonder if there was more. Then I'd set it aside again. It was just another story my wife knew I'd work on from time to time when I got the urge to write.

It wasn't until 2025 that I finally decided to give it breath—to stop thinking about it and start building it. That quiet, private story evolved into this novel. It didn't become the story I expected it to be when I started. It became the one I loved writing.

And Still We Stood is no longer just a dream. It's a reflection of faith, of doubt, of collapse, and of the people who still choose to stand when it would be easier to fade.

I never expected to share this with anyone. But maybe it was never just for me.

And this is only the beginning of the story.

Acknowledgments

This book would not exist in its present form without the keen eye and steady hand of Stephanie Taylor. Her insight, attention to detail, and thoughtful guidance helped me see the story more clearly and bring out the best version of it.

I am also grateful to my family, whose patience and encouragement carried me through the long hours at the keyboard. To my friends and early readers, thank you for your enthusiasm and for reminding me why this story mattered in the first place.

Finally, to every reader who has chosen to spend their time within these pages — thank you. Your willingness to step into this world is the greatest gift an author could ask for.

PROLOGUE

This was never about chaos. Chaos was only ever the means.

The American experiment had gone on too long. It was resilient, unwieldy, and—most maddening—built on ideals that refused to die. So, they adapted. They buried themselves deep, not in politics but beneath it.

They killed a president once. No fallout. Even when the truth leaked, they buried it in theories, noise, and time. The Kennedy hit was a lesson: power doesn't need to scream. It just needs to outlast memory.

They fueled riots when peace held too long. Stoked outrage when unity took root. They feared Reagan for the compromises he made to keep the country together, not the policies he implemented. They feared 9/11, not because it wounded the nation, but because it united it by giving an enemy outside the U.S. to focus on. They feared leaders who refused control, those brash enough to crack the scaffolding they'd spent decades building.

Every time America remembered who it was, it hit harder.

Unity was the enemy; the path to break the nation was through division.

They tried dividing the country in many ways: race, economics, political parties, and even by separating people through a pandemic. But beneath it all, something older still held. Forgiveness. Compassion. That unyielding kindness. It didn't come from law or culture. It came from faith, specifically, the kind rooted in grace. The kind that said always to give a second chance. In truth, that didn't bend. Christianity had been diluted by politics, mocked in entertainment, and misused by pulpits. But the real thing, fundamental belief in Christ, still lingered, and it was not only inconvenient, it was dangerous.

They couldn't kill ideas, but they could kill symbols, silence pulpits, and strip belief down to slogans and fear. Political parties were messy, too tribal, too unpredictable. Faith, though… faith could be drained slowly, until nothing living remained.

They knew their history, knew civil war would only unite people again. The goal was control—final, invisible, a dictator without a face, a regime without a name.

And they were almost there.

They were sure they had finally found the right group. They knew they had the right plan.

ONE

James sat motionless on his bed in the nearly empty room that should've held so many cherished childhood memories. The last beams of sunlight slipped through the blinds and striped the worn hardwood floor like fading ghosts. The bed beneath him creaked softly with each shift of his weight, the old frame too familiar, too silent. The once comforting noises in the house now sounded like the place was breathing its last breath. The air was still, tinged with the scent of wood polish and linen that hadn't been disturbed in days.

This had once been a warm place, filled with life. Now it felt hollow, like even the walls had forgotten how to carry laughter.

He thoughtfully twisted the gold ring he wore on his right ring finger. It was just a half size too large, but he couldn't bear to have it adjusted. It was what it had always been: strong, sturdy, worn, and meaningful. He would not change that now.

He had worn it since the day his father died in the hospital six months ago. It wasn't fancy, just a simple gold band with an etched cross at the broadest part. James had always been fascinated by it, and when he stood in the hospital that day, he vowed to never be without it.

His last memories with his father were always there, never far, never faded: the sharp smell of antiseptic, the metallic tinge of blood that clung to the air like it had soaked into the paint. The light buzzed faintly above the bed, steady and cold, while he stood at the edge of the room, staring at his father's hands and wondering if he could take one more step.

He had been seventeen. Just three months from graduation. Three months from finally taking flight. But his father wouldn't see any of it, wouldn't cheer at graduation. Wouldn't see James begin his life. Wouldn't know the man he'd raised alone.

His father had always been solid. Present. A man of few words and unshakable faith. He'd filled every room with quiet strength from the moment James' mother passed away. From that day forward, it had just been the two of them, James and the man who never once let him feel like something was missing.

Standing there smelling the blood and antiseptic, seeing him lying so still, had pulled James back to the night his mother died. She was pregnant at the time and he recalled how excited everyone had been leading up to that night. How excited he had been. He was about to be a big brother. The house had buzzed with joy and laughter for days. Warm. Alive. Ladies were over for the baby shower. The pink. The bows. His mother's smile. The lightness in his father's voice. A lightness James would never forget or hear again.

James had been four. Old enough to remember the smells, the sounds. Old enough to know he was going to have a sister. His mother had smiled more in those final weeks, even through the pain. She'd stayed in bed a lot. He didn't understand it then; it was just that something was hard, and his father said her body was tired.

Then the night came. His father woke him gently, whispering something about it being time. Time for his baby sister to arrive. Grandma was already there, ready to stay with him. Everything would be fine by morning, his father promised. He said it with calm eyes and a voice filled with love, a voice that gave James a calm and unshakable faith. It let him drift right back into a safe and loving dream.

It seemed like only a moment later when Grandma came in. She was crying as she scooped him into her arms. She held him close and whispered, "It will be okay. Everything will be okay." But her voice shook.

James didn't understand. Was he in trouble? Why was Grandma picking him up? She'd said he was too big for that now. Why was she crying?

Why wasn't Mommy there? Why wasn't Daddy there? Where was his baby sister?

James saw a man standing at the front door as they entered the hallway. The light from the living room was too bright for his sleepy eyes, and his tears blurred everything. Grandma kept whispering to him, rubbing his back, but the fear crept in. Something wasn't right.

Hot tears dripped from his chin onto Grandma's shoulder. He didn't know why he was crying; he just knew something had changed.

The man at the door didn't move. He looked big. His face was serious but kind. He had on a uniform like Daddy's.

"I'm sorry, son," the man said softly. "I'm afraid your parents were hurt tonight."

"Hurt?" James didn't understand. Hurt how? What did that mean? Nothing could hurt his parents.

The man knelt a little now, meeting James' blurred gaze. His voice was soft but full of something James couldn't name, like sorrow wrapped in strength.

"There was an accident," the officer said, his voice rippling with compassion. "Another car hit your parents' car on the way to the hospital. Your parents were hurt. They are at the hospital."

His daddy said he was taking Mommy to the hospital, and he would get to see his sister in the morning. Was it morning yet? He wanted to see his sister, his daddy, and his mommy, too.

"It will be okay. Everything is going to be okay," his Grandma whispered, holding James tighter. Her voice cracked as she repeated the words, like they might come true if she said them enough. James felt her arms tighten around him.

"I'm going to take you and your Grandma to the hospital to see your parents."

James wanted to go, but he couldn't move. He was still crying, though he didn't know why. "Hurt?" What did that mean? Was Mommy crying too? Was Daddy helping her? Was his baby sister okay?

Tears streamed from his Grandma's eyes, but he still didn't understand. It was more than his four-year-old brain could take in. His daddy was the strongest man in the world. Nothing could hurt him. Nothing.

The whole way to the hospital, his Grandma held him in her arms. James stayed curled tight in her arms, still crying.

Then his daddy was there, opening the door to the squad car. Tears in his eyes, his father reached for James, and James moved quickly into the safety of his Daddy's arms.

"Sorry, Sarge, I got here as quickly as I could," the police officer said as he stepped out of the car, voice tight, holding back emotion.

"It's okay. Thank you for bringing them," James' father choked out. "I just couldn't leave them."

His father was badly scratched on one side of his face. James saw a couple of stitches, and most of that side of his father's face was swollen. One of his arms was bandaged and in a sling. He held James in the other.

"What happened, Daddy? What's wrong with your face? Where is Mommy? Do I get to see my sister now?" he asked, starting to cry again.

"James, I am so sorry. Mommy and I were in a car accident, and your Mommy got hurt badly. She and your sister are with God now," his father said slowly but clearly, tears falling from his eyes.

Grandma let out a sharp, low cry. "I am so sorry, son. I am so sorry, James. Your Mommy was the best of people, and she loved you so much."

James didn't remember much else about that day.

Over the years, James came to understand what had happened: about a block from the hospital, a drunk driver ran a red light and T-boned his parents' car. The vehicle slammed into the passenger side—the exact spot where his mother sat. The impact crushed the door inward, trapping her.

She gave birth in the ambulance, but his sister was stillborn, or as his father had told him, his sister just took her first breath in heaven rather than here on earth. His mother was gravely injured, and complications from the birth caused her to hemorrhage. Despite the paramedics' efforts, she died shortly after arriving at the hospital.

His father had stayed with her the entire time, steady, reassuring, never letting her know he knew she was dying. He held her hand until her last breath. Only after the officer arrived at their home to bring James and his mother to the hospital did he allow the doctors to tend to his injuries.

Now it was his father who lay dying.

"Son," he said from the hospital bed, reaching over his broken body with his one good arm. The shotgun blasts had done too much damage. The doctors couldn't fix it. He had lost too much blood. "I want you to have this. Remember, God will always be with you."

He slipped off his wedding ring and placed it in James' hand.

As the tears ran down James' face, he slipped the ring on his right ring finger and whispered, "I love you, Dad. I always will."

"I love you, son." Those were his father's final words.

James had later learned his father had been the first to arrive on the scene of a 911 hang-up call. Backup was on the way. As he reported his status to dispatch, a shotgun rang out, ripping through the static of the radio. The shot slammed into his vest, shredding his radio and knocking him to the ground. It didn't penetrate, but the force was enough to stun him. He may have lost consciousness. No one ever knew for sure.

When the second officer arrived, the scene was chaos. The gunman stood fifteen feet from James' father, shotgun raised. As the officer slammed his car into park, the suspect fired again. This blast struck James' father across his exposed side, tearing through him.

The officer yanked the AR-15 from its rack, braced himself in the doorframe, and fired. Two rounds hit the gunman just as he turned.

The man staggered a step toward the officer and tried to lift his weapon again.

The officer fired once more. The third round struck the gunman in the head, dropping him.

Without waiting for backup, the officer sprinted to James' father, kicking the shotgun aside as he passed. His father was barely conscious. Somehow, the officer managed to drag the 6'4", 250-pound man into the squad car and race him to the hospital himself.

James looked at the ring again. A reminder. A promise. Those moments, those losses, had carved something permanent into him. The months that followed would set the course of his life.

His father had raised him to be strong, to protect those in harm's way. That calling had taken root early, but now it burned with clarity. James wanted to honor the legacy his father left behind.

At the same time, the house felt like a tomb. He was crushed, confined in the emotional wreckage of all he had lost. Every room whispered memories he wasn't ready to relive. He couldn't breathe in that silence anymore. He needed out. He needed freedom.

And so he prayed and came to peace with it. He would join the military and become a pilot. Growing up in Ventura, he had spent his childhood watching the planes fly out of Point Mugu, their roar etched into his memory. When he was six, he told his father, "One day, I want to fly those planes." The dream had never left his heart. He would rise above the wreckage and find meaning in the sky. He believed God was behind him.

His grandma moved in. The house felt empty. Hollow. Faded. Haunted.

James' father had been everything, present and anchoring. He prayed over his son in the mornings, helped with homework in the evenings, and comforted him through nightmares at night. Now James was the one praying, each morning and every night, seeking God's guidance and peace, strength in his weakness.

The chief of police had pulled James aside at the funeral. "Son, if you need anything, you can let me know. Your father was a good officer. A great man."

He took the chief up on that, using his connections to earn an appointment to Annapolis, the Naval Academy.

He needed to get out of that house, out of the silence and ghosts. He needed something new, something above it all. Freedom, maybe. Or just distance. The sky would have to do.

And now, the day had come. His last night in the house where so much had ended. Tomorrow, he began a new chapter. One, he prayed, that would hurt less than the first. One with purpose. Clarity. With the chance to help other families hold on to what he had lost.

* * *

Sam leaned closer to the softly glowing monitors in the cramped, windowless cabin. His eyes scanned a roster of incoming appointments for the Academy's newest class.

Most were predictable—polished, recommended, optimized. And then he saw a name that made him pause.

Sarah J. Whitaker.

No connections. Slightly older than average. Unremarkable on paper. Late application. Impossible to get an appointment.

He had read the file five times before approving it. No one ever asked why or noticed.

He leaned back in his chair and stared into the darkness above. It had been months ago, late January, maybe February. With a few keystrokes, a record was modified without flair.

And he still wasn't sure why he had done it. Not exactly.

But he trusted his instincts. He always had.

In that isolated cabin, far removed from everything, he had made a choice. Even now, it felt like the beginning of something much larger.

TWO

James stood on the house's front porch where he'd grown up, staring out at the street softened by a heavy marine haze. The sky hung low, thick with gray June gloom that seemed to settle over Ventura like a weight rather than a blanket. A faint, salty breeze came off the ocean, bringing the damp scent of seaweed and wet pavement.

His grandmother, wrapped in a thin cardigan against the early morning chill, stood beside him. She hadn't said much, but her silence held the same weight it always had, steady, unspoken love shaped by years of holding together what remained.

"You'll do fine," she said, voice low but even. "You always do."

James nodded once and pulled her into a hug. She fit snug in his arms, but there was strength in her grip—the kind born of grief endured, not avoided.

At the curb, Lieutenant Rios waited by the car. He had been his father's field training officer when his father was a rookie, retired now but still built like he wore the badge. He didn't call out or wave. He just stood there with his hands in his pockets, posture straight, and eyes respectfully down.

James turned and walked down the porch steps, wood worn pale by sun and time, and didn't look back until he reached the car. His grandmother stood exactly where he'd left her, one hand resting on the porch rail, watching him go. Not crying. Just watching.

LAX was chaotic. James expected the lines, the overhead calls, and the impatient shuffle of too many people crammed into a space that had never been meant to be this crowded. He moved through it like a ghost: security, boarding, five hours of hum and altitude. Somewhere over the middle of the country, he watched the clouds roll by beneath him and tried not to think about what tomorrow would bring.

The plane touched down at BWI just before five. By the time he left the airport and got into the back seat of a waiting cab, the air had changed—thicker and wetter. He rolled the window down halfway but regretted it almost immediately. Everything seemed to cling to him.

The drive to Annapolis was lonely. The cabbie didn't talk, which suited James fine. Trees lined the highway, unfamiliar and green in a way California never was. A different kind of stillness settled in the closer they got to the Academy, a stillness that felt like the air was holding its breath.

The hotel was plain, the kind of place made to be forgotten. One bed, beige walls, a buzzing air conditioner never quite stopped rattling. James dropped his bag, sat on the edge of the mattress, and let the silence catch up.

Tomorrow, it would begin. Uniforms. Orders. The first real step toward a future he'd chosen without feeling like it was his.

His fingers found the ring on his right hand, twisting it slowly, absently, just as they always did when thoughts got too loud. The weight of it was familiar. Grounding.

He lay back on the bed, hands folded on his chest, eyes fixed on the ceiling. He didn't know when he finally fell asleep, only that it came slowly and never all the way.

James woke to the buzz of his phone alarm vibrating against the nightstand. 0530. The room was still dark, the curtains drawn tight against the early morning light. For a moment, he lay still, unsure if he'd actually slept or just closed his eyes and drifted somewhere in between.

He dressed in silence. Khaki pants. A plain navy polo. Running shoes with double-knotted laces. He checked the mirror briefly, not to fix anything, but to ensure he hadn't missed a detail. Regulations were clear, and James had no intention of showing up out of step.

Outside, the air was already warm and thick. It was not hot, but it was close, with that clinging East Coast humidity that felt like a damp cloth against the skin. He checked out of the hotel with a nod to the clerk and joined a small cluster of others out front, waiting for the Academy shuttle. Some tried to make small talk. James stood off to the side, watching the sun rise over the rooftops.

By the time they reached the gates of the Naval Academy, the place was alive. Cadre in crisp uniforms barked orders over the clatter of rolling suitcases and the murmur of nervous families. Plebes, first-year Academy students, stood in clusters, wide-eyed, fresh-faced, awkward in their goodbye clothes. No one looked ready. Maybe no one ever was.

He gave his name at the table, received a folder with his first schedule and identification badge, and was pointed to the first station. No welcome speech. No pause to reflect. Just movement, fast, impersonal, and efficient.

"Next group, follow the red line. Don't stop. Eyes forward. Move."

The first stop was the barbershop. James had cut his hair short before coming, high and tight, just like the packet had instructed, but it didn't matter. The clippers buzzed indiscriminately across every scalp, leaving nothing but skin and stubble. By the time they were finished with him, the back of his neck burned faintly from the blade.

He didn't speak. None of them did. Just a line of boys turned anonymous, one cut at a time.

Next came the gear issue. Uniforms, PT clothes, socks rolled tight into pairs, a canvas laundry bag filled with navy blue shirts, belts, covers, and insignia still in plastic. They moved down the hallway like packages on a belt, halting, signing, receiving, and moving again.

James caught a glimpse of himself as he passed a mirror, head shaved, shoulders squared beneath the weight of a uniform he hadn't put on yet, eyes tired, jaw set.

He barely recognized the reflection, because it looked exactly like someone he'd seen before.

His father.

He blinked once, then kept walking.

The rest of the day moved like a machine, quick, loud, unrelenting. Dress. Form up. Move. Shouts barked from every direction, cadences called, commands given, and obeyed without hesitation. Every plebe carried a map of the Yard, folded, crisp, never opened. You followed the line. You followed the voice. You followed the system.

They learned to march clumsily. They ate their first meal under watchful eyes, backs straight, forks raised and lowered in unison. They began to eat when told. Every piece of food on every plate was eaten. It was tradition wrapped in discipline and snapped into place faster than James had believed possible.

Few plebes spoke during the hours, James was silent. By late afternoon, the bravado had drained out of even the loudest ones. The sun beat down, sweat soaking through cotton. Everyone looked tired. Everyone looked the same.

In the evening, they assembled by company and stood shoulder to shoulder on Stribling Walk. The flag rippled in the breeze above them, and the shouting stopped for the first time that day.

The Oath of Office came without fanfare. Just words, memorized, repeated, and solemn. And yet, as he spoke them aloud, something settled where all the grief had lived.

…to support and defend the Constitution of the United States against all enemies, foreign and domestic…

The moment was brief. The consequences wouldn't be.

That night, in Bancroft Hall, he lay in a room with three other exhausted plebes, the lights off, the walls thin. The only sound was the creak of the bunk and the weight of breathing. The day echoed behind his eyes too fast to hold, too sharp to forget.

James stared up at the ceiling and waited for sleep to come.

This time, it did.

James' first year at Annapolis was challenging in ways he hadn't anticipated. He could handle discipline, long days, relentless schedules—he'd been raised on routine and endurance. What unsettled him was how small he felt in it all, as if he'd been set adrift.

He did what was expected, always on time, in formation, uniform sharp, room regulation-perfect. He memorized protocols and the chain of command as if they were scripture. Where others adapted, some even thrived, James endured.

The other plebes built friendships in the margins and learned to game the system's edges: whispered jokes during formation, improvised drills to amuse themselves during downtime, laughter in defiance of the stress. James rarely laughed. He respected their resilience, even envied it, but grief gave him no such relief.

His classmates noticed. At first, they tried to bring him in, with roommates throwing him nods, upperclassmen offering encouragement, and the occasional chaplain drifting by with a question disguised as casual interest. But James had already learned how to be alone in a crowded room. That steady calm carried him through funeral plans and empty dinners.

He attended the mandatory events, football games, unit functions, and the occasional group outing. He was often around the others in his class, near but always just out of reach, always half a beat outside the rhythm. He knew it, and others felt it.

It showed. But to most, it just read as focus—maybe a little shyness— the kid who was too serious to be part of the crowd or too shy to try. He hovered at the edge of it, close enough to see, never close enough to join.

In the cracks of the day, late-night study halls, moments after meals, the few hours before taps, he stayed folded into himself. While others played cards or swapped stories, James reviewed flashcards, organized notes, folded laundry with perfect precision, or just spent time in prayer.

But the days added up, and the system wore down even his distance. Eventually, there was comfort in knowing what was expected and when. The chaos of I-Day gave way to rhythm: March. Eat. Study. Drill. Sleep. He moved through it with precision and with confidence. The nerves faded. His hands became steady when called on. He could recite code, find his way to anyplace on campus, and fall into step as if born to it.

Still, his desire for stillness never left. He found himself seeking it in the strangest places, beneath the sound of others' voices, in the corners of the wardroom, in the rhythm of drills done well.

Most Friday nights, the common area buzzed with energy, college football reruns, mock debates, and exaggerated stories from home. James would sit nearby, close enough to feel the warmth of community but never quite stepping into it, book in hand and notebook open. Wanting to be included, but unsure how to return to something he'd forgotten how to need.

He was disciplined, focused, and on track. He ranked near the top of his class. But everything he did still felt like it belonged to a version of himself that had gone missing somewhere back in Ventura.

When Christmas leave came, one of the only real breaks plebes were granted, he went home to see his grandmother. The old house hadn't changed. It still creaked in the same places, still smelled faintly of wood polish and the dust of too many quiet years. But the silence that had once comforted him now pressed too tightly against his ribs.

He loved his grandmother. That was never in question. But the house, the life they'd once shared all felt like it belonged to someone else. Someone he wasn't sure how to be anymore.

Toward the end of that first year, while studying for finals in the library, he noticed her, Midshipman Whitaker. He'd seen her there before, usually seated a few rows away, silently focused like the rest. But she registered differently that day for reasons he couldn't quite name.

James mainly lived in his own world, class schedules, drills, internal checklists, but something about her caught at the edge of his awareness. Maybe it was the way she moved through the shelves with certainty. Perhaps it was just the first time he had let himself look up.

They didn't speak. His priorities were fixed, his defenses still drawn. But when she glanced in his direction before disappearing behind the stacks, he held her gaze just a second too long.

Whitaker. He'd seen the name before on rosters and during drill but never connected it to a face, until now.

Finals came and went. If he had to guess, James performed well in the top ten percent, but didn't check. There wasn't enough time.

Summer orders arrived almost immediately. Training blocks, underway drills, and travel between bases. There'd be a short window of leave, but not long enough to justify the trip home. Or at least, that's what he told himself.

The silence that awaited him at home was more than he could bear, so avoiding it was easy to justify.

THREE

The monitors glowed softly in the dark.

Sam sat still, one leg tucked beneath him, coffee gone cold beside the keyboard. A few windows were open, routine traffic, system logs, nothing out of place. He toggled through the windows with careful rhythm, until the one he wasn't supposed to have open filled the screen.

WHITAKER, SARAH J.

Midshipman 4th Class

No demerits. No standout achievements either. Solid marks. Respectable physical scores. Not overly social, but not withdrawn.

He read through the latest evaluation notes, tracking the familiar rhythms. Early morning muster. Academic blocks. Watch rotation. Her schedule laid itself out like a map he already knew. He could picture it without trying, when she'd be in Bancroft, when she'd be running PT, when she'd likely collapse into her bunk at 2300.

It wasn't an obsession. It was insurance.

He didn't expect gratitude and didn't want it. But he had pulled her into this world. Invisibly. Illegally. Untraceably. And if she failed now, it couldn't be because the system looked too closely.

He flagged the line that tracked her assignment path. There was nothing concerning yet. Surface warfare was trending with a likely East Coast billet. That would do.

He closed the window then paused. His eyes lingered on the dim outline of the screen, already refreshed and gone.

Not too loud. Not too bright. Not too reserved, either.

She was holding.

For now.

But he knew better than anyone how quickly things could change.

* * *

The second year began with the same rhythm. James still spent most evenings alone, either in his room or tucked into a corner of the library, while others took liberty weekends as a chance to blow off steam. He used the time to study, think, and breathe outside the pressure.

At first, his roommates assumed it was just plebe habits lingering, discipline that would fade once the pressure eased. They invited him along a few times. But before long, it became clear—James preferred the solitude. It was simply who he was. Then one day, as James was leaving the library, she walked in.

"Leaving so soon?" she asked, a hint of amusement threading through her voice. "You're the only one I know who spends more time here than I do."

He stopped and turned toward her. He recognized her at once, Whitaker, the woman from the stacks. And now she was speaking to him.

"You're in here a lot?" he asked.

She nodded. "Most evenings. You never notice anyone."

Her tone was soft and curious.

He smiled slightly, holding back a chuckle. "You're probably right," he said, surprised she had noticed that much about him.

There was a pause long enough that either of them could have walked away. Instead, she shifted her books to one arm and glanced toward the far wall, where the low hum of the vending machine blended with the quiet of a few small tables tucked near the back.

"I was supposed to study," she said, still looking past him. "But I wouldn't mind taking a few minutes off. If you feel like staying."

James blinked, surprised she had spoken to him, more surprised she wanted to spend time with him. He already knew he wanted to be there, wanted to know her, though he hadn't been ready to ask. He gave a slight nod. "Yeah. I could stay."

She smiled, small, almost shy, and turned toward the back corner. He followed, certain for once he belonged exactly where he was.

They sat with coffee, trading a little conversation. For the first time in years, James felt good simply being near someone.

They discussed their classes, professors, and Academy routines. Yet for the first time, James felt truly at ease across the table from someone. Welcomed for who he was, seen. Even at home, with his father, he had carried the sense of being measured against someone else, his father's reflection, or the mother he barely remembered, but never simply himself.

At first, he only knew her as Whitaker. That's what everyone called her, formal, distant, like everyone else at the Academy.

But she became Sarah over time through shared tables, late-afternoon coffees, and more casual conversations than he could count.

And he became James.

They began going out of their way to spend time together. Study sessions aligned, tables turned into shared ground, and conversation slipped easily into the spaces between assignments.

And slowly, the small talk gave way to real stories.

He told her about Ventura: the cool ocean air, a city safe enough that a cop could live and work there without constantly looking over his shoulder. The conversations were casual, simple memories he enjoyed sharing, and the way she listened opened a door that drew him closer to her.

She told him about Chicago's South Side. The constant noise. The corners you avoided after dark. How people seemed to expect you to earn their respect before they bothered to know your name.

James felt the unspoken draw, the steady comfort of someone who listened and truly heard him amid the harshness of Academy life. With her, even quiet moments carried meaning, a subtext that hinted at something beyond friendship.

Days bled into weeks and weeks into months. They marked time by small routines: the worn table by the east-facing window at Drydock, the soft thump of books placed side by side in the library, the familiar rhythm of walking back across the Yard. Just being near her gave him calm.

Once, during a long lull in a study session, she glanced up and said, "For as much as we talk, you don't let much out."

James considered it for a moment. "Yeah, I think I've just learned to carry it all."

Another afternoon, as she leaned forward to mark something in his notes, James noticed the slim silver cross resting just below her collarbone.

"That's beautiful," he said, his voice softer than he meant. "Does it mean something to you?"

She touched it absently, thumb brushing the surface. "It was a gift. From people who changed my life. It reminds me of them… and of what I believe."

James turned his hand slightly, letting the light catch the etched cross on the ring on his finger.

"I think I get that," he said. "This was my dad's."

She nodded.

At night, as he prepared for lights out, James often found his thoughts circling back to her. She was different from anyone he had known before.

20

She made him feel safe, and that let him be more open than he had ever been.

During their first liberty weekend together, the conversations shifted from casual to more intimate. While most of their classmates spilled into bars and crowded hangouts popular with midshipmen, James and Sarah wandered toward the waterfront, coffee in hand, and found a shaded bench overlooking the harbor.

With the restraints of the Academy temporarily lifted, they found themselves free to talk.

James spoke first, his voice low, "My father was the anchor in my life. He taught me faith through action. Every morning, with his first cup of coffee, he'd pray for me, for wisdom, for help being the father I needed, and for me to find my way in the Lord. Then again, at night, he'd pray the same prayers. For him, it was as natural as breathing. I didn't realize it at the time, but his example grounded my faith. I accepted Christ when I was eleven. I've always tried to follow Him faithfully. I know I fell short—especially when I was sixteen or seventeen—but I always came back. That foundation has carried me through every hurt and heartache in this life."

"I guess I've always believed," he said. "But following's a different thing. I've struggled with that part."

Sarah nodded, taking a long sip from her cup before answering.

"I didn't grow up with any of it," she said. "Church wasn't even on the radar. But when I was nineteen, I had this friend drag me to some young adults thing at her church. I almost didn't go back."

"What changed?"

She smiled, soft and a little wistful. "When I was nineteen, a pastor and his wife came into my life when I needed God the most. They just… saw me. Didn't try to fix me. Just cared. They became like family."

She reached up and touched the silver cross at her neck.

"They gave me this the day I was baptized. It reminds me of them but also of what I found."

James studied her for a moment. He could've said a hundred things, but none of them fit. So he offered the only one that felt honest. "I think I needed to hear that," he said.

They let the quiet settle between them, not as an ending but as part of a rhythm they began to fall into. The weeks that followed carried the same pattern—classes, study sessions, stolen moments. About a month later, another liberty weekend drew them back to the harbor, coffee in hand, where the conversation deepened again.

James told her about his parents, how his mother died when he was four, too young to understand it, but old enough to feel the absence. How his father never really recovered, though he tried to hide it. He talked about growing up under a man shaped by duty and grief—his father, a hero shot in the line of duty. Despite everything, he believed his father never regretted giving his life to protect the people of the city he loved. He mentioned the sister he never knew, the one lost at birth, but never far from thought. The one he still hoped to meet someday.

Sarah listened, eyes earnest, hands wrapped around her coffee like she understood the cost of saying those things aloud.

Sarah told him, "I never knew my father. He left my mother before I was born—might not have even known she was pregnant. I never asked.

"I always loved my mother. She did the best she possibly could. She struggled to keep a roof over our heads and food on the table. Sometimes, the food just wasn't there. I tested her every moment of my teenage years, but I always knew she loved me. And I always loved her.

"So when the day came that she told me she had brain cancer, I suddenly found myself—at sixteen—watching her slowly waste away. That day, I stopped testing her. I dropped out of school, took my GED, and went to work. I waitressed in the evenings and worked at a coffee stand in the mornings.

"Before long, my mother needed help with almost everything. That became my third job—caring for her whenever I wasn't working. But there was no other choice. I knew in my heart it was what I had to do.

"I never asked her what the diagnosis really meant. I don't know if the doctors told her there was a treatment that might have extended or even saved her life. I never wanted to know. Maybe there never was. But sometimes I think—now, looking back—that she couldn't bear to spend all we had and more on just a chance."

Her voice stayed steady, carrying both peace and strength in the plainness of her words.

"It was about a year after she died," she said softly, "that my friend dragged me to that church event. I almost stayed away. But that's where I met the pastor and his wife. They didn't push, didn't ask for more than I could give. They just kept showing up, week after week."

Her voice stayed steady. "That's when it started to feel real—that maybe God saw me after all."

James nodded, his voice low. "I think He does."

A quietness lingered between them, the breeze drifting in from the harbor. People passed behind, talking and laughing, but James felt a peace beyond it.

What he felt was more than friendship—something deeper, more valuable. Patient, earned through the hardship of openness.

As schedules shifted and Academy demands changed, that depth endured, though it grew more slowly. Some weekends they shared, others slipped past with only a word or two, yet the bond held.

When they talked, they were honest. Both were focused and driven in their own ways. James had wanted to fly since before he could spell the word. Sarah was chasing something harder to define—perhaps dignity, perhaps a sense of worth no one could take away.

Whatever their relationship was, James held it where it stood, and Sarah seemed content to do the same.

Even after graduation, with assignments pulling them in different directions and their lives branching outward into the vast and uncertain world, James never forgot the harbor conversations or what they meant—the feeling of being seen at last.

FOUR

Sam adjusted the brightness on the lone monitor in the darkened room, the screen's pale glow casting angular shadows across the concrete walls. The system hummed, more analog than digital, held together by a dozen kinds of paranoia and too many sleepless nights. It looked rough, but it was clean. And safer than it had any right to be.

Names scrolled by, faces, commissioning assignments. He paused when hers came up.

ENSIGN SARAH WHITAKER

Designator: 1830 – Naval Intelligence Officer

He exhaled slowly and leaned back in his creaking chair. That hadn't been her first choice. Maybe not even her second. But it was the one that stuck. In this world, sticking mattered more than dreaming.

"Too smart for signals. Too grounded for ops," he'd said once, back when she was just a profile in a database full of unknowns. "She'll adapt. She always does."

* * *

Sarah and James graduated and entered the Navy as officers, each taking a different path. James went to flight school, beginning what would become nearly two years of intense training before earning his wings as a C-130J pilot. Sarah was assigned to Naval Air Station Jacksonville (NAS Jax) as an 1830 Naval Intelligence Officer, stepping into a role that would completely shape her career.

Her first assignment was paperwork-heavy, briefing summaries, intel routing, endless acronym-stamped forms. She spent more time squinting at screens than doing anything that felt like real work. But her name got noticed. That was something.

The years that followed were a blur of orders and airports. For Sarah, it was a season of movement, always posted, always present, always to the next place or assignment before she could be comfortable with her current one. Intelligence took her deep: cyber teams, forward-operating bases, submarine-force assignments. Each rotation felt like its own story, disjointed then, but strangely cohesive in hindsight. She learned the language of silence, briefings coded in posture, and missions that never made headlines.

She didn't rise fast. But she rose well, the kind of officer people simply trusted.

James, finishing flight school nearly two years later, took a different path, one fueled by grief and an unrelenting drive to excel. He volunteered. Again and again. Wherever a pilot was needed, he showed up: cargo runs, medevac rotations, high-risk transport flights into places few wanted to land. He made himself useful. Indispensable. Unforgettable.

Their paths crossed just enough to remind them they still mattered to each other—an occasional email, a rare call, one brief visit. But mostly, it was five years of becoming who they would have to be when everything finally broke.

Sarah was eventually assigned back to NAS Jax in Jacksonville, Florida. At first, she didn't understand the reassignment. She had been excelling; the kind of assignments every intel officer wanted seemed to fall into her lap regularly. And now, NAS Jax? It felt like a demotion. Had she screwed something up?

She'd only been on base a few days when she heard him say, "You here a lot?" She turned, a smile already forming.

James.

They spent the evenings together for a few weeks, reviving old memories and growing close again. Closer than before. Their bond had been forged in shared glances across the Yard, casual talks after study hours, and the kind of mutual understanding that merely required them to be near each other. Now, after five years of almost no communication, it felt alive again.

He told her he had only been on base a few weeks. He mentioned a woman named Trish once, casually. A civilian contractor. Loud, lively, impossible to miss.

"We grabbed dinner a few times," James said, his tone light. "She was fun. Smart. Knew how to work a room."

Sarah raised a brow. "That's a compliment. But?"

He gave a slight shrug, tracing the rim of his cup. "She came on strong. I think she expected me to match her pace. I didn't.

"I met her at a bar just off base, she walked right up to me and struck up a conversation. Her energy was impossible to ignore. She's just one of those people who walks in and feels like they belong anywhere they are and always get noticed. She noticed me, and I was interested. But by the third time they got together, mostly just casual meetups, she'd leaned in close, fingers brushing my arm, and asked, 'Are we finally done pretending we wouldn't end up in bed?'"

James chuckled as he continued, "I guess I paused. Too long, apparently. She laughed it off, stood up, and joked about finding someone less hesitant. She didn't call again. Neither did I. She's... not subtle. Nice. Just... not my speed."

Sarah met Trish the next morning outside the admin building, tall, radiant, with the kind of presence that made people notice without meaning to. She was already mid-conversation with someone else when she glanced over and spotted Sarah stepping out of the side door. Her eyes flicked once, uniform, posture, face, then past her, toward the tarmac where James was helping a crew offload gear.

Something in the glance sharpened.

Later, they crossed paths again in the cafeteria line. Trish slipped in beside her like they'd already met.

"You're new. Intel, right?"

"Yeah," Sarah said, keeping her tone neutral.

Trish nodded, scanning her tray like it was evidence. "You and Callan know each other?"

Sarah hesitated, just a beat. "Yeah. We go back a ways."

A smile tugged at the edge of Trish's mouth, suspicious, maybe a little jealous.

"Careful with that one," she said, voice low. "Men like him don't date. They… marry. Or pray about it until they vanish."

Then she winked and walked off like she'd just handed over a classified file.

One evening, barely two weeks after she had arrived, James broke the news. The Navy being the Navy, she wasn't surprised. He was being deployed and then reassigned to Point Mugu when he returned.

It felt like another near miss to Sarah. She wanted more, but now that chance was slipping away again—not quite a couple, but closer than ever. But rebuilding the bond, so strong, so close… losing that, however undefined, hit hard. Like a mission scrubbed before launch, it still left wreckage behind.

In those first weeks at NAS Jax, she had really just focused on James and had met few other people.

The base had its own language, its own pulse, one she had started to learn years before, but now found she had to relearn. Aircraft howled overhead at all hours, echoing through the hangars and across the cracked pavement like a warning. The scent of fuel and salt lingered in the air, clinging to uniforms and skin. New arrivals were a constant; wide-eyed and eager, or already burned out. Sarah wasn't sure which one she was. Her reassignment here had first felt like exile. Then James had made it feel right. Now it was something else—lonely and sad, set against the restless energy of the base. Officers moved with the same clipped efficiency as the enlisted. Salutes were sharp. Conversations were brief. And Sarah felt both invisible and constantly watched.

But there were moments, casual exchanges, brief encounters, bits of conversation that stuck for no particular reason. Sometimes she'd pass the same young sailor sitting on the curb behind the barracks, phone pressed to his ear, always saying the same thing, "No, I'm listening, I just don't know what you want me to say." She would keep moving, but she always noticed.

Trish quickly became a constant.

The morning after James deployed, Trish stepped into line next to Sarah like an old friend in the middle of a conversation.

"Callan. I swear, I was ready to jump his bones right there in the parking lot, then the man practically handed me a Bible and wished me a good night. What's the story with you two?"

"Nothing. We're classmates from the Academy. Nothing romantic, just friends."

"Yeah, when friends look at me like he looks at you… let's just say it doesn't usually stay platonic."

Uncomfortable with the conversation and unwilling to engage further with a woman who looked entirely capable of going into detail, Sarah nudged the topic elsewhere.

"So why are you here? If you planned to work around the military anyway, why not just enlist?"

Trish smirked, but the expression faded quickly. "I'm not exactly the type to follow every order or walk the straight line. But pilots are my thing. Always have been. Working here keeps it casual enough that no one calls me a jet bunny to my face."

Trish looked Sarah up and down, evaluating her, then moved on. "So, intel, right? Probably makes you the smartest person in the room. Guess that explains why you keep Callan at arm's length."

Sarah had laughed, but it felt like a probe disguised as a joke. She felt like Trish had been more interested than she let on, and she might have been a bit jealous of the time James and Sarah spent together in the past couple of weeks. Like she was trying to decide if Sarah and James were more than Sarah was letting on. To Sarah, they were, and that was the problem. To James? She doubted it. She would never say it, but suspected he signed up for the deployment despite, or maybe because of, the fact they were growing close.

Her quarters were small but clean, sterile in the way military housing always was, with fresh paint over old dents and laminate wood over creaking concrete. She kept her things in order, and she kept herself in order. But the sense of being watched was always present.

She found herself thinking through her career, the choices she had made, and the missed chance with James. Maybe that encounter with Trish nudged something loose and made her reconsider what she'd been holding on to. The next day, she started noticing the men on base in a different way. About six months after arriving at NAS Jax, she slipped into something new.

She hadn't meant to. But there was a relief in letting go of what might've been, a release from the ache she'd carried since graduation. Letting herself feel something again was survival.

Will Hamlin was charming to the point of disarming. He had that rare confidence that was felt when he walked into the room. Polite when it mattered, irreverent when it didn't. The first time they really talked, he noticed the crease in her brow before she even realized it was there and said, "Careful, Whitaker. That look'll get you promoted and aged ten years all at once."

She'd rolled her eyes. But he'd said it like he meant it.

He was a contractor, mostly in logistics, but he carried himself like someone who'd seen more than he said. You could hear the weight between the lines if you listened closely. Once, when a junior officer joked about cushy assignments, Will just said, "Not all the wars are on paper," then changed the subject.

He made her laugh. He made her feel steady, in a world that didn't stop spinning. And he made her feel accepted for who she was. That part mattered more than she let on.

He started bringing her coffee without asking. He remembered the kind of protein bars she liked and kept one tucked in his pack for when her meetings ran late. He called her "Whit" like it was shorthand for something more intimate.

She never mentioned James to him. She knew she felt too deeply for him and found sharing it difficult. She feared sharing it would chase Will away.

For a while, she let herself believe that the lightness Will brought to her was love.

Maybe it wasn't the kind that lasted, but it was real. It was hers. And for the first time in a long time, she let herself be chosen.

And maybe that was enough, not forever, but for then.

Their relationship deepened quickly. Will listened when she spoke, or at least, he looked like he was listening. He made plans. He made promises. Six months later, he asked, and she said yes. It all happened so fast she had to stop and think whether she'd even sent a message to James. Eventually, she did. She wanted him there. He was the closest thing to family she had.

The timing worked out. James wrote back and said he'd "be honored to attend."

Later, she would look back at that message and wonder what he really meant. But at the time, it felt perfect.

The wedding was beautiful. Her pastor performed the ceremony, and James arrived just as promised. He didn't draw attention to himself, but when she looked out across the crowd during the vows, she caught him smiling.

It was a small smile. Just enough to steady her. It reminded her of those moments at the Academy, when he'd nod across the mess table or silently slide his tray to make room. There was pride in it—a blessing.

He mingled only briefly, offering polite congratulations, never clinging to any group, but Sarah didn't mind. When they spoke, he said just enough: that she looked radiant, that he was glad to be there. And he meant it. She could see it in his eyes.

Before he left, she spotted James talking with Will near the bar at the reception. Will had already shed his jacket and rolled up his sleeves, a beer in one hand, the other resting lazily on the counter. He looked relaxed, maybe too relaxed. But Sarah let it pass. The night was perfect. Everything felt like it was falling into place.

James reached out to shake Will's hand.

"You're a lucky man," he said. "You married one of the best women I've ever known."

Will smiled, clearly riding the high of the night. "Yeah. I still can't believe she said yes."

James nodded. "Just take good care of her. She deserves the best."

His voice carried a calm warmth, like an older brother giving his blessing. Will lifted his beer in a loose salute. James smiled back, gave Sarah one last look across the room, and disappeared into the crowd.

In that moment, she believed she had everything: the man she loved beside her, and the only person who had ever truly seen her, smiling in the background like family.

FIVE

On his flight back to California, James' mind replayed every moment of the wedding and the reception. Watching her stand and say 'I do' to Will. She'd glowed. Peaceful. Like she'd found something she hadn't even known she needed. And maybe she had. He was happy for her. He was. That was the part that hurt the most.

His note to her had said he was honored to be there. But watching her promise forever to someone else had carved something permanent out of him. Not regret. Not exactly. Just the weight of a door closing that had always been slightly ajar.

By the time he arrived at Point Mugu, he'd tucked it all away, folded and pressed it like one of his old uniforms: clean, kept, but no longer worn.

Shortly after the wedding, James relocated again, this time to Joint Base Lewis-McChord, just outside Tacoma. The air was different there; it was damp, pine-swept, and always threatening rain, but something about the routine felt good. Predictable. He'd always been good with routine.

On Sundays, he started attending a small church near the base. He had always made it a practice to find a church at every base. He tended toward small churches, as that was what he had grown up in. So when he found the small church just a few minutes from base, it felt like home the moment he walked in.

That's where he met Christina. She was a greeter, one of the first faces people saw when they stepped through the doors. She had a natural, understated beauty about her, but what struck him was her smile.

The first time, she offered him a bulletin and a smile. The second time, she remembered his name. By the third, she'd asked if he wanted to sit with her and her family.

He said no, politely, and she didn't seem to mind. When he deployed a few weeks later, she handed him a note the Sunday before he boarded the shuttle. It was simple. Just a few lines:

You seem like someone who carries more than he lets on. If you ever want to talk, email me. Or don't. I'll pray for you either way.

The note was kind, and it meant something to him. However, he barely knew her, so while he kept it and considered emailing her often, it stayed folded in his pocket. But about a month into deployment, after a long night on the tarmac in Qatar, the engines cooling and the desert wind scouring the edges of his flight suit, he opened the note again. He breathed in slowly, exhaled heavily as he typed the address.

Hi Christina,

You probably don't remember me. Or maybe you do and wish I hadn't written. Either way, thanks for the note. You were right. I carry too much. It's not all heavy, but it piles up.

Hope things are going well stateside.

—James

He almost deleted it three times before hitting send.

She replied the next day.

Of course, I remember you. You're the only one who didn't blink when my little cousins used your boots for a napkin on Easter Sunday.

Things here are good. Rainy. Church potluck went nuclear again, never let two deacons argue about whose banana pudding counts as "from scratch." Pretty sure Mrs. White is still sulking. Send help.

And yeah, you carry too much. But you don't have to carry it alone.

His plan was to send a simple note back if she had replied. But as the sound of her voice came into his mind while he read the note, everything changed. She was so different from the noise of deployment, so grounded, it pulled things out of him.

A week later, he wrote:

There was once someone—a friend. Not more, but… not nothing. We lost touch. She got married. I thought I was fine until the wedding. I smiled; I meant it. But something about that day still hasn't let go of me.

Is it stupid to grieve something that never really existed?

Christina answered that night.

Not stupid. Brave.

Some of the hardest things to let go of are the ones no one else saw you holding. But if it mattered to you, it mattered. That's all the reason you need.

That changed something. It gave him a place to rest the ache. She asked the right questions and gave him the extra encouragement he needed when it mattered most. She remembered Sarah's name, and encouraged him to tell her anything that he wanted to, that he needed to talk about.

By the time his deployment had ended, he could hardly wait to see her.

She was waiting in the back of the sanctuary the following Sunday, with no clipboard and no name tag this time. Just her. Same smile. Same steady presence.

He hugged her before he even realized he was going to.

They started meeting up after church, first for coffee, then the occasional dinner, and then long walks through Tacoma's wet streets, where the conversations ran deeper than either had planned.

It had rained for three days straight.

James offered her his jacket as they walked from the church parking lot, but Christina shook her head and pulled her cardigan tighter like it was armor. "If I take your jacket, you'll try to offer me your shoes next. Let's admit you've got a hero complex and move on."

He smirked. "And you've got a martyr complex."

"Only on Sundays."

They stopped beneath the eaves of the coffee shop, water dripping steadily from the tin roof. She wrung her braid out, then looked at him thoughtfully.

"You ever feel like you're still waiting for life to start?" she asked.

He thought for a long moment. The streetlight buzzed behind her. "I used to think it started when you found someone," he said. "Now I think it starts when you stop trying to prove something to people who aren't even looking."

She nodded, lips twitching. "That's a very James answer."

"Good or bad?"

She tilted her head. "Right."

She lived in a second-floor walkup that smelled like rosemary and old books. The living room was half windows and half houseplants, ivy, succulents, and a fiddle-leaf fig that dominated the corner.

James stopped by occasionally to drop off groceries or walk her dog when her shifts ran late. She always offered dinner, but he never stayed past ten. He felt it inappropriate to be seen leaving a woman's apartment late at night, even ten was on the edge for him.

One evening, she stirred something on the stove, apron dusted with flour, hair pinned up messily.

"You know this is burning, right?" he asked from the doorway.

"No, it's just caramelizing."

"It's tomato soup."

She laughed. "That's why I'm the optimist in this relationship."

Dinner was simple. They sat at the table, prayed over the meal, and talked as if the world outside was on mute. When it was time to leave, she walked him to the door.

At some point, just before he stepped out, she said, "Promise me something."

He turned. "Depends what it is."

"If I go first, don't close off. Don't go numb. Let it hurt, but don't live in it."

He blinked. "Christina, you're twenty-seven and invincible."

She didn't smile. "People always say that right before the plot twist."

He just reached for her hand and held it longer than usual. He smiled, shook his head, and turned to leave.

Another afternoon, while they were walking, the sun was warm, the kind of ordinary Saturday heat that made the world feel steady. James walked beside her, paper bags in hand, his eyes squinting at the sidewalk ahead. He wasn't a talker. She seemed to like that about him.

He suspected she hadn't meant to start leaving things at his place at first. A book here. A note there. One day, her favorite coffee made its way onto his shelf, and he took it as a hint. He brewed it without comment, the next time she came by. That was how he showed care, not with grand gestures but small, deliberate acts. Thoughtful. Steady. Intentional.

She called it "soul fatigue," the way she sometimes came home too tired to speak but too wired to sleep. He understood. He had his own name for it, "the fog." It would settle in behind his eyes after a hard week or a memory he was struggling with. He always came back to it, eventually, when he was ready. The story would surface in the middle of a relaxed evening or over coffee the next day. The weight would shift. He trusted her with it.

They'd talked about Sarah many times over the months. She helped him understand what he felt about her better, understand how important she had been and would always be. It became a corner of his life he'd made peace with. His father came up often, more than she seemed to expect. The man's shadow stretched long in James' memory. His mother, too. The stories were gentler, but there was loss there. His sister. His grandmother. Names layered with silence and sorrow. So much hurt in one life.

She had her own past. Scars she didn't wear on the outside. But enough pain to recognize it in someone else, he saw it in her as well. She didn't try to fix him; instead, she stayed with him. She prayed with him, for him, even when he hadn't shared what it was that was hurting him.

And he never tried to fix hers, either. When she shared pieces of her story, the hard ones he could have rushed to solve, he simply listened.

He prayed with her and in the evenings, on the walks back to his apartment, he would pray for her more. He understood the log in his own eye and the splinter in hers. He knew he was not whole. He let her be honest without trying to rescue her.

Somehow, their broken places just lined up—and made room for healing. The laughter filled in the gaps. With her, he could breathe. He didn't have to be more or less than he was. He made space for her without asking her to carry him.

One late afternoon, walking down the street toward his apartment, she looked over at him. He shifted the bags in his arms as they rounded the corner. There was something there, in her eyes.

She stopped. "Let's just do it."

James paused mid-step, one foot still forward. "Do what?"

"Get married."

He blinked.

"Not someday. Not after one more deployment or career shift or cross-country move. I love you. I trust you. I don't want to keep hitting pause on a life we already have."

She didn't need him to kneel. She didn't need fireworks. Just this: the warmth of the sun, the honesty in her voice, and the look in his eyes when he realized she meant it.

No fear. No hesitation. Just that steady "Yes." And in his chest, something finally exhaled.

She smiled.

So did he.

And they kept walking, together, no longer waiting.

The ceremony was small: friends from church and a couple of officers from his unit. It was small, simple, and beautiful. They wrote their own vows, and James' hands were steady as he said them.

Sarah wasn't there.

She was deployed with a submarine group somewhere under the Atlantic, with no surface communications or warning. He'd sent the invite anyway, knowing it would never reach her in time.

It stung more than he expected, but he understood. The Navy didn't pause for weddings, funerals, or anything in between.

Looking back on it later, he realized he hadn't needed her there to feel her presence. She'd been part of the man he'd become, the man Christina chose.

SIX

Sarah's life moved on, new orders, new rhythms. They still spoke occasionally, but more and more, she learned about James secondhand from mutual friends who mentioned he was overseas again or tagged photos from yet another base in a new time zone.

Sarah seemed stuck in time while James was always moving. Three months after the wedding, she received his email. She was happy for him, genuinely. Meanwhile, while she'd been deployed, Will had quit his job without telling her. All he would tell her was, "Wasn't the right fit."

While the time on the sub had been good for her experience, it had come at a time when cracks at the seams of her marriage were already beginning to show. Will quitting his job meant for months he had sat at home drifting.

Men just do better being busy, she thought. Will's months at home had resulted in months of day drinking. So when Sarah was finally home again, they would argue every day about the drinking, about his not looking for a job. He would respond by claiming he could not find a job, but it was clear there was no job he was willing to do. Then, there was the added stress that she seemed unable to get pregnant, they had tried for months before her deployment.

Then came the call.

His grandmother, his last living relative, had passed in her sleep. She was old and the decline had been slow, but it still shook James in a way nothing else had. After his father's death, she'd been his last anchor. He rarely spoke about her, but Sarah remembered the softness in his voice whenever he did, the way he smiled almost to himself when her name came up.

He only asked if she could come.

She said yes before he finished the question.

Will came with her. He had insisted, despite her hope that he would stay at home, allowing them some time to reset apart.

James met them at the airport, standing just inside the terminal with his hands in his pockets. His uniform was neat, his posture solid, but his eyes looked older, like sleep had been optional for weeks.

"Thanks for coming," he said, offering Sarah a brief hug and nodding to Will.

Will returned the nod and offered a firm handshake. "Wouldn't miss it. Sorry for your loss."

"Appreciate it. Christina wanted to be here, but a two-hour car ride back-to-back with a six-month-old didn't sound like a good time for anyone." James' voice was steady, but a little distant.

Sarah had no idea James was a father. Her distance from him had grown.

Outside, James led them to his car. As they approached, Will moved to the rear driver's side door and opened it.

"Let me get your door for you, babe."

Sarah paused for half a second, her eyes flicking to the empty front passenger seat long enough to register it. Then she offered a smile and slid into the back.

The door shut gently, but the message lingered.

Will walked around and slid in beside her without a word, settling into the seat like it was the obvious choice.

The drive from the airport was quiet. Will made a few polite efforts, asking about the weather and the expected turnout for the service, but mostly, he stayed silent. Sarah watched him from the corner of her eye. He was just… managing things. Lately, he seemed more like a man performing stability than living in it.

When they arrived at James' childhood home, Christina stepped onto the porch with the baby in her arms. She was effortlessly stunning, and everything about her seemed to shine. Warmth radiated from her as she crossed the driveway, quick on her feet but steady and completely at ease.

She came straight to Sarah and pulled her into a hug before she could react. It was warm, unguarded, the kind of embrace that slipped past her defenses. In that instant, Sarah felt what she hadn't known she was missing—a sister's embrace, long overdue, and desperately needed.

"It's so good to finally meet you," Christina said, pulling back with a bright, genuine smile. "James has told me so much about you. I feel like I already know you, like you're this long-lost sister I've been waiting to meet. You mean the world to him, Sarah. Truly."

Her voice carried only kindness. Sarah wanted to cry because she so needed that hug, that kindness, and that love.

She shifted the baby slightly in her arms. "Can you say hi, Wyatt? This is Auntie Sarah."

Sarah smiled, genuinely. "Wow. You are exactly the kind of woman I always imagined would finally steal James' heart." She turned to James. "You really were blessed to find her."

James nodded. Even with the loss still hanging in the air, he seemed lighter than she'd ever seen him. Standing there beside Christina and Wyatt, he looked… settled. Grounded. Christina's presence had taken something heavy off his shoulders.

Then Christina turned to Will. Sarah had noticed him admiring her a little too obviously, the way his eyes lingered for a beat too long.

"And you must be Will," she said warmly, though her tone carried slightly less joy. "It's a pleasure to meet you."

Will shook her hand. "Thanks. Good to meet you, too. I've heard… very little about you. Or James, for that matter." The words were measured, but the edge was clear—a dig at Sarah.

Sarah ignored it. She was here to support James, Will was here for his own reasons. Tonight would be about James, Christina, Wyatt and memories of James' grandma.

Christina turned back to her. "James was going to get you a hotel, but I insisted you stay here. We've got plenty of space, and honestly, it's so much better than any Holiday Inn. Plus, it gives you and James more time to catch up." She paused, then smiled teasingly. "But if you'd rather have the hotel, we're happy to cover it."

Sarah jumped in before Will could open his mouth. "No, this is great. I'd love to stay. It'll be good to talk with you more… and get to know Wyatt."

That evening, they all sat around the living room and talked. Wyatt babbled happily from Christina's lap.

Sarah thought the baby might've said more than Will.

At the service, Will stayed close. From the moment they arrived, it was clear he was uneasy. He watched James with guarded eyes, answered questions quickly, and never strayed far from Sarah's side. When she knelt beside the casket for a silent prayer, his hand rested on her shoulder, just a little too tightly, like he was bracing for something.

After the final words were spoken and the crowd dispersed, Sarah glanced around until she spotted James near the cemetery's edge, standing alone and overlooking the low hills beyond. His hands were in his pockets, his expression unreadable.

She walked over, Will trailing a few steps behind. They stood beside him in silence. Christina was a short distance away, holding Wyatt and gently thanking guests as they passed. The wind tugged at Sarah's sleeve, cool and steady.

James continued to look out at the view.

"Do you think you'll ever have kids?" he asked quietly.

It was just a question dropped into the stillness, like a stone into deep water. The question tore at Sarah, she had so long prayed for a child. Now she hoped she never had one, not with Will. They were already breaking, a child years ago may have shored them up, but now it was more likely to tear them further apart.

Sarah glanced at him. The words caught in her throat. She could feel Will stiffen beside her, his posture going rigid.

"We'd like to," she said at last. "But… sometimes these things don't happen the way you hope."

James nodded and continued to stare out toward the horizon.

Sarah felt like something had shifted in that moment. In the silence, she knew James understood.

After they returned to the house, they enjoyed some light conversation, but James was clearly lost at the moment. Both James and Will retired early, and after Christina put Wyatt down, the house was still. The baby monitor buzzed softly on the kitchen counter.

Sarah stood barefoot by the sink, rinsing out the last of the dinner dishes, letting the warm water run slightly longer than necessary. Christina came in quietly, tying her robe around her waist and brushing a few stray curls behind her ear.

"Not tired?" she asked gently.

Sarah gave a half-smile. "Not yet."

Christina poured two mugs of leftover decaf and handed one to her. "Night like this… I get it. Everything feels louder somehow."

They sat at the small table James had built with his grandfather in high school. Christina traced the grain of the wood with her finger, then looked up.

"James was talking about you tonight," she said. "After dinner. Not in a weird way," she added quickly, smiling. "He just… he worries. Said he knows how much having kids meant to you. How hard this all must be."

Sarah exhaled slowly, hands wrapped around her mug. "He always sees more than I want him to."

"You hide it well," Christina said. "But not from him."

There was a long pause before Sarah spoke again.

"Will's not… happy. He hasn't been for a while. He left the field two years ago. He used to be a contractor, always busy, always moving. But when he came off the road, something changed. He just sort of… stalled out. Can't seem to find his footing again. He hasn't in almost a year."

Christina waited, saying nothing as Sarah found her voice again.

"He's angry all the time. Picks fights. About nothing, laundry, tone of voice, and how I looked at him. And when he's not angry, he's just… gone. Like I'm sharing a house with a ghost who slams doors."

Christina's eyes softened. "That sounds… exhausting."

"It is," Sarah admitted. "And I don't even know how to be mad at him for it, because I know he's hurting. He's lost. But I'm still here. Still trying. And I don't think he even sees me anymore."

They sat in silence for a while—just the hum of the fridge and the faint creak of the house settling.

Christina finally said, "You know, James told me once you were the first person he ever really trusted with the truth about himself. That he felt safe with you before he even knew what that meant."

Sarah looked up, surprised.

"He never said it like he was holding onto you," Christina said. "Just that he owed you a kind of honesty. He said it changed him. That's why I wanted to meet you. Not just because you mattered to him, but because anyone who helped make him who he is… had to be worth knowing."

Sarah was speechless, unable to find words to respond.

But she nodded. Slowly. Gratefully.

Christina reached across the table and gently squeezed her hand.

"I'm glad you're here."

Sarah looked down at their hands, at the steadiness in Christina's grip. There was so much care and love in her voice. Steady and unwavering.

Christina's voice softened even further. "You don't have to carry all this alone, Sarah. I know I'm technically just the wife," she added with a slight grin, "but James and I, we care about you. Deeply. You've been part of his life longer than I have. And now, you're part of mine too."

Sarah swallowed hard, trying to find something to say. Christina's grip softened even more, gentle, warm, steady. It must have felt like when she used to hold her mom's hand at the end.

"We pray for you. For Will. Regularly. Not just in passing. We'll keep praying. And if you ever need us for anything, you call. Doesn't matter what time. Doesn't matter why. We'll be there."

Sarah blinked back the sudden sting in her eyes. "You're kind, Christina. I'm not sure I've done anything to deserve it."

Christina's expression grew serious. "You did everything," she said. "If you hadn't been who you were for James, he never would've let me in. You're the reason he could love me the way he does. You gave him that trust. That healing."

She squeezed Sarah's hand again, firmer this time. "You're part of our story. Whether you realize it or not."

There was truth and grace in her voice.

The kind of grace Sarah needed to feel right now.

For years, she'd wondered what it would feel like to see James with someone else. Now she knew. It was a soft ache mixed with something akin to peace.

SEVEN

Three months after the funeral, Sam sat in a small cabin with no windows that no one would ever find. The data confirmed it.

After months of partial pings, masked communications, and dead-end probes, the signal came through, clean, organized, and deliberate.

They were moving.

Sam sat back in the old swivel chair, its joints groaning under the motion. The screen glowed in the dark, casting long shadows across the cluttered desk. Maps, drives, code fragments, timelines—everything was converging.

It's real.

It's coming.

And it's big.

He rubbed his eyes, then leaned forward again, tapping through the latest compiled profile. Not the attack—he didn't have the details yet—but the movement pattern, the coordination, the language. The hidden group was always careful, masked behind shell fronts and proxy governments. But this... was different. This was precision. It had fingerprints.

Not his.

That mattered more than anyone would ever know.

Sam had been embedded in their systems for years, just watching. Tracking. Leaking when he could. Rescuing when it was safe. He wasn't one of them. And the deeper they moved, the more convinced he became that this wasn't a power grab. This was a purge. A reckoning. Or worse, a power grab disguised as a purge.

He stood, stretched, and crossed to the wall where the photo board hung, faces pinned, lines drawn in colored thread. Most of it was digital now, but he liked the visual anchor. It kept him grounded.

His fingers drifted to a picture near the edge. A woman in uniform. Strong jaw. Sharp eyes. The kind that had learned to survive rather than trust. Sarah.

He'd kept tabs on her since she surfaced as an applicant to Annapolis. A handful of people in his network had crossed her path, some intentionally, some not. Her name kept popping up. She wasn't loud. Wasn't reckless. But she endured. And that made her dangerous to them.

Or valuable to him.

He tapped the photo lightly. "Please don't be where this lands."

His gaze shifted to one photo over. Will.

One of Sam's old contractors, briefly. Smart. Capable. And unstable. After he left the private side, Sam had watched him bounce to the public sector, then out entirely. Always discontent. Always trying to reinvent himself, but never from the inside.

Will had walked away from everything he'd tried to offer. Not just jobs or contracts. Paths. Doors most men would never even see, placements in firms, advisory posts in secure holdings, even command of assets Sam kept off the books. High trust, low visibility. Tailored to Will's skillset. To his ego.

But it had never been about Will.

Sam had offered those doors to give the man balance, to keep him grounded enough that Sarah wouldn't get caught in his collapse. If Will could land somewhere, anywhere, it might spare her the fallout.

But he couldn't, or wouldn't, stay rooted.

And people like that didn't spiral alone.

She married him. She was still with him. Sam crossed his arms, eyes narrowing. And she didn't deserve what was coming.

He turned back to the terminal and encrypted a message. Short, targeted. One of the embedded safe lines. Not to Sarah, not yet, but to someone close to her.

He couldn't stop the wave.

But maybe, just maybe, he could get the right people off the shore before it hit.

* * *

The uniform shirt was unnecessary. James knew it, but he buttoned it anyway.

There was a more casual option in his bag, one of those base-issued polos, but something about seeing Christina again made him want to look like the man she fell in love with: clean, upright, and put together.

He checked the mirror, ran a hand over his jaw. Still smooth. The last shave had been this morning, but he no longer trusted time. Three months overseas had trained him to treat every moment like it might slip away unnoticed.

He reached for his phone.

One new photo.

Christina had sent it from the terminal: Wyatt asleep across her lap, open-mouthed and barefoot, one tiny fist still gripping a graham cracker. The caption read:

"Your son. I swear he gets taller every layover."

James smiled and let the image sit on the screen for a moment. Wyatt was almost one now. Walking. Babbling. He knew James' face, but only in pixels. Only in waves and echoes through a screen.

Now he would know the man.

Christina had stayed with her friends during the deployment, just outside Indianapolis. Easier that way. Her friend had helped with Wyatt and given Christina the companionship she needed. He'd offered to fly out there, to go to them instead of making her haul a baby cross-country alone. But she refused.

"No," she'd said. "Come home. Let's start there. We'll meet you."

So here he was, home. Or close enough to taste it.

He'd landed at Camp Pendleton two days earlier. The transport crews were cycling out fast, but he'd been one of the last to offload, waiting on a backup shuttle to get him north. Today, he drove to L.A. in a borrowed car, gear still packed in the trunk, wondering what it would feel like to hold his son again. To feel Wyatt's weight in his arms. To smell Christina's shampoo. To not have to count days anymore.

He checked the time. United 2247 should be wheels down in minutes.

He grabbed his bag, slung it over his shoulder, and stepped into the noise and chaos of LAX.

James stood near the pickup zone outside Terminal 7 at LAX, just past the security line where the crowd thinned. It was early afternoon, and the Southern California sun reflected off everything: glass, pavement, windshields, like the whole world had been lit a little too bright.

He rechecked the arrivals board, even though he knew the flight by heart.

United 2247. Landed. Taxiing to the gate.

The buzz of traffic moved in waves behind him. Families gathered at curbs with signs and balloons. A little girl sat cross-legged on a suitcase, eating gummy bears one at a time.

James shifted his weight and glanced at the secured perimeter beyond the terminal doors. The TSA had pushed the waiting zone back again. There were too many policy updates and threats. The jetways were beyond his field of vision—just layers of glass, barriers, and heat.

His phone vibrated.

Christina.

"Just landed. Wyatt's asleep again, of course. Can't wait. 🖤 *"*

He smiled, chest loosening for the first time all day. He tapped a reply.

I'm right outside. Just look for the best-looking guy in uniform.

Before he hit send.

The air shifted before the sound.

A low, dense pressure rolled through his chest, like a change in altitude that came too fast. Heads turned. Birds lifted from the trees in a sudden wave.

Then came the blast.

A flash. A soundless roar. Then fire.

The explosion erupted from behind the terminal, a wall of orange and black climbing skyward. A second later, the shockwave hit, shattering glass, alarms wailing, and throwing bodies like paper.

James had time for one thought: *No.*

Then the force slammed into him.

He hit the ground hard, the back of his head cracking against the pavement. People were screaming. Running. Sirens blared from somewhere too far away. The sky burned.

James tried to move, but the world was tilting, spinning, collapsing inward.

Then everything went black.

* * *

Sarah sat at her desk, staring at a report she had tried to read three times. The base was quieter than usual, at least for a Wednesday afternoon. The chatter on the operations floor had thinned to a low murmur, and the ceiling fans above spun with the slow confidence of machines that had survived too many heat waves.

Her phone buzzed.

She flipped it over and saw the name: Christina.

ATL layover. We survived the first leg. Wyatt tried to baptize a bagel.

[1:03 PM EST]

Sarah smiled, a real one, before she could stop it.

She typed back:

Please tell me you got video.

Also, please tell me there was cream cheese involved.

[1:04 PM]

The reply came almost instantly.

It's all in the cloud now. Holy cream cheese everywhere. He's in his spiritual awakening phase. 😇

Sarah leaned back in her chair and let the warmth linger. For weeks now, Christina had been the only person who reached out without an agenda, no rank, no explanations, just gentle and undeserved love.

Their emails had started as updates while James was deployed, mostly about Wyatt. But somewhere in the last month, they'd become something else. Longer. More personal. A kind of shelter.

Christina asked how Sarah was sleeping, if she was eating, if she needed to talk.

Today, for the first time, Sarah had responded honestly.

Some days, I don't even recognize him anymore. I feel like I'm married to a thunderstorm. Just waiting for the next strike.

Christina's response had come two minutes later.

You are still you. Don't let his storms make you think otherwise. I'm praying for you. And when we get settled, I want you to come visit. Or I'll come to you. I mean it. Any time. Any reason. You won't go through this alone.

Sarah had stared at that message longer than she meant to.

She'd typed back:

Thank you. Truly. I don't even know how to explain how much that means right now.

She never got a reply.

It was maybe an hour later when the base went silent in a different way.

The kind of silence that comes when too many screens refresh at once. Heads turned toward monitors. Hands froze over keyboards.

Someone on the far side of the room said it first.

"Was that LAX?"

Sarah blinked. "What?"

A tech turned the volume up on the internal news feed. Flames. Smoke. A terminal engulfed.

"Breaking news out of Los Angeles International Airport—what appears to be a massive explosion…"

She was already standing before the anchor finished the sentence.

The ticker scrolled past the bottom of the screen—United Flight 2247 among the names flickering in early manifest data.

Her heart stopped.

She knew that number.

She knew that flight.

Christina. Wyatt.

Sarah instinctively grabbed her bag and walked out of the building. The heat of the sun hit her face as the breathless rush of the world tilted under her feet.

She was on the line with her CO before the front gate was in sight.

Orders blurred. Faces passed in a rush. Someone handed her a tablet somewhere in the chaos, and someone else nodded her toward the flight line.

Sarah moved like she was underwater, slowed, muffled and floating above the ground.

The C-130 had been scheduled anyway. It was a supply run to Point Mugu: communications gear, emergency kits, and a few rapid-deploy logistics teams. A quick call to her CO and back-channel approval from a friend in ops added her to the manifest.

By the time they lifted off, the sun was dipping across the western sky, casting long shadows across the tarmac. She didn't know what time it was in L.A., only that Christina's flight had landed.

And then exploded.

The C-130's cargo bay vibrated around her, metallic and loud, but empty in all the ways that mattered. She sat on the bench near the rear wall, strapped in, her helmet loose in her lap, and her flight jacket half-zipped.

The crew stayed forward. The others in the bay—logistics and airfield security—left her alone. Maybe they'd been briefed. Or maybe they just recognized the look.

Her hands stayed clenched around her phone. The screen still showed Christina's last message:

You won't go through this alone.

Sarah read it for the fifth time. Then the sixth.

The words blurred.

Wyatt had barely turned one.

And Christina—the kind of woman who noticed when your voice shook, who followed up two days later when you lied and said you were fine, and who talked about faith like it was an anchor, not a duty.

They were gone.

Sarah stared at the aircraft's wall, at the rivets, seams, and paint-scratched panels, and tried to find her breath.

If James was with them…

She shut that thought down.

She didn't know. Not yet.

If he'd been inside, he might be on a list. If he'd survived, he might be one of the nameless in the hospitals. There were already hundreds listed. Some with names. Some without.

She had to find him.

And if she couldn't—

No.

She would.

The aircraft's hum filled her chest. The hours stretched. Nothing but wind and metal and the sound of her heart ticking forward one beat at a time.

The C-130 rolled to a stop at Point Mugu just after 2100 hours. As soon as the ramp began to drop, she grabbed her bag and headed for the edge of the tarmac.

A man in flight gear met her halfway.

"Lieutenant Commander Hamlin?"

She nodded.

"Chopper's ready. Pad three."

That was all he said.

She followed without a word.

The Seahawk was already spinning up, its rotors turning slowly and steadily. She climbed in, strapped down, and pulled the headset over her ears.

She was the only passenger.

She should've asked who arranged it, and why it was already waiting. But the question never made it to her mouth.

Her thoughts were elsewhere.

Christina was gone—the explosion too massive, the fire too fast. She'd seen the footage repeatedly in the ready room, on the tablet, on a dozen screens. No survivors had been pulled from the wreckage of that plane.

Only bodies.

And James…

Could he have survived?

She knew he was meeting them, but where would he have been? On the concourse, the curb, or inside? Was he close enough to die, or far enough to live? All she could think about now was what came next.

Hospitals. Triage centers. Morgues.

If he were alive, he'd be hard to find. If he weren't…

She closed her eyes and leaned her head back against the bulkhead. The hum of the helicopter filled her chest, loud and steady.

She prayed silently.

Please don't make me look for him on a list.

Please don't make me find him on a table.

EIGHT

The Seahawk touched down hard. Sarah was already moving toward the tent across the tarmac and through checkpoints. No one dared question her. She was a military intelligence officer, and the look on her face told people not to mess with her.

She'd been standing in the operations tent for nearly an hour.

Names. Codes. Overlapping jurisdictions. Triage lists that were two hours out of date before they hit the printer. Whenever she asked about James, she was pointed to a different table. A different hospital. A different maybe, each one further from an answer.

She stepped outside and leaned against the side of a comms trailer, the smoke-salted wind biting through her uniform. Her eyes burned.

Her phone was still silent.

"Lieutenant Commander Hamlin?"

She turned. A man stood a few feet away in civilian clothes, with a police badge clipped to his belt and shoulders squared like someone who could end a bar fight on his own.

"Yeah," she said. "That's me."

"Name's Roland. Long Beach PD. You've been looking for a Navy pilot, Callan, right?"

Sarah straightened. "Yes. James. Have you—?"

"He's alive."

Her breath caught.

"Unconscious. Head injury. Came in about thirteen hours ago. No ID on him at first, wallet and phone were gone. They found tags during triage and logged him later. Your name didn't get linked in time. Comms are a mess."

She blinked. "How did you know where to find me?"

Roland's voice stayed flat. "Someone knew you were here. Said you'd be looking. I wasn't officially assigned, just told to make sure you got to him."

She studied him. "Who told you?"

He shrugged. "Friend of a friend. Doesn't usually leave instructions. Just dots to connect."

That was all he offered.

The SUV parked beside the tent was already running. Roland turned and started walking.

She followed.

Inside, he kept his eyes on the road. City lights slid past the windows.

"St. Mary's," he said. "No visitors allowed, technically. But your uniform'll open the door. He's in recovery. Awake, but incoherent, far as I know."

Sarah stared straight ahead, hands clenched in her lap.

"You knew I'd come," she said, the weight of it catching in her throat.

Roland was slow to answer. "Someone knew you were here."

* * *

At first, it was just noise.

A monitor beeping somewhere to his left. Soft voices. A door opening. A door closing. Something humming overhead.

He tried to move, but the world stayed still. Heavy. Too bright.

Where…

His mouth was dry. His limbs ached. The air smelled like disinfectant and plastic, and something beneath that…burnt metal, maybe.

He blinked against the light, the ceiling sharpening into focus one fluorescent flicker at a time.

A hospital.

The thought landed like a dull weight. His ribs hurt. His head felt like it had been split open and re-stitched by someone in a hurry.

Why…?

His mind reached, and the images came in flashes. LAX. The terminal. He'd been as close as security allowed… waiting, watching for Christina and Wyatt. Phone in hand. Sending a text…

The blast.

His heart lurched. He tried to sit up but only managed a groan.

A nurse appeared at his side instantly. "Easy, Lieutenant. You've been fairly out of it for the past thirteen hours or so."

Lieutenant. So they knew who he was.

"Wh…what happened?" His voice came out hoarse, barely above a whisper.

"An explosion at LAX. You were lucky. Concussed, but mostly just banged up—no internal bleeding. Moderate contusion. You were completely out for about an hour but have been pretty foggy since then. You've got a few stitches and a hell of a goose egg."

James blinked slowly, fighting through the haze. "Christina… Wyatt…"

The nurse's expression shifted. Too smooth. Too careful. "You've got someone here to see you."

The door opened before he could ask again.

And then she was there.

Sarah.

In uniform. Eyes red-rimmed, but standing tall, steady—barely.

As their eyes met, the truth passed between them. He already knew.

She stepped closer. Silence and the unbearable stillness of grief and friendship colliding.

She reached for his hand.

His fingers closed around hers, trembling.

The weight of it… the silence, the hospital, the broken pieces of his life pressed in around them.

Her voice cracked as she said it, barely more than a whisper, "I'm sorry."

His throat tightened, but he stared at her. For once, he just let it be there, between them.

And for the first time in his life, he let someone else carry the loss with him.

$* * *$

The hallway outside James' room was too silent.

Machines beeped softly behind the closed door. She'd left him only minutes ago, asleep again, worn down from the shock and the sedatives. They had not spoken, silence between them had said everything.

She walked to the end of the corridor and leaned against the wall, arms crossed tight over her chest.

Her phone buzzed as it reconnected to the network… Finally, it had been off for hours, dead half the flight, and had been ignored the rest.

One missed call.

Will.

She stared at the screen, heart sinking.

Time stamp: nearly twelve hours ago.

Just one voicemail. Eight seconds.

She pressed play.

"Where are you?"

Will's voice. Ragged. Unmoored.

She left Florida before she had told him anything had happened.

She didn't mean to hide it. She just… hadn't known how to explain. Naval Intelligence. Coordinating with local authorities. It was a lie, one she could live with.

She swallowed and dialed.

It rang. Picked up on the third try.

"Hey," she said quickly. "I'm safe."

A beat.

"Where are you?" Will's voice was sharper now. "I woke up and you were gone."

"I was deployed. LAX. Intel wanted someone on site… they needed coordination, civilian interface. I couldn't call until I landed. It all happened fast. Cell signals have been down."

"Why you?" he asked. "There are bases closer. People closer."

She closed her eyes. She didn't know what to say; no matter what she said, it would end badly.

"I don't know. I got the call, and I went. That's my job."

Silence stretched.

"James is out there, isn't he?" His voice dropped. "He was flying back. You knew that."

"Will—"

"Did you go for him?"

The question landed like a punch. It was a fair question. Her answer would only make things worse.

"I went because they sent me."

"Right."

His voice cracked on that single syllable. She could hear it… the thing breaking.

"Will, I didn't do this to hurt you. I just… I didn't know how to say it without making it worse."

"You made it worse already. You chose him and did not even tell me. It has always been him."

He hung up.

Sarah stood frozen, the line dead in her hand.

For a few moments, she sat unmoving. She had nothing left in her to call him back and fight more; she just could not muster the strength. She had been wrong, but he overreacted. Then, mechanically, like someone waking from a dream, she turned and walked back into James' room.

He was still asleep, his face pale beneath the bruising. Machines hummed gently around him. She sat down in the chair beside him, folding her arms on the edge of the bed and lowering her head.

And for the first time since everything began, she let herself cry broken tears.

The tears gave out before the grief did. Her body, wrung out and aching, finally gave in. She fell asleep there, head against her forearm, the weight of the day pressing down like a blanket soaked in concrete.

When she awoke, she rubbed her eyes and reached for her phone. One new text.

From Will: I'm sorry.

That was all. She stared at it for a long moment, her breath catching. Something in her chest folded in on itself. Then her phone buzzed again — a call this time.

Unknown number.

She answered, already knowing.

"Mrs. Hamlin?" The voice was calm. Clipped. Too professional. "This is Sergeant Rivera with the Jacksonville Sheriff's Office. I'm calling regarding your husband, William Hamlin. I'm sorry to inform you—he was involved in a single-vehicle accident earlier this evening."

The words shattered her. They just kept falling. Like a ceiling giving way.

She loved Will. For all his faults, for everything he'd become, she still loved him. And as much as she hated what he had done to them, the words still crushed her already devastated heart.

Sarah was silent. The world had gone very still, like the space between heartbeats.

"From what we can determine, he appears to have lost control and struck the center divider at high speed. Emergency services responded, but…" A pause. "He was pronounced dead at the scene. I'm very sorry for your loss, ma'am."

She closed her eyes, a hand pressed to her mouth.

Was it her fault? Did he get angry? Drive too fast, lose control? Or was this how he decided to end it? Was there something she could've said—something she could've done—to stop it? But now it was too late. Whatever answer there was, it died with him.

And that was when the second edge of the blade finally fell.

Her phone was still in her hand, screen dark, when it buzzed again.

A different number this time.

She hesitated. Her body was lead. Her mind, smoke.

"Hamlin."

A beat of silence.

"Mrs. Hamlin, this is Roland." Flat. Matter-of-fact. Like earlier. Like nothing had changed. As if the world hadn't collapsed under her feet.

"Yes," she said slowly. The word barely held shape.

Why is he calling me? How did he get this number?

"I was told to call you," Roland said. "A friend asked me to pass a message. Said you should look at X. Said it's important."

The call ended before she could even form a question.

She stared at the screen.

A message. Another one. From someone who already knows too much. Her mind reeled.

Why me? Why is someone watching me? Who's pulling the strings?

Fear tangled with sorrow, coiling tight in her chest. Every nerve frayed— every breath like glass.

Her thumb hovered for a beat. Then she opened the X app.

The top of her feed was already autoplaying. A shaky cell phone video. Screams. A blinding light. Then fire.

The LAX explosion. But not any footage she'd seen before.

This was different. Planned. She had watched the explosion a dozen times—news clips, security feeds, overhead drone loops.

But this…This video had been waiting. Someone had been filming the plane. The moment. They knew. They were ready.

She watched, breath caught in her throat, as the wave of fire erupted across the screen.

And then, mid-frame, the video had paused.

Frozen in black. Overlaid in stark white letters.

WRATH

NINE

Sam never intended to disappear, not at first. In the early years at the NSA he still believed he could work inside the system, that if he stayed long enough he might slow the tide. But the deeper he went, the more clearly he saw where it was heading, and by then the choice felt less like defiance and more like inevitability. Disappearing was not a whim; it was survival, and it was logic.

When he finally walked away, there was no dramatic gesture to mark it. No staged death, no midnight escape into the wilderness. He signed the paperwork, handed in his badge, and left through the same doors he had walked through every morning. On the outside it looked ordinary, almost anticlimactic, but that was the point. The act of leaving needed to draw no attention at all.

The building began quietly. First it was the markets. He had always understood people and the rhythms they produced, and the markets were simply those same rhythms captured in numbers. He studied how trends looped into one another, how sentiment bent supply and demand, and when he placed his money against those patterns, the returns came. With the returns came freedom. With freedom came reach.

Once he was wealthy enough to move beyond the markets, he turned toward acquisitions. He avoided the firms that made the news and instead bought the ones no one noticed. Small retailers hidden inside supply chains. Tooling shops that kept manufacturers running. A handful of obscure technology firms, defense subcontractors buried in spreadsheets that only auditors ever glanced at. Piece by piece, the structure grew—raw goods, production, distribution—all stitched together in ways that, from the outside, looked like coincidence. Within five years he had infrastructure. Within ten, an empire hidden in plain sight.

The logic was simple. If you wanted to move people unseen, you owned the buses. If you wanted to hide data, you controlled the wires it rode on. And if you needed an aircraft to vanish without a trace, you owned the airport, the logistics hub, the camera supplier, and at least two cleaning crews. He never explained it that way to anyone else, of course. But when he studied the map of what he controlled, that was the shape he saw.

Wealth alone, though, wasn't enough. He needed distance, insulation, so the trail of acquisitions looked less like orchestration and more like the scattershot portfolio of a billionaire with strange whims.

Alaska was never a fallback. It was sanctuary—the last stretch of wild where satellites blinked and fiber lines faltered. There he built a base, not a bunker. Nothing paranoid. Just quiet, cold enough to turn away guests, remote enough that no one arrived by accident.

The "home" the world saw was a log fortress set high in the mountains, more than ten thousand square feet of handcrafted excess. Stone and marble hearths. Massive windows. Top-end appliances and furniture. Solar, wind, and geothermal backups. It looked like indulgence. In truth, it was a decoy—an excuse for the bandwidth and the energy draw.

Even the logs weren't logs. They were steel cores clad in real wood, every piece hauled in by truck and fully documented. The windows carried the same deception, triple-layered and bulletproof, opaque from the outside but flawless from within. When an installer remarked on how odd it was that you could see out without being seen, Sam filed suit. The court ruled in his favor, labeling them defects. That was all they were meant to see. No one guessed he had drawn the specifications himself—or that he owned both the manufacturer and the builder.

Security looked impressive enough: cameras, motion lights, alarms, every bell and whistle expected of a half-insane recluse billionaire. But the real defenses didn't show. Weapons caches hidden in unlikely places.

Tracking programs and micro-cameras with motion sensors. Laser grids and automated emplacements that could turn the property into something no one wanted to approach.

Beside the house sat a small cabin. During construction he had lived there, and later it became storage—at least that was the impression. A snowmobile stood out front. A workbench crowded with tools and fuel cans filled the space. To a casual eye it was ordinary. But the true entrance lay underground. Sam had learned he worked better above ground, so he built a false wall and left just enough space for a narrow office where he could bury himself in work without stepping into the main house. A network of tunnels tied cabin and house together, hidden veins running beneath the snow.

Even when he wasn't inside, thermal scans showed him there—heat signatures pacing halls, cooking in the kitchen, sitting at a desk. All fabricated. Heating pads built into floors and furniture glowed in shifting patterns, mimicking presence. Sometimes they lit up from the couch, sometimes from the bed, always enough to keep the illusion alive.

Beneath those tunnels lay the true heart of it all. A geothermally regulated climate. A thousand-foot well pulling pure water. Computing power enough to rival an NSA regional hub—minus the AI. That was too uncontrolled. Sam didn't trust code that thought for itself. He wanted eyes only where he chose to look. Scripts traced threads he flagged, custom logic stitched them into connections, and his mind did the rest.

The centerpiece was a five-acre underground farm, the part he considered most remarkable. It had taken a decade of experiments— shoring walls against collapse, building hydroponic rigs, simulating seasons—to get it right. Once perfected, he left it dormant. It wasn't for now. It was for the end. They said five acres could feed scores, maybe a hundred if rationed. For the fifteen or twenty he meant to shelter— family, the ones he trusted—it would be enough.

The world thought the threat was chaos. It wasn't. It was erosion—slow, surgical, the kind that wears a suit, sits for interviews, and smiles while freedoms vanish one checkbox at a time.

Now the pace had shifted. The chatter changed—coordinated, deliberate, large. You don't work where he worked or dig where he dug without learning to smell smoke before the flames.

He had names. Maps. Purchase orders. Intercepted memos that shouldn't exist. Something was coming. Others whispered about it. He prepared for it.

His network wasn't designed to make him rich or grant him power, though it did both. It was built to save the remnant—to pull out those the system meant to erase, framed, discredited, disappeared. Those were the people his network sought to shield.

His sisters widened that reach. Through them came others who still believed in something larger. People too honest to be bought, too sharp to be fooled. Pastors, engineers, administrators in places that mattered. They didn't see the full web. They didn't have to.

Churches became proving grounds. Sam never demanded loyalty, but he had no patience for laziness or compromise. He watched—who stepped forward, who stayed when it grew difficult. The pattern reminded him of the parable: the master who gave servants little, then more when they proved faithful. Sam followed the same logic.

When they proved themselves, he opened doors. A position in one of his firms. A quiet push into a larger company. Sometimes he was the angel investor who gave them the seed money for a dream.

He never backed CEOs or boards—too visible. He worked two layers down: regional VPs, mid-level controllers. People close enough to see the gears turn, far enough not to be crushed when they stopped.

These weren't soldiers. They were watchers, gatekeepers, ordinary men and women living ordinary lives. Sam helped them, and in return they were willing to help when the call came.

And help them he did. He funded a child's surgery when insurance refused. He paid for legal defense when someone decent was trapped in red tape. Always within the law. Always for the marginalized, the ones the system had failed. They didn't forget. When he needed small favors, they answered.

Early on, the network stumbled. He had trusted records, not patterns. Someone can look flawless on paper, but until pressure comes you don't know where they'll crack. And when they fold, they don't just fail—they destroy.

He had safeguards, yes, but safeguards drew questions. Too many threads and someone starts to trace them. That was when he changed everything. No more quick integrations. No early trust. He watched for months, years, sometimes decades. And when he moved, it was slow, deliberate, layered beyond any audit's reach.

William Hamlin was a pilot program. He came in partway, given tools and support but not the full scope. Sam wanted to see what pressure would do. Hamlin didn't hold. A good man, but brittle, too shaped by what the world told him to be.

Sarah was different. She didn't break. Didn't cave. She endured—scarred but steady. Not perfect. But tested.

* * *

Frank Jameson was a Marine's Marine. Force Recon. Hard-charging. Steeped in discipline. He'd served in every hotspot from Bosnia to Fallujah and still had enough bark to run three-mile drills with twenty-year-olds until his last tour. His son, Samuel "Sam," was not the man Frank had hoped to raise.

The first "camping trip" with Frank happened when Sam was ten. Frank made it sound like an adventure, just the two of them, "the men of the house," heading into the woods to rough it like real Marines.

Frank was stationed at Fort Leonard Wood at the time. A couple of his buddies rolled up in a battered Humvee, trading stories and laughing like they were already on a mission. They drove for hours, deep into the Ozark backcountry, no roads, no signs, just pine and gravel and the hum of engine noise.

When they stopped, Sam climbed out, stiff and nervous. Frank handed him a pack that was clearly too heavy and said, "This is where we start."

The Humvee drove off, leaving a dust cloud and silence behind.

They hiked for miles, over ridges, through brush, until they reached a flat spot near a spring-fed lake. They set up camp, and Sam was too tired to be afraid as night fell. Yet.

Frank handed him a .22 rifle the next morning and said, "We need meat. Let's go."

But less than an hour into the hunt, Frank slipped on a mossy rock and fell hard. The crack of bone was unmistakable.

Sam panicked, but Frank didn't. He barked orders, his face pale but steady. "Help me up. Splint it. You remember how."

Somehow, Sam did. They limped back to camp. Frank couldn't walk after that. For the rest of the week, it was on Sam to hunt, boil water, and keep the fire going. He caught rabbits, skinned them with trembling hands, and boiled water in a dented tin cup. Every task was watched and evaluated. Not once did Frank thank him. He just nodded or grunted, as if checking items off a list.

When the Humvee returned a week later, Sam nearly wept with relief. He'd been sure they wouldn't make it, certain the splint wasn't enough and infection would set in, that Frank might die right there in the dirt.

Then Frank stood. No limp. No wince. Just a straight back and a smug look.

"You were right," one of the Marines called. "Kid kept you alive."

Frank clapped Sam on the shoulder. "Told you he could do it."

Later, in the truck, Sam didn't say a word. His father's leg had never been broken.

It had all been a test.

That became the template. Every year, Frank took him farther into the woods. By twelve, Frank stopped coming along, just dropped him off, and drove away. At fourteen, the rifle got replaced with a knife. At sixteen, no gear at all.

By the time Sam turned eighteen, he wasn't scared of the woods. He was scared of becoming his father.

When he told Frank he wouldn't be enlisting or joining the Marines, the silence that followed was worse than any explosion. Frank didn't yell. He just turned, walked out of the room, and didn't speak to him for three days.

They never fought. Not really. But they never truly reconciled, either.

Sam loved him. Or maybe he loved the idea of him… the myth. But the man? The man had taught him survival, not trust, not affection, and certainly not warmth.

His mother never raised her voice. In a house where silence was punishment, her love was peace. She prayed while folding laundry and quoted Scripture like it was breath. Sam never told her, but he memorized every verse she whispered. That's where it started, faith—before the NSA, before the betrayal. She planted it. What he saw later made it unshakable.

He graduated from high school at seventeen. MIT took him in on a wild bet. He broke their record—the fastest completion of a BA and Master's in cyber systems: two years, three months, eleven days. He slept on benches, ate from vending machines, and didn't miss a single exam. He wasn't trying to break the record. He was trying to start his life. College was just another barrier. And for better or worse, Frank had taught him how to face a barrier: move fast, push through, and never stop trying.

He'd learned not to trust the surface story, not after four years inside the NSA. He hadn't joined out of patriotism. He went in because it was the best place to learn the rules, so he could one day play outside them. Cyber-intelligence, pattern tracking, forensic telemetry, he absorbed it all.

And when it was time, he left. Not abruptly. Slowly. He built a mental break, months of small behaviors, disjointed thinking, and erratic patterns. Enough that when he asked to get out, they didn't fight it. He wasn't a threat. He was unstable. They let him go.

And sometimes, he dreamed.

Dreams that came sharp, insistent. More warning than whisper. He'd long since stopped questioning the source. They were from God. He was sure of it. Had been for years. And when they came, he listened.

One of them was about her.

Sarah J. Whitaker. He'd seen her name before, just a line on an application list from the Academy. He was scanning through applicants, half out of boredom, half out of habit, and then there it was. A whisper he couldn't place. He moved on. Tried to ignore it.

Then he dreamed. A corridor. Fire on the walls. Sarah, bleeding, alone and reaching for something that wasn't there. He woke up with her name on his tongue.

That was enough.

He started watching, not interfering. Not at first. Sarah was sharp and driven. More than capable of making it on her own. But he knew how the system worked. If you have a GPA that is too high, you get groomed for things you didn't choose. Too low, and the doors you needed stayed shut. He kept her right in the middle… safe. Untouchable.

Then came James Callan.

Another name he wouldn't have cared about, except for her. Her scores dropped 2.86% over the next few months. Not a lot. Not enough to raise alarms. But to him? That was a red flag waving on a hill. James meant something to her. So he took a closer look.

James had a story. Most did. But he made you stop scrolling. A clean record. Loss. Faith. Depth. Without Sarah, he would've stayed in the static. But with her? Sam needed to know if he was an asset or a liability.

She chose James. He noted that. Noted how she steadied when he was around. But life didn't play fair. They were never on the same trajectory. And that made them fragile.

The more accomplished Sarah became, the more dangerous her path could be. Sam needed her to land in intelligence. Not command, not special operations. He couldn't risk visibility. He needed her to know things, not be known for them.

So, he nudged. Pushed doors open invisibly. Made sure her rotations touched sub operations, cybersecurity, shipboard protocol, human terrain, and chain-of-command anomalies. She needed range. She needed to see the whole board. Because someday he'd need her to understand why it was collapsing.

Her marriage to William Hamlin?

A disaster. Lovely man, deep convictions, but too brittle. Sam gave him jobs when he left the military subcontractor world, offers through shell companies, places where he could have found purpose. He declined and chose to spiral instead. And now, he was dragging Sarah with him.

That almost broke the plan.

Almost.

But Sarah wasn't easy to break. Not truly. Sam had come to believe that was precisely why the dream came about, why she mattered.

Because now, it was happening.

He didn't know what it was, not the exact contours. But he knew the pattern. Threads being pulled. Systems twitching in the dark. The tempo of the silence had changed.

Something big was coming.

The catalyst.

And he wouldn't be able to stop it.

But he could catch it.

The alert tone pulled him out of his thoughts, clean, sharp, and deliberate. A single chime, buried beneath the hum of air handlers. Not random. It never was.

Sam's hand hovered above the keyboard, fingers frozen mid-command. The screen blinked once, then stabilized… ten alerts stacked by severity, all system-detected unless otherwise noted:

LAX Terminal 7 – ALERT • Structural Failures Detected • Multiple Thermal Events Detected • Explosions Detected (Multiple Sources)

LAX Command Node – ALERT • Response Loop Disruption • Internal Security Reporting Offline

LA Cell Tower Node 332 – ALERT • Signal Drop Detected • Physical Damage Suspected (Proximity to Blast Radius)

Power Grid Sector 14B – ALERT • Surge Event Logged • Partial Outage Detected (No Confirmed Cause)

ATC Network – Pacific Southwest – ALERT • Regional Node Failure • Emergency Fallback Routing Active

LAX Inbound Traffic – ALERT • All Arrivals Suspended (FAA Feed) • Holding Pattern Issued (Externally Confirmed)

Flight 2247 – Gate 72A – ALERT • Communication Loss • Proximity to Terminal 7 – Event Correlation Suspected

Flight 882 – Gate 72B – ALERT • Transponder Drop • No Response to Tower • Structural Loss Detected

Flight 619 – Gate 71B – ALERT • Combustion Warning • Total Loss Suspected (Unconfirmed Source)

Flight 1932 – Taxiway – ALERT • Tower Contact Lost • Transient Ping Only

He scanned the list once and then again. The system didn't draw conclusions—that wasn't its job. It reported, and he interpreted.

Terminal 7 wasn't confirmed as the epicenter. Not flagged, but the pattern pointed there.

And the pattern was correct.

He didn't move for a full ten seconds.

Then, slowly, he stood.

This was the first domino.

It had begun.

He scrolled through video feeds, news streams, internal surveillance cameras, and traffic cams, watching and analyzing. It wasn't just Terminal 7—not exactly.

It was Flight 2247.

The aircraft had just arrived. Hadn't even reached the gate when it exploded, nose still rolling when the fire engulfed it.

That wasn't random.

A domestic flight. Prime time. Ideal for maximum psychological impact. This wasn't just a terrorist attack. It was the first move. The purge, whatever it would look like, had begun.

A new alert chimed. Different tone. Higher priority.

One of his primary assets was diverging from expected behavior.

He pulled it up: Sarah.

She was boarding a C-130J scheduled to depart hours earlier, bound for Point Mugu.

Why?

She wouldn't be needed at LAX. That wasn't her zone of responsibility. Something else was pulling her in.

He opened her orders. Scrubbed her recent communications. Ran his tracing algorithms through all external and internal data channels.

There. Flight 2247. Logged in her call history.

Christina.

James' wife.

James would've been at the airport if Christina had been on that flight. Or close. And Sarah was going after him.

That made sense.

She was a malfunction in his system for now. Emotions. Unpredictability. But if he could keep her from going off-script, stabilize her… she'd return to form.

He needed her stable. The world as they knew it was coming apart, and he was still the only one who saw it clearly.

He pinged local transit hubs and rerouted a military helicopter to be on standby at Point Mugu. Discreet. Unnoticed. Ready to receive her.

Then he turned to the next task: finding James.

He entered a complete profile: name, biometric description, known identifiers, and tagged it for distribution. First responders. FEMA. Law enforcement. Anyone active in the LAX zone. The system would flag any match.

Nothing.

Next came the hospitals.

He pushed the profile through medical channels within a 100-mile radius—still nothing.

He moved to fallback networks, ones he didn't activate often: nurses, intake staff, a few hospital administrators, and people he'd helped years ago.

They didn't know who he was. Not really. Just that when they'd needed help, an anonymous donation for college, a few months' rent, a surgery for a family member, someone had stepped in.

Now that someone sent a simple message:

Hey. It's been a while. Could you do me a small favor? Let me know if you see anyone matching this name or description. I think he was at the airport today. He's a dear friend.

Simple. Easy. Nothing that would draw attention. They wouldn't question it. Wouldn't think twice.

But they'd act.

Because when Sam asked for something, people listened.

The text came in from a nurse at St. Mary's, one of Sam's soft contacts.

Your friend has a bad concussion, but should be okay. They're moving him now to the ICU, not sure where he'll end up. Things are crazy here.

James. Found.

Sarah, meanwhile, was still at LAX, probably tearing through every available manifest, security list, and casualty register. Likely not finding him. Communications in the area were still down or jammed. The window for clean resolution was closing.

Left alone, she could spiral.

Every hour without answers deepened the emotional strain, and the longer that lasted, the harder it was to pull her back into operational stability.

He needed someone on the ground.

Sam pulled up his proximity index; primary assets within fifty miles. Most were civilians. A few military. He filtered by access potential.

Fire personnel? Problematic. Too essential. Couldn't walk off duty.

LAPD? Out. No movement permitted.

Then… Roland. Long Beach Police Department. Off-shift today. Trusted.

Sam made the call himself. No signal routing. No intermediary. Just direct.

Roland answered on the second ring. "Yeah?"

"I need your assistance," Sam said. "You know I wouldn't ask if there was another way."

Silence. Then, "Go."

"Lieutenant Commander Sarah Hamlin. Navy. Female. Mid-thirties. Five-eight, about one-eighteen. Brown hair, long, but pinned up in a military style. Officer blues. She responded to LAX, but she's not with a team. She's looking for a man, Lieutenant James Callan. Navy pilot."

He paused just a beat.

"He's alive—St. Mary's ICU. The place is locked down, so no visitors. But someone in uniform, her rank... she can get in."

"I'll find her."

"She doesn't know me. Don't explain. Keep it vague."

"I know how to handle it."

The line went dead.

Sam exhaled. That was the last piece. Now it was up to Roland.

He stared at the darkened screen, its glow still faint against the far wall. The alerts had stopped for now.

He leaned forward, elbows on the desk, hands clasped. The geothermal hum beneath his feet usually brought comfort. Now it just felt like pressure rising from the earth.

He had contingencies and scenarios mapped out. He'd run simulations, set triggers, build tools, and recruit people, but not like this, not this fast. Not this soon.

He'd known something was coming. The patterns told him. The dreams had hinted. But dreams didn't carry timestamps.

He'd lost a node. Temporarily, maybe. But Sarah was spiraling, and that made her unpredictable. James was out of play. Vulnerable. One of the few anchors she had left. And the system, the one he'd built with his own hands, over years of sweat and paranoia, had just been punched in the teeth.

Sam leaned back in his chair, jaw tight. His shirt clung to his back. He hadn't noticed until now. Sweat, cold and sharp, soaked through the fabric. He closed his eyes for a breath, then another.

"I wasn't ready," he whispered. Not for this.

But… ready or not… he had to move.

Before he stood, another alert lit up, low priority, but tagged for review.

A post on X.

He pulled it up—just a grainy, handheld video of the LAX explosion. From a phone, it seemed. But something was wrong. The person filming wasn't surprised. They were already watching, already focused as if they'd been waiting.

Then the fireball.

Then a cut to black.

Then one word:

Wrath.

Anonymous account. No bio. No history. Created twenty-four hours ago. One post. Sam's linguistic tracers had flagged it within minutes. Biblical tone wrapped in precise, modern language. Not AI. Not random. Human. Intentional. Designed to sound ancient and feel current.

That was it—the announcement.

TEN

James had been released that morning. There was just a clipboard, a signature, and a nurse with tired eyes telling him to take it slow, like she actually believed that was possible.

Sarah drove. He was glad she did.

The house in Ventura, just minutes from Point Mugu, looked older than he remembered.

When Christina and James moved back after the assignment came through, it felt like a gift—living in the place again. For the first time in years, it felt like more than just a shelter. It felt like home. After his mom died, so much of the love seemed to seep out, like the house itself had died. His dad held it together as best he could, but when he passed, the silence turned cold. The place became a shell—a haunted one.

But Christina… she brought warmth into everything. Her laugh, her ridiculous insistence on seasonal decorations, and the way she filled the rooms with light, music, and life. And when Wyatt came, the house finally seemed to give the years a second chance. There were toys on the stairs, tiny socks in the laundry, and the sound of little feet slapping the floor. For a while, the place felt sacred.

Now it felt… abandoned—a grave with walls.

Sarah was already out of the car. At some point, she'd opened his door, standing there with her steady patience. He moved slowly, carefully. His body hurt, still stiff from the cuts, the bruises, the smoke… but the real damage was the guilt. The endless reel of what-ifs.

He'd let Christina talk him into going straight home from his deployment. She and Wyatt were flying back from her friends' place in Indianapolis. Said it made more sense that way. At the time, it did. But he kept thinking… what if he'd said no? What if he'd insisted they all travel together? They could have been on a flight earlier or later… anything but that flight.

What if he'd been there?

If they'd all been on that plane together, maybe they'd all be in heaven now. At least then they wouldn't be separated.

But he held on to the fact that they would be together again one day in heaven. And for whatever reason, God still had plans for him.

He stepped out slowly. Too slowly. He hadn't even realized how long he'd sat there until Sarah's hand brushed his arm. With her help, he crossed the threshold into the shell of what used to be the most joyful place he'd ever entered.

Everything smelled the same: lemon oil, coffee, something faintly floral from Christina's old reed diffuser. The air felt frozen. Fresh but… like the house itself had paused, unsure how to go on.

Sarah had been here before. She'd held Wyatt, laughed with him. Sat on this couch, barefoot, talking with Christina late into the night. She and Christina had gotten close. He'd been grateful for that. Christina used to call her when she was worried about Will, about deployments, about whether she was doing okay.

Will.

He thought the man was self-centered and uncaring. He'd tried to be nice to him for Sarah. But she had deserved better. Will always seemed brittle, like a man carrying too much pride and too little joy. Christina used to say they needed to pray for him more than judge him because Sarah saw something in him that they didn't.

Whatever she'd seen, it hadn't been enough.

He stopped by the counter, his hands bracing on the edges like he might fall through the floor. The words came out before he could stop them. Maybe they'd been waiting there all along.

"I'm sorry, Sarah. I'm sorry to burden you with my injuries… my pain. You've lost so much, too. You shouldn't have to carry me now." He hesitated, then added, "You must be hurting too… all of this, and Will, too."

She blinked, as if the words hit harder than she expected. A tear hovered in the corner of her eye.

"Thank you, James," she said softly. "But there's no other place I need to be. Nowhere I'd rather be. Family is built for times like now. And we're family."

He stared at her. Admiring her strength, thankful for her words.

She was right, of course. They were family… family that had chosen to become family. An unspoken bond that would last—standing through time, distance, and circumstance. It had survived much and only grown stronger.

She walked into the kitchen to avoid stillness. He knew that motion. Until he had met Christina he had lived it. He had spent years perfecting it… staying busy to keep the pain at bay.

She needed to face her grief. He knew it. But he was too broken now to help her do that.

James made his way over to the couch. When Christina and James moved in, Christina had replaced nearly every piece of furniture in the house. The sofa she chose was comfortable and large enough for him to lie on. He had fallen asleep there in the evenings, watching some show with her more than a few times.

Sarah brought him fresh coffee and set it in front of him. She sat on a chair nearby, and they just sat there in silence, listening to the creak of the old house, both lost in thought.

He'd thanked her for the coffee but never drank it. By the time he touched the cup, it was already cold. He didn't care about the temperature. The cup was one of Christina's favorites.

Sarah had no way to know that. She'd just grabbed one.

It took him hours to touch it.

Sarah dozed. James emptied the cup into the sink and rinsed it out. He turned around, walked to the couch, grabbed a blanket, and covered her with it. She stirred slightly and drifted back into sleep.

He headed upstairs to their bedroom. He knew he was no more likely to sleep there, but he had to face the room eventually.

And he was so glad Sarah was there.

She had always felt safe. Made him feel he was safe when she was around.

And right now, having that safety was what he needed most to face his fears.

James had paced through the house most of the night, finally falling asleep on the still-made bed in the master bedroom. He only got a couple of hours of sleep. It was still dark when he woke up.

He wandered into the backyard and settled on the deck steps to pray for peace, comfort, and God to get him through yet another dark time. That's where Sarah found him, plate in hand; fried eggs, toast, and bacon. She set it down next to him with a cup of coffee in a plain mug from the old set they rarely used, then sat silently in a deck chair.

The sun was just starting to rise, the dark sky giving way to pale light. It was a beautiful time of day, calm enough he could hear the faint rush of waves, only audible in the morning when the city was still. A cool breeze moved the light fog across the yard. It would have been perfect if everything weren't so wrong.

He sipped the coffee and picked up a piece of bacon.

"It feels dead here," he said solemnly. "So much history, so much pain. All my childhood memories are in this place, but all I can feel is the pain."

She got up, the chair's legs scratching faintly on the wood, and moved to sit beside him, placing her hand on his.

"She was so alive. She brought so much love into every place she was, just by her mere presence. Wyatt... he had so much life to live..." A stray tear rolled down his face. "You know me. You know how hard I tried to keep people out. I ran from the pain. I paused with you... stopped for a moment in history and just saw you. Your strength. Your beauty. You became my family. My sister. More. But after the Academy,

I shut people right back out. Ran. Flew. Took every deployment I could find…

"Then she was there—a beacon of love. I couldn't resist. She was like you; she never pushed, was just there. Helped me face my demons but never pushed me to. She accepted me for the broken person I was, never trying to change or improve me. Now she and Wyatt are gone. One day, in heaven, I'll see the man my boy was meant to be…"

A long silence passed.

"Christina once told me," he said, "that people who say God won't give us more than we can bear are taking 1 Corinthians 10:13 out of context. It's about temptation. Not suffering."

He swallowed hard.

"It's 2 Corinthians 1:8 and 9. Paul's talking about being in Asia. Said they had burdens beyond what they could carry, despaired of life itself. I feel like that now…"

Sarah rubbed his back lightly, just listening.

"Paul went on to say God gave them that burden to break them. So they'd turn to Him. To find strength in Him when their own failed. He knows we can't be happy in this life without Him. Can't even survive it without Him. He wants us to seek Him. I need His strength right now… more than I can say."

Tears had started to run down Sarah's face again. He turned to see her and smiled faintly.

"Thank you so much for being here with me. I needed someone. Really… I needed you."

He stood, picking up his plate and mug, and walked inside.

The rest of the morning passed mostly in silence. James had spent much of it in prayer, asking God to carry him through and make him a better man, a man more reliant on Him. He prayed for Sarah, too. He worried about her. She was where he'd been a decade ago: full of hurt, stuffing it down, avoiding it. Maybe to protect herself. Maybe to protect him. He wasn't sure. But he prayed for her just the same.

"You should eat," she said in a hushed voice rough with concern and exhaustion.

82

"I'm okay. Just not hungry right now."

There was a trace of resolve in his voice… maybe even peace. God had granted him that much. A small measure of stillness. A faint, solid belief he would see his family again one day. That God still had plans for him.

"You can't just shut down," she said. Then, softer, "She wouldn't want you to."

He looked at her. Eyes hollow. Voice flat.

"I'm not. I'm trying to find peace. And reason. You can't fix me, Sarah. So stop trying."

It came out sharper than he meant. The edge surprised even him. But the grief was raw, and his skin was too thin.

He saw it hit her. Saw something shift in her eyes… pain, twisted tight into anger.

"I lost them too, James," she said, her voice rising. "Not the way you did, I know that. But Wyatt… he—"

He stood suddenly. The chair scraped hard across the floor.

"Don't." His voice cracked. Hands clenching into fists. "Don't pretend this is the same."

"I'm not pretending anything! I was there. I held him. I loved him—"

"You loved him?" he snapped. "You were passing through. You saw him a handful of times—"

"I saw him enough!"

"You barely knew him!"

He stepped toward her. Anger rising. Uncontrolled.

Sarah's hands were trembling. She stepped back, bumping a side table near the window. A small vase tipped, pushing over a picture frame that Christina had loved. It had sat on her kitchen counter the first time he visited her apartment.

Time slowed.

The frame fell, wood cracked, and glass was scattered across the tile. The picture skittered away, face down.

They both froze.

James took a step back. The rage drained from his face.

"That wasn't your fault," he said softly.

Sarah's expression was a mixture of horror and sadness.

"I scared you," he added. "I didn't mean to."

She turned, walked past him, and picked up her bag. Slid the strap over her shoulder. Silence.

He stared at the broken frame and said nothing more. He was too emotionally drained.

Sarah walked to the door.

James saw her moving, and remained silent. He didn't even move. Just stared at the broken frame, as if it held everything he'd just lost... again.

ELEVEN

The last time they had seen each other was the day she walked out of the house. A few texts had passed between them; short, polite, carefully worded. He invited her to Christina and Wyatt's memorial. She asked him to go to Will's. Neither came. Too much was going on during a time of too much healing.

It was okay with her that their excuses were lies.

The investigation into the bombing had gone cold—no new leads, no arrests. *Wrath* had been the only claim of responsibility and hadn't resurfaced. The world moved on; nervously at first, then almost eagerly. Memorials were held. Interviews faded. Politicians made speeches about "resilience." But with only *Wrath* to blame, the blame seemed to linger.

Sarah had gone back to work within days of Will's funeral. Trish had shown up, uninvited, standing solemnly near the back. Afterward, they talked. Briefly, but that was enough.

Now, they talked often, sometimes about work, but more often about everything else.

Sarah said little at first to her coworkers or her superiors.

She showed up. She worked. She went home.

Her work was flawless, but her eyes were hollow. She felt like a placeholder—present but mentally elsewhere.

Trish clocked it by the second day. "Okay," she said, flopping into the chair across from Sarah in her office, "are we talking grief shutdown or just general loathing of humanity? Either way, I brought snacks."

She dropped a protein bar and a pack of sour gummies onto Sarah's desk with all the delicacy of a dropped grenade.

Sarah blinked. "What is this?"

"A peace offering. Also, possibly dinner. You're starting to look like a hungover scarecrow."

That was how it began.

Trish treated her like someone who'd taken a hit and needed to get back up, occasionally with help, occasionally with sour gummies.

They talked about cafeteria coffee ("actively hostile"), the comically outdated base software ("I think this program predates Moses"), and the time Trish accidentally launched a drone sim in the wrong briefing room ("Technically not my fault. They left it armed.").

And somewhere in the middle of all that, Sarah started breathing again. Will came up once.

"He was a good man," Sarah said gently. "At least… he tried."

Trish raised an eyebrow. "Yeah, I remember Will. Tall, broody, allergic to eye contact?"

Sarah gave a weak smile. "I was around him a few times. Heard about him from friends, too."

She took a sip of her coffee. "You can't lie to me, Whitaker. He was a broken man, cosplaying confidence. Ran from success like he owed it money."

Sarah blinked, then huffed through her nose. "He had some good in him."

"Sure. So does spoiled milk—doesn't mean I'm drinking it."

That one got a real laugh.

"Look," Trish added, "I'm not saying you were wrong to love him. I'm just saying… You didn't break him. He showed up that way. You just gave him a soft place to land, and he bailed like safety was a trap."

Something in the way she said it, calmed Sarah, made her believe that it may be true.

"Besides," Trish said, smirking, "if brooding were a virtue, Batman would be a saint."

That was Trish, and it helped.

A week later, Trish ambushed her outside the intel building.

"Tell me you own something that sparkles."

Sarah squinted at her. "Like… a pin?"

"Like a dress. Or heels. Or joy, Whitaker. You know… something that doesn't come in grayscale. I'm rescuing you from yourself."

Before Sarah could argue, she was already being pulled toward the lot.

That night, Trish took her to some off-base hole-in-the-wall that smelled like tequila, cheap perfume, and bad decisions. It had neon lights, loud music, and a dance floor that pulsed like a heartbeat. Sarah hated it until she let go and loved it.

They danced. They drank. Trish shouted over the music about her favorite pilot exes and the superiority of rum over vodka. Sarah talked little but laughed more than she had in months.

At one point, breathless and glowing under the strobe lights, Trish leaned in and shouted, "See? You're not dead!"

Sarah just shook her head, smiling. But somewhere beneath the smile, a tiny part of her agreed.

Later, at the bar, a guy in a flight jacket caught her eye: tan skin, easy grin, oozing with confidence. He offered a drink. She said yes.

They talked, barely. When he leaned in and touched her hand, she let him. When he leaned further, she let him kiss her.

It was awkward and more than she was ready for.

She pulled back before it went further, muttered something unintelligible and ducked out the side door.

Ten minutes later, Trish joined her outside, heels clicking on the concrete.

"Well," she said, handing Sarah a bottle of water. "At least he was cute. But good thing you stopped it… he was only an LT Another good part about not being military. I can have fun with him tomorrow, and the military does not care, but you and him… firing line, baby."

They started walking, the glow of the bar fading behind them. After a few steps, Trish nudged her with an elbow. "You know, though, I do know some places where the guys aren't all military. We can hook you up with some stress relief that won't get you court-martialed."

Sarah rolled her eyes, concealing a small grin. "Maybe another time. I need to work in the morning."

* * *

James had been cleared to return to duty a few days after the memorial service.

He'd spent a fair bit of time thinking over his next move. He was close to recommitting for another four years. The military always made it overly enticing: bonuses, career stability, and the illusion of forward motion. But he felt like it was time to move forward, away from the military.

He had joined out of duty, something his father had drilled into him… and out of fear—fear of stillness, fear of grief. The military gave him both direction and cover.

Christina had helped him grieve his father. In doing that, she'd somehow prepared him to face losing her.

He remembered that conversation early in their relationship.

He'd dropped by unannounced, and she was trying to heat tomato soup. It was burning, "caramelizing," she'd claimed, completely deadpan.

Dinner had been barely edible, the grilled cheese somewhere between "well done" and "rescue mission."

Her cooking never improved, but she always insisted it would… eventually.

Afterward, sitting on the floor with their paper plates and scorched sandwiches, she'd gone silent for a moment. Then said, "Promise me something."

He looked up. Her face was completely and uncharacteristically serious.

"If I go first… don't close off. Don't go numb. Let it hurt… but don't live in it."

That was the only conversation they had about it. But it had stuck with him.

The day of her memorial it played in his mind like a command.

He had to feel the pain but also move through it. Move on. Part of that meant change.

He had held onto his parents' house like it could bring them back. And the temptation to do the same now, to keep the house because it had been his and Christina's… was strong. But shortly after the memorial, he put it up for sale. He knew it was time.

The timing worked. He had one more deployment… it would be his last. He chose to leave the military and security behind. He would carve a new path for himself.

He was trying to figure out what came next when he overheard two mechanics talking on base.

"Yeah, they're a good group. Most of those military contractors are just trying to get rich. This one's different. Still contracts, but all the profits get funneled into relief, homeless programs, women at risk, and disaster zones. Word is, the guy who owns it is some crazy-rich ghost who doesn't take a paycheck. Just wants to do good."

The other mechanic had chuckled. "Yeah, sounds great. Probably fake."

"Nah, they're real enough. Look 'em up if you want."

James caught the name. Later that night, he looked them up.

He dug into their reputation. The stories. The interviews. The absence of anything flashy or self-promoting.

And then, he reached out.

* * *

It had been nine months since Sarah had spoken to him.

They'd exchanged the occasional text or email, brief check-ins, nothing heavy.

The relationship had retreated to the protection of silence. Like a dog that had been smacked on the nose, still loyal, still watching, but wary.

So, when her phone rang and James' name appeared, she was both happy and nervous.

"Hey, stranger," she answered, trying to keep it light.

They exchanged pleasantries. He sounded good; whole, like he'd finally let the weight fall off without handing it to someone else to carry.

He told her he'd sold the house. That stunned her.

He had grown. This time for real.

Then came the bomb. "Yeah, so… my term's almost up. I'm not re-upping. Taking a job with this little contractor group. They do a lot of good; they reinvest everything into relief projects. Homeless outreach, disaster response, stuff like that. I feel like I can do more good there than I can in uniform."

There was a pause.

"I wanted you to know before it happened."

She had always figured James would be a lifer. The kind of guy who hit twenty years and kept going because the uniform fit too well to take off.

But he sounded different now. Resolved; if this brought him peace, she was glad for him, even if part of her wanted to argue for him to stay in the military.

* * *

Sam had pored over everything for months.

He never found the connections. He never understood why it had been LAX or Flight 2247. Eventually, he'd stumbled on a small clue he thought might lead somewhere: the word *Wrath* had seen a spike in usage. Of course, it exploded after the attack, but there'd been a twenty-five percent bump three weeks prior. Not huge. But enough to chase.

He'd spent a month, maybe more, down that rabbit hole. Nothing to show for it. Maybe the group had intentionally left it there, just enough to waste investigators' time. Or maybe it was just noise.

What he hadn't expected was the silence. Maybe he'd been wrong. Perhaps it was just a random terrorist attack. His gut still told him it wasn't. He still believed the deep state was pulling strings, but the lack of follow-up gnawed at him.

Why stop after one event? Why go dead?

Maybe they'd evaluated and decided it had failed. Or maybe the next move was just too well hidden. It was six months after the attack when he got a standard tracking ping. A pilot likely not re-upping had waited too long to confirm. He always liked to know. Military pilots were good pickups.

Then he saw the name: James Callan.

Sarah's… whatever he was to her, he mattered. And he wasn't just anyone. Only eight years in the cockpit, but flight time like a twelve-year vet. Plus, if Sarah trusted him, that was enough for Sam.

Sam reached out to a contact on base, a mechanic. He told him to find a way to drop the name of the group nearby. It was casual, indirect, and without red flags.

Two days later, James reached out to Sam's contractor company without knowing it.

A few months later, Sam caught a familiar pickup in the subtle channels. The pattern was the same, and the digital footprints were the same. It was time to brace again.

Wrath chatter was climbing. Predictably, with the anniversary coming. But something about it felt colder this time. Quieter. Like breath held in the dark.

Nothing real.

Yet.

TWELVE

Three months later, on the anniversary of the Flight 2247 bombing, tens of thousands turned out for the biggest of the "We Remember" events.

Held at Allegiant Stadium in Las Vegas, it was billed as a fundraiser for the families of victims and others "impacted by the tragedy." But everyone knew what drew the crowd.

The event was hosted by household names, the kind of stars Los Angeles claimed as its own. The lineup promised a once-in-a-lifetime collision of genres, the biggest names in music sharing a single stage. Stadium-filling rock bands played beneath marquee pop idols, all leading to the world's reigning superstar—fresh off another record-shattering global tour. Every seat was full. Outside, the lines still coiled around the blocks, fans desperate just to hear the echoes spill into the night air.

The red carpet felt like Oscar night. Every major name within reach of Southern California made an appearance. Politicians. Celebrities. Musicians. Influencers. All "there for the cause." All live on camera.

When it happened, the concert was already over two hours in. The host cracked a final joke, teased the crowd, and introduced the superstar.

At 8:45 PM, the main headliner walked on stage. The stadium erupted. She waved, smiled, and took her place at center stage. The lights pulsed. Then... something burned through the roof. It didn't draw much attention at first. The cheers were too loud, and the lights too bright. Some, who noticed the bright flash, thought it was part of the show.

Even when people saw the first blazing lights dropped from above, people mistook them for pyrotechnics.

Then the screaming started. The type of screams that froze your blood. That would never leave your mind.

Flames spread across the crowd. Bodies lit up like matches. The stage, engulfed.

There was a sharp cry from the star, one short scream cut off mid-breath... captured on every screen in the stadium.

And then the feed went black.

At the exact moment, 10:45 PM in Houston. The port was still. The day's business was long over. Just the hum of machinery, the clink of metal, and the soft rhythm of waves slapping the docks.

Then... chaos.

From above, a small drone banked silently over the Ship Channel. In a single pass, it dropped a cluster of thermite charges—maybe twenty in total. They hit storage tanks, fuel lines, and valve clusters, and everything ignited.

Where the thermite touched, steel melted. Flames shot thirty feet into the air. Fuel detonated. Chemical tanks erupted. Pipelines burst like overripe fruit. A chain reaction rippled across the terminal. What had been one of the country's most secure, strategic civilian ports became an inferno in seconds.

The night sky turned orange, and the fire kept spreading.

Ten hours later, almost to the minute, a video dropped on X. Split-screen: Vegas and Houston.

Flames. Screams. Silence. Then... black. One word, white letters in the center of the screen:

"Is"

* * *

The call came just after midnight Eastern.

Sarah was still in uniform, sitting on her couch in the dark, television muted, eyes locked on the crawl at the bottom of the screen. When her secure line buzzed, she answered immediately.

"Lieutenant Commander Whitaker. Temporary assignment; Joint Task Force Raven support out of the Pentagon. Pack light. Orders are inbound."

Within fifteen minutes, she was on base at NAS Jax. The brief was short, clipped, and surreal. Two simultaneous attacks, one in Las Vegas and one at the Port of Houston. She was told to wait for further orders and directed to a classified viewing room. There, she was given access to the earliest available footage: ground-level cell phone clips, some overhead video, and one shaky angle from what looked like a local chopper.

She watched silently, her mind moving, filtering, analyzing, sorting chaos into pattern.

Sarah's last few years had been complicated; high performance, strong results, but a stalled track. She'd been stuck at her current O-4 rank longer than expected, shuffled between deployments, caught in limbo with no clear path forward. This felt different. Deliberate. Like someone had pulled her file on purpose.

She got the second call, and within the hour she was on a plane. Temporary assignment to the Pentagon. Joint Task Force support.

When she landed in D.C., the Task Force had already located higher-resolution feeds. Someone had traced the origin of the Vegas drone to a rooftop launch at the Mandalay Bay Hotel, barely a block away from Allegiant Stadium and high enough to provide a clean line of sight. The drone's path was clean, direct, and unwavering. It breached the roof with what appeared to be a microthermite charge just as the popstar stepped onto the stage. The delay was surgical: four seconds of hover then release.

She watched the footage again at Joint Ops, this time in high definition. The star's silhouette against the spotlight. The flash. The fire. The scream. Then blackout.

The drone was recovered mostly intact. The frame was custom, military-style maneuverability, and commercial camouflage. Internals were a mess: burned, scrubbed, and stripped of any traceable hardware. But the drop system had been upgraded. Precision targeting. Multi-point stabilization. Whoever had built it knew what they were doing.

Houston was different.

The damage was immense, but the footage was limited. Most of what they had came from static security feeds. It showed a burst of flashes across the docks, flames licking skyward, and metal melting in place. The few aerial views were smoke-obscured.

Only one video followed the drone clearly: the anonymous post to X, uploaded just before dawn. No name, no account history, just the title "Is." It showed the device banking low over the ship channel, dropping thermite in methodical bursts—one tank, then another, maybe twenty charges in all. Each hit sparked perfectly, controlled and brutal. The video cut to black as the port lit up behind it, flames mirrored in the water, the skyline turning molten orange in silhouette.

The drone was gone with no trace. It could have been abandoned in the bay or retrieved. So far there were no signs of it.

Sarah watched that one, too. Over and over. What disturbed her wasn't just the destruction… it was the intent. Vegas had been personal. Artful. A scalpel. Houston was industrial. Calculated. A hammer. But both… were precise. Timed. Measured. Simultaneous.

For Sarah, the six months that followed felt like trench work: intelligence combing, data sifting, and lead chasing, which led nowhere. Sarah gave everything to it. The Task Force reviewed the footage frame by frame. Analysts broke down the drone design. Linguists and social media scrapers scoured metadata and post history. Nothing stuck.

And yet, the signatures were too familiar.

The video had the same structure, precision, and timing. It was also the same kind of X-posted video, with one haunting difference: this time, the word was "Is." The font was the same, the fade-to-black was the same, and the three-second pause was the same. It mirrored the Flight 2247 video exactly.

She found one anomaly. An uptick in the word *Wrath* across major platforms about three weeks before the first bombing. Enough to be noticeable, but low enough to evade direct detection before the Flight 2247 bombing. A twenty-five percent bump… exactly twenty-five percent. It gave her hope… for about a month but turned out to be another dead end. Or perhaps carefully planned to lead investigators down a path that would go nowhere.

"Is" was harder. Too broad. Too saturated to isolate.

In six months, she came to a single conclusion: This had to be the same group as the 2247 bombing, *Wrath*. They were still out there.

THIRTEEN

Following the sale of his house, he had moved onto base. But after leaving the military, he settled into a tranquil home near Helena Regional Airport in Montana. The company let him live wherever he wanted, as long as he could store a plane at a nearby airport. Helena Regional was perfect. It was home to National Guard air operations, and it offered what he needed without the hassle of a major hub.

The week before the anniversary, he decided to return to Ventura for a candlelight vigil held at Christina's and his old church.

He'd seen the promos, the celebrity lineup, the headlines. Part of him thought about going to the tribute concert. Vegas was a quick trip by air, and his company would've covered the fuel, but the idea of watching a tribute to the dead felt… off. Manufactured. His grief needed peace.

The service was small, held in a chapel in Ventura. Candles lined the front. Christina and Wyatt's names were included on the memorial banner beside dozens of others. The pastor spoke softly about memory, loss, and hope beyond death. James stayed seated long after the service ended, long after the last of the congregation had slipped out into the cool night.

It was nearly midnight when he stepped back into his hotel room.

The TV was on before he could stop himself.

Flames.

Smoke.

He dropped onto the couch, stunned, the remote forgotten in his hand. The footage was poor—cell phone videos, shaky angles—but it was enough. The stadium was a wreckage of fire and smoke. The stage was obliterated, and bodies were burning in the crowd.

And then the headline shifted.

Port of Houston: Simultaneous Attack.

He leaned forward.

Again?

The next morning, the company contacted James. They needed him to fly supplies from various airports nationwide to assist with medical shortages in Las Vegas and critical materials for Houston. By that afternoon, he was already airborne.

The first supply run was to Vegas: water, med kits, spare generators. Then, Houston: wound dressings, fuel, satellite phones. He flew in whatever they needed, whatever they could load, logging hours again like it was wartime. Every time he landed, it was chaos: makeshift command centers, burned-out infrastructure, roads crawling with volunteers and the National Guard.

The rhythm became familiar—load, fly, unload, pray, repeat.

He wasn't wearing a uniform anymore, but the work felt sacred in its own way. He was trying to help people at a time they needed the help the most. Volunteers lined up at the hangars anywhere he landed, sometimes with more heart than training, but James loved the compassion of every volunteer. He taught them how to strap down cargo. Showed them how to balance the weight. Took kids up in the cockpit when asked, let them see the world from above, even just for a moment.

At night, he returned to the silence of his house.

Sometimes, after a run, he'd land just before dawn, peel off his gloves, and sit for hours on the tarmac before driving home. The ache in his chest was still there; he knew it would always stay. But flying helped. The air still made sense.

Once, a young pilot asked why he didn't return full-time, sign on, rejoin the fleet, and put the uniform back on. James only shook his head.

"This is where I'm needed now."

After a few months, the relief flights slowed. He returned to the core work his company usually handled. The job was easy, but he still flew missions, usually to the Middle East, carrying supplies or transporting contractors heading out for their rotations.

It was a very different life from what he had ever imagined. But he enjoyed it all the same.

* * *

Sam hadn't watched the concert live. It wasn't his thing. He'd known something would happen; he could feel it in the pattern shifts, the signals under the noise, but even he hadn't predicted how theatrical it would be.

It wasn't the fireball that shook him. It was the precision.

Within minutes, his secure feeds lit up. Two cities. Two strikes. One moment. Same method, different intent. A public stage incinerated. A port, one of the country's most vital, was reduced to molten metal and shattered pipelines.

Ten hours later, the X video dropped, just like last time. It had the same framing, the same font, and the same deliberate silence before the final flash of white letters.

"Is"

He'd confirmed that the original *Wrath* video wasn't random. The metadata had been clean, but too clean. Artificial. A redacted fingerprint left on purpose. This new one was smarter. Uploaded from inside a spoofed subnet routed through three foreign ISPs and a compromised satellite transponder over the Atlantic.

He didn't know who had filmed it. Like everyone else, he only knew they wanted it seen.

The footage from Vegas showed everything: every drop from the drone, each twist of its path before it punched through the stadium roof. The drone itself was a one-off, custom-built, and its control signature was unfamiliar. It didn't match anything in his offline archive of U.S., Chinese, or Russian designs—not military, not commercial, but something in between.

The stadium drone had been recovered. Mostly slag. Its guidance package was melted, its motors fused. But someone had worked on it and refined it. Sam spotted a unique cooling shunt design tucked near the rear armature. It shouldn't have worked. But it had. He would've given anything to get his hands on it, but he couldn't.

Houston's drone was never found—only the trail it left behind and the video.

"Every drop," he muttered, watching it again, not for the first time… and not the last. The thermite had been deployed with such control and spacing. No human pilot could've managed it, not like that. It had to be algorithmic. Pre-programmed with target overlays and reaction conditions. Like a scalpel.

He noticed Sarah had been reassigned. He didn't interfere. Not this time. She needed the chase. So did he. In the end, they both came up empty. No trail. No face. Just smoke. No chatter on the encrypted boards. No fingerprints on the tech. The media swirled with theories: foreign plots, radical cells, rogue insiders. Sam didn't believe any of them. *Wrath*, if that's what this was, didn't operate like terrorists. They didn't crave fame. They didn't release manifestos. They struck with purpose, then disappeared.

Sam knew how to look deeper. The three weeks before the original 2247 explosion, usage of *Wrath* had spiked… not by much, but enough. The kind of microtrend that people miss. He had thought it a coincidence. Now he wasn't sure. Before this latest hit, there was nothing. But afterward, the same post-pattern emerged. It was like someone whispering through the code. But "Is"? That was harder. It was everywhere. It meant too much to too many. How do you search for a whisper in a crowd of echoes?

By month six, the Task Force Sarah had been attached to had nothing left to chase—no real evidence. No suspects. No group had claimed it. Officially, the case was open, but unofficially, it was cold.

Sam knew the enemy was waiting.

And so was he.

* * *

As the leads dried up, the Task Force was reduced in size and scope, as it became very clear there was little to be found. One by one, those temporarily assigned were sent back to their regular duty stations with advice to be ready to be back if any further data surfaced. Sarah found herself heading back to NAS Jax, frustrated. She felt like there was more, but the Task Force, meant to unjam information, was a logjam.

Sarah's return to NAS Jax was just a reassignment memo, a return to her old office, and the discreet thrum of routine. It was mid-August when the orders came through, nearly ten months since the twin attacks. She was rotated off the Joint Task Force at the Pentagon with polite appreciation and a vague promise to be kept in the loop.

Sarah would continue working on any leads she could find and reviewing everything the Task Force allowed her to see. But Trish had other plans.

She appeared outside Sarah's office before she'd even had time to boot her computer, grinning like she'd won something. In her hands was a small paper gift bag decorated in glittery pink flamingos and sun-faded hibiscus flowers.

"Welcome back to the land of humidity and questionable cafeteria coffee," Trish said, offering the bag like a ceremonial relic.

Sarah looked at it, then at her. "Should I be worried?"

"Oh, definitely. I almost kept it for myself."

Inside was a gaudy plastic cat figurine—the motion-sensor kind with the waving paw—and a handwritten note tucked underneath: "Too sharp to be Pentagon safe."

Sarah snorted a proper, caught-off-guard snort that made Trish beam with pride.

"Don't say I never gave you anything," Trish added, already backing out the door.

It was stupid and small and oddly perfect.

FOURTEEN

Sarah started the day like any other Thursday. Early. Restrained. With the kind of Florida heat that clung to your skin before the sun even crested the trees: wet, slow, and building.

She'd been in the office since six, clearing reports, reviewing message traffic, trying to stay ahead of the wave she was sure was coming. *Wrath* had been silent for months, but the silence felt unnatural now, like the last breath before something cracked.

She told herself the calm was good, that it meant the country was holding, but she knew the riots continued, the unrest at having no real group to blame simmered.

The door creaked open behind her.

"I brought a bribe," Trish said, stepping inside with a cardboard carrier of iced coffee. "And before you say it, yes… It's the real stuff. From base Starbucks, not that gas station espresso water you pretend to like."

Sarah looked up. "What did I do to deserve that?"

Trish smirked. "Nothing. But I need you in a good mood before I poke the bear."

Sarah narrowed her eyes. "What kind of bear?"

Trish dropped into the chair across from her. "Heard James relocated to Montana."

That landed just hard enough.

"Flying a fancy LM-100J now," Trish continued. "Civilian side. Contractor gig. Low-profile company, top-level access. Rumor is the thing's a beast; sleek, fast, and customized like you wouldn't believe. Not a bad gig if you can get it."

Sarah continued to watch her, knowing she would get to her point eventually.

Trish leaned back and studied her. "You know this is probably your only window to get a break. After the anniversary, you're going to be buried again. It could be months before you see daylight."

"I'm fine."

"You're stalling."

Sarah's voice cooled. "I have work."

"You always have work. That's your shield. I'm just saying… It's been almost two years. You haven't seen him. Haven't talked to him. But you are always thinking about him. Maybe it's time."

Sarah picked up her coffee, and just held it. "It's not that simple."

"It never is," Trish said. "But that doesn't mean it's wrong."

She stood. "If you're going to crash, do it somewhere under the radar. Take a weekend. Breathe. Go see him. You never know when that option's going to disappear."

She smirked. "And hey… worst case? A couple nights of guilt-free Montana sex, cause you know… what happens in Montana no one ever cares about… You could do worse."

She left the coffee and walked out without waiting for an answer.

Sarah sat alone, fingers around the condensation-slick cup, heartbeat steady but heavier now.

A few minutes later, she opened her email. She searched his name. And she stared at the blinking cursor.

* * *

James was still in awe of the LM-100J.

Months earlier, the company had contacted him directly, asking him to bring his C-130 to their central hub in Grand Junction, Colorado, a small but well-positioned base nestled against the Rockies and close enough to western supply lines. Far enough from scrutiny.

The company was medium-sized—maybe ten planes in the air at any given time, under a thousand employees total—but it moved like a unit twice its size.

He'd expected a routine inspection. Maybe some upgrades. Instead, when he landed, he was greeted on the tarmac by a young woman he only half-recognized: Mary. They'd exchanged a few emails. He could not recall her title, but her stance said she, like most employees of the company, was a trained and dangerous person.

She shook his hand briskly. "So, we've had a couple of new hires recently," she said. "And since you're one of our more senior and most active pilots, the company's decided to reassign your bird to one of the new guys and give you something a little… newer."

She led him into a hangar. And there it was. A brand-new LM-100J, gleaming under the overhead lights like a gift.

James stopped cold. He'd seen the specs and heard stories. To his knowledge, Lockheed had only ever produced five. But this… this was his first time seeing one in person. This was brand new off the production line, so the company had to order it from Lockheed.

"You're kidding," he said under his breath.

Mary smiled. "Welcome to the upgrade."

He'd only flown a handful of missions in the new bird; supply drops, logistical runs, a run to the Middle East and back. But the plane itself was incredible. It felt like the C-130J he'd flown for over a decade; just clean, tight, nimble, and fast. FAA regulations were strict; civilian aircraft couldn't carry active defense systems like flares or ECM suites. The plane lacked the armor of its C-130J sister, which led to the improved control. The default avionics package was similar to a long-range commercial freighter.

But the upgrades this one had? They were subtle. Integrated. It flew like a C-130J tuned for instinct. Everything was more responsive, more fluid. More alive.

Then came the notice: a crew would arrive for a "routine" inspection.

James had logged maybe fifty hours in the aircraft. He was surprised, he knew an inspection would happen early in the flight hours, but fifty seemed overly cautious. However, the company had likely sunk $150 million into the plane, handed it to him with no strings, let him park it where he wanted, and even positioned a co-pilot close enough to fly regularly with him. It made sense they'd want to ensure their investment was being maintained.

He expected four or maybe five people to inspect systems, likely just sweeping through the avionics suite and the maintenance logs. What showed up was a thirty-person crew and a mobile operations rig the size of a food truck, for a "routine" inspection.

James swung by the airport a week later to check on the progress. He was expecting they would be wrapping up and wanted a quick walk-through to see how things were going. But what he found looked more like a pre-deployment tear-down than a civilian maintenance check. The crew was deep into every system: hydraulics, avionics, and engine bays. Panels off, diagnostic rigs running. He'd have thought the aircraft was heading into a combat zone.

He stood near the nose of the plane, chatting with the lead mechanic about the timeline.

"She's solid," the man said. "Should be ready for flight testing by midweek. But we've still got work to do on the environmental control and some custom wiring. Not exactly off-the-shelf gear."

James nodded, only half listening now. His attention had shifted. Someone was walking toward the hangar—a woman. And in the backlight of the open bay, he recognized her.

Sarah.

He froze.

He broke from the conversation and started walking, fast at first, then slowing, wondering if he was really seeing what he was seeing. His smile grew with every step.

She looked different. The same. Tired, maybe. Or maybe he hadn't seen her in so long that memory had softened the edges.

"Sarah?" he called out, almost laughing the word.

* * *

Sarah's stomach clenched. This might've been a mistake. She had wanted to call him, but in the end decided not to, so James had no idea she was going to show up. She had landed, rented a car, thrown her bag in the backseat and drove to the hangar. She still heard the last words they'd thrown at each other almost two years ago. Remembered walking out of his house without so much as a word.

The grief had torn them both raw. Christina and Wyatt. Even Will. That night... it had been a moment that was bound to happen. Will had been right, she had placed James over her own husband in the moment and that choice had most certainly been the final straw for Will. She felt the weight that night and had pushed James just the right way to get the reaction she had long regretted getting.

She stood in the middle of the hangar, her heart pounding, her windbreaker sticking to her arms. The hum of equipment, the clank of tools—it all felt distant, muffled by the rush of blood in her ears.

She hadn't known what to expect. Seeing him smiling at her, walking, almost jogging toward her was certainly something she had wanted but was unprepared for. She froze in the moment with a terrible hope rising in her. She tried to smile and failed.

"Hi," she said—subdued. Useless. But it was all she had.

And then... he was there, right in front of her. Before she could say anything else, before she could brace for whatever this was going to be, he wrapped his arms around her. It was real, solid and she felt loved.

She embraced the moment, relief coursed through her as she pressed her face to his shoulder, breathing in grease and cold mountain air. His arms wrapped around her like they'd never let go. For a second, she let herself believe that everything had led back to this.

Her throat tightened. A tear slipped free before she could blink it back.

"Hey," he said, his voice low, warm. "Took you long enough."

She almost laughed, almost hit him. *You could've come too,* she wanted to say. *You knew where I was.* But all that came out was a half sob, half laugh.

"Yeah," she said. "I know."

He held her until she let go of him. She stepped back, wiping her eye with a fast brush of her hand, like maybe he wouldn't notice. She was sure he did, but he let it pass. Instead, he nodded toward the truck.

"Come on. You hungry?"

She hesitated. Then nodded. "Starving."

The conversation on the drive was muted, only a few questions on how each was doing. A couple of wrong turns gave them something to joke about. She teased him about the state of his truck. He teased her about still walking like she was bracing for a promotion review board. In that strange way, it was easy when things were broken too long to be brittle anymore.

The place was small and smelled like maple syrup and fresh coffee. It had worn floors, mismatched chairs, and a waitress who smiled like she already knew them and called them both 'Hun'. It was the kind of café only locals came to.

Sarah slid into the booth as if she were still nervous to be there. James sat across from her, arms resting on the table, letting the silence stretch.

She finally looked up. "This feels weird."

He raised an eyebrow. "The café?"

"No. You and me. In the same place again. After everything," she said, rolling her eyes. He knew what she meant.

James leaned back and let out a slow breath. "We were always going to end up back here. Well, not Montana, but together. Sooner or later."

The waitress brought menus and coffee. Sarah stared at hers, unsure whether to drink it or hold onto it for stability. After a beat, she wrapped both hands around the mug and breathed it in, like it gave her permission to exist.

"You look good," he said, finally, and meant it.

She glanced up, surprised. "You too. Lighter."

"Montana'll do that."

They ordered: him, the omelet; her, toast and eggs. The talk stayed on safe ground. She asked about the plane and his flying schedule. He asked about Trish and the new command structure down at Jax. Their words tiptoed around the grief.

When their food came, she finally smiled. "I didn't think I'd be able to eat."

"You always could," he said, grinning. "You just forget until it's in front of you."

That made her laugh. A small one. Real. And just like that, the nerves vanished and she felt like she was home again.

The coffee was warm. The eggs were decent. And for a moment, it felt like the world had paused.

James seemed so much happier than Sarah had ever known him. It was good to see he had actually let go of things. He had stopped carrying around all the hurt. She doubted it was gone, just no longer holding him down.

FIFTEEN

She caught something outside the window as they sat there, enjoying awkward silences and coffee just slightly better than the coffee on base. Two dark SUVs rolled up across the street. Tinted windows. Purposely discreet. Government-like, but not government tags. Three men and a woman got out. Two men stepped into guard positions while the woman walked into the restaurant and held the door until the 3rd man walked in after her. Sarah was sure they were not government; they had to be contractors.

The man was older, maybe fifty, wiry but moved like he was nineteen, easy and full of energy. His clothing was perfectly pressed and looked expensive. He walked like he was listening to music or dancing. A couple of fast steps followed by a slow step or two, and then fast again. His head stayed steady, facing forward, but his eyes roved everywhere. The casualness of his entrance was a strange flip from the seriousness his three guards carried. He never acknowledged his guards, almost as if he was unaware they were there. But Sarah suspected he was aware of every detail of every moment in a way normal people never were. Once inside, he glanced around like he was looking for a friend. James turned around to see what Sarah had been staring at.

"Wow," he breathed. "How do they know I am here?"

The man crossed the café without acknowledging a single other person. Straight toward their table.

James set his mug down. Slowly. The man stopped beside them, nodded once, and looked straight at Sarah.

"Hi, Sarah," he said, tone easy. Familiar. "Mind if I join you?"

Sarah blinked, confused that James seemed to know who these people were and yet the man had addressed her not him. The man looked at her calmly. The calmness felt measured, calculated, like someone who already knew the answer to the question he'd just asked.

The woman at the door stood, unmoving but appearing to nearly be floating. Trim, composed, she stood watch like she had a job to do and had already done it. Sarah turned toward James, but he was already looking at the man. He cleared his throat, eyes still on the stranger.

"Sarah… this is… what, the owner? …Of my company."

The man offered his hand like it was the most natural thing in the world. "Sam Jameson." Sam smiled slightly. It was meant to be kind, but felt practiced. Then he gestured toward the booth. "We should talk."

Sam didn't waste time.

"You booked a flight," he said, voice low but even. "I saw you were not very far away, so I thought I would meet you. You showing up here gave me a rare chance. A good one."

He glanced once at James, then back to her.

"I've known about you a long time, Sarah."

She stiffened. His expression remained unchanged, but the movement from his eyes told her he noticed.

"I pushed for your appointment to the Academy. Had to work around a few people who didn't think you were the right fit. But I knew you were."

Sarah said nothing. Her brain was running three speeds behind her pulse.

"I've trusted people to pass you pieces. But I also knew I couldn't keep doing it forever, not without you and eventually everyone, questioning everything. Sooner or later, the silence would turn into suspicion." He let that sit.

"I'm here because I don't want that. I want you to know who's been on the other end of the line. Who lined up the helicopter. Who sent Roland, and I need you to trust that when something comes through, it's not noise or misdirection."

James was watching, half-alert, half-intrigued.

Sam's gaze softened just slightly. "I trust you. I trust him too," he added with a nod to James, "but you; I've watched you long enough to know your character."

Her throat was dry. Every part of her screamed to ask a thousand questions, but her instincts told her that was precisely what he expected. He'd answer each one as deliberately as he'd planned this meeting.

Sam reached into his coat pocket and pulled out a receipt. It was folded once and worn just enough to show it wasn't fresh off a printer. He slid it across the table, barely brushing her hand.

"You're smart. You'll figure it out."

Sarah unfolded it slowly. It was a Starbucks receipt. From the airport. Her airport. The same café she'd stopped at before the flight. Same coffee. Exact name on the order. Same timestamp. Her stomach dropped.

He hadn't been bluffing. He hadn't just found her. He'd been tracking her, step by step.

"Just a little proof," Sam said, flatly. "That I see you. That I've seen you. For a long time." He paused. "You're important to me, Sarah. And important to God."

Then he turned to go.

The woman was already holding the door.

"Start with this: search social. Track usage of the word *coming*." He paused halfway across the room, turning back. "You're smart, you will figure it out."

Then he turned and walked out.

Sarah stared at the receipt in her hand as if it might have burned through the skin. James leaned back in the booth and exhaled slowly.

"I was told he was eccentric," he said, tone dry. "Starting to think that's not quite the right word."

Sarah gave him a look, but the corner of her mouth twitched. The tension eased slightly.

James glanced at her.

"So, where are you staying?"

She hesitated. "I booked a hotel. Just something nearby."

He raised an eyebrow.

"A hotel? Nah. You should stay at my place."

She blinked. "Are you sure?"

He smiled that gentle, grounded James kind of smile.

"Plenty of room," he said, the corners of his eyes crinkling. "You won't believe what you can buy up here for what I got from selling my parents' house." He paused, just long enough for the moment to carry weight. "And I promise… no yelling this time."

Sarah laughed, shoulders easing. "No yelling," she agreed. "Not this time."

James took her back to the hangar first, insisting she at least see the plane before they headed out. The sun was fully up now, streaking across the aluminum skin of the LM-100J like someone had buffed it with gold.

He walked her through every detail like he was showing off a classic car. New paneling. Custom systems. The way she moved in crosswinds. The absurdly smooth landings. He spoke with a veiled affection that reminded her of who he'd always been: someone who noticed the small things. Who cared more about the mission than the medals.

They grabbed lunch at a diner in town—one of those places where no matter what you order, it will be great, as long as it was a burger. They talked easily. Nothing heavy. Just life. What it had been. What it had become. How the world felt now—crooked, off-kilter, and barely holding on.

Sarah had missed this, the bond between them was still easy after all this time. The way he looked at her, like the ground steady under their feet had never changed in all these years.

When they pulled up to the house, she was surprised by how normal it all felt: a long gravel driveway, a wide porch with creaking wood, wind through the trees. It was just a home built for someone who finally wanted to live.

"So," he said, parking the truck. "Welcome to Montana."

She smiled. "Thanks for the detour."

James grabbed her bag from the back. "Let me show you the guest room. You'll have the whole wing."

She raised an eyebrow. "There's a wing?"

He just grinned. "Told you. California money goes a long way up here."

They stayed in that night. James grilled steaks out back while the breeze rolled off the hills, dry and cool. Sarah stayed in the dining room, watching him through the screen door; tongs in one hand, drink in the other, grinning at the flames like he was still twenty and they had just met. Twelve years now, and a lifetime of problems through both their lives. And still this felt like it had always been here.

Dinner was simple but perfect: steak, grilled corn, and roasted potatoes. It was the kind of meal you only made for someone who mattered.

They ate outside. Just wind and conversation.

"So," she said after a while, "what do you know about your employer?"

James leaned back in his chair. "Not much, honestly. Ex-NSA, I think. Might be pushing billionaire status, but lives like a ghost somewhere in Alaska. Big house."

Sarah blinked. "That's… not unsettling at all."

He laughed. "Yeah. The only person I've ever seen face-to-face is Mary; she's the one who held the door. And even then, barely. A couple of emails before that. She met me at the hangar, handed me the plane keys like I'd won a contest."

"Why stay with it?"

James thought for a second. "Because they keep doing good. Disaster relief. Missing persons. Medical supply runs. I don't know how much money he pours into it, but I've seen what it does. It's worth it."

Sarah leaned forward, elbows on the table. "You ever think we'd end up like this? Montana. Peaceful. Still breathing."

James smiled faintly. "I used to think I'd never make it past thirty."

She looked over at him calmly. "Yeah. Me too."

A pause stretched between them, full of everything they hadn't said in years. Grief. Distance. Regret. The pieces they'd held onto, and the ones they lost.

They sat silently for a long moment, the quiet between them filled with comfort.

"You seem lighter," she said eventually.

"I am," he said. "Not because it hurts less. Just... I know who I am. Maybe for the first time."

She turned to face him. "And who's that?"

He met her eyes. "Someone who still loves you."

Sarah reached for his hand. Held it. Let it be enough for tonight.

The morning came peacefully.

Sarah woke at sunrise, the kind of early that arrived unplanned but welcomed her anyway. Montana light filtered through gauzy curtains, pale and gold. For a minute, she just sat on the edge of the guest bed, barefoot, heart full.

The house was still. Just the soft creak of the floorboards as she padded toward the kitchen.

She found eggs. Bread. Some overripe peaches on the counter. There wasn't much else in the kitchen, but it was enough. She'd eaten worse on deployment. A quick breakfast took shape: scrambled eggs, toast, and a pan of sliced peaches caramelized in butter.

James stepped into the kitchen mid-yawn, hair tousled, bare feet on tile.

"Well, that's a sight," he said, voice rough with sleep.

Sarah smiled over her shoulder. "Don't get used to it."

He grinned, grabbed two mugs, and poured coffee without asking if she wanted any. Of course she did. They ate quietly, both of them too comfortable to fill the silence. It was familiar, almost like they'd done this a hundred times.

When they finished, James washed the plates while she dried. He looked over. "Still need to get you back to the hangar."

"Yeah. Car's there." She hesitated. "I wish I could have stayed longer."

"I know," he said. "I want you to stay longer."

On the drive, James asked, "So, what are you up to these days?"

"Working the *Wrath* cases," she said lightly, "But I feel like I run into another logjam every move I make. The whole idea of these Task Forces is that we work together and share everything, but it all feels so… filtered."

The road curved along a low ridge, morning mist clinging to the trees. When the hangar came into view, Sarah felt something tighten in her chest.

James pulled in beside her rental and left the engine running.

She turned to him. "Thanks. For everything."

He looked at her for a long beat. "Don't let it be another two years."

She looked back at him and said, softly, "I never stopped loving you either."

She leaned in. Kissed his cheek. "Now don't make me regret saying that."

And then she was out, bag slung over one shoulder, the smell of peaches still on her fingers as she walked to the car.

When Sarah returned to base, the first thing she did before she even unpacked was run the search. Not just once, but through three different intel tools, each parsing the last 72 hours of social media chatter across public and private datasets.

Sam had been right. The word *coming* had spiked by twenty-five percent, the same as before the first attack. Same usage patterns. The same regions were lighting up. Different tone, though. Darker. Sharper. She tracked it to when it started. Three weeks before the anniversary…

She flagged it, logged the spike, and passed it up the chain. The alerts ticked higher—just slightly—enough to shift posture without raising alarms.

A few days later, Trish dropped by as usual, coffee in hand and smirk in place.

"So," she said, drawing out the word like it had a hidden story, "how was he? I mean it. As big and rugged as I think? I mean, Montana."

Sarah blinked. Then shrugged, half-humoring her. "Montana is beautiful," she said plainly. "James is doing well." Her voice was even, measured, trying to answer clearly, seriously. She knew better than to argue. If Trish had decided something had happened, then in her mind, it had. Anything Sarah said now would only sound like denial. So she left it there.

SIXTEEN

A few weeks later, the lead technician connected with James and let him know the plane would officially be ready to fly the next day. Mary was waiting at the hangar when James arrived. She greeted him with a clipboard and a smile, as if everything was perfectly normal.

"Some additional systems were brought online during the maintenance cycle," she said. "Let me walk you through them."

She showed him each of the new upgrades. Most of it had been dormant before; flagged as pending or under development. Now it was all live. The AI co-pilot was sleek, responsive, almost anticipating his inputs—like the next generation of flight assist systems, years ahead of what he'd trained on. The tracking systems were more precise than anything he'd flown with—systems that felt like they belonged on classified aircraft, not a civilian freighter. This likely crossed a line for the FAA, which he guessed was why it had been offline.

Most of it, he realized, had to be custom work—integrated off the books, without waiting for regulators. Risky, but brilliant. And it worked.

James glanced around the cockpit one more time, still amazed. The systems felt sharper now. Alive in a way he could feel, even if the technology was beyond him.

He turned to Mary. "Just how many of these planes did the company order?"

"Five."

He raised a brow. "Are they all like this?"

Mary gave a quick laugh. "Heavens no."

"Then why is this one?"

She hesitated for just a second, enough to let the air shift. "He said you're important. And that you're important to Sarah. And Sarah… is important to him."

James sat with that for a moment.

"He wanted you safe," she added. "As safe as he could make you."

James looked back at the controls and then out through the windshield toward the hangar doors. Sharp, clear morning light spilled in, catching on every sleek surface like a spotlight.

For years, he'd flown for people who barely knew his name. In the military, you were more a number than a name. Now, someone had gone to extraordinary lengths, because of who he was and who he mattered to. That did something to a man. He thumbed the harness latch and sat back momentarily, letting it all settle.

James had thought of Sam as some cold, calculating mind moving pieces on a board. Maybe, James thought, he was just a man who never quite learned how to act around people. A man who cared in the only way he knew how.

James gave a faint smile. "Well," he murmured, "guess I better live up to the investment."

* * *

The evening before the anniversary, the Task Force, along with various heads of departments across nearly every branch of law enforcement and military, briefed the Joint Chiefs. The briefing was short, tense, and measured.

120

Across the secure line, senior officials from each major base and agency reported readiness levels, threat conditions, and intel gaps. The tone was serious, facts shared at a brisk but organized pace.

Near the end, Sarah's name came up.

"Lieutenant Commander Whitaker, US Navy Intelligence, identified a linguistic anomaly three weeks ago, a widespread increase in the use of the word *coming* across social platforms. A twenty-five percent rise, sustained."

Someone on the call muttered, "Still no link?"

"No. That's the thing," the briefer said. "No coordination, no central pattern, no traceable source. It's not coming from new accounts, bots, or foreign actors. It's ordinary users. Different states, different ages, different beliefs. All posting it."

A beat of silence.

Someone added, "If it weren't so persistent, we might call it a coincidence."

But nobody said it was.

The next morning, Sarah was awake earlier than usual.

She had slept poorly, too many half-formed thoughts bouncing around in her head, but she was at the office before six. The sun hadn't fully risen, and the base was still nearly lifeless, but tension filled her every muscle. It felt like holding your breath as you watched a vase falling off the counter.

She reviewed the briefing again, reading and re-reading the same lines, and watching the timestamps on her screen tick by.

At 8:03, Trish walked in, holding two cups of Starbucks and wearing that unbothered smirk she always saved for moments that needed cutting through.

"Morning," she said. "Figured you'd already poisoned yourself with the office sludge. Thought I'd save your stomach and your soul."

Sarah reached for the cup without looking up. "Reloading already."

"Atta girl."

The Task Force meetings dominated her day. They were held every two hours and reported the same thing: no new developments, leads, or threats they could act on—just the same steady hum of unease.

Tension thickened as the hours wore on. She could feel it in the hallways, in the clipped conversations, and in the sideways glances. Social media was flooded with speculation, fear, and jittery countdowns.

Many businesses had closed for the day, not by mandate but by choice. Streets were muted, and offices were empty. Even without a new attack, whoever was behind the last ones had already left their mark. The country held its breath.

The secure conference room at NAS Jax was cold and hushed, lit only by the glow of wall-mounted screens and the soft blue light from embedded table consoles. Sarah sat at the far end, eyes fixed on the Pentagon video feed. The room was full of familiar faces, senior analysts, and command staff, all gathered for the final anniversary readiness briefing.

The latest update had just wrapped. Sarah sat motionless, back straight, watching the Pentagon feed as chatter filled the room. Someone from Homeland dismissed the earlier social media findings.

"We've seen the *coming* spike flatten out. There's no clustering, no account overlap, and it hasn't risen again in the last 48 hours. It could just be… linguistic drift. A cultural echo."

She thought, *flatten out. It had been flat for three weeks, not 48 hours—flat and twenty-five percent higher than expected.*

Someone else chimed in. "Anniversary effect. People reflect. Get dramatic online. Doesn't mean it's a signal."

Sarah wanted to scream at them. She just stared at the screen, jaw tight. She knew what she'd seen. A twenty-five percent jump in usage, across unrelated users, across platforms. Not bots. Not AI-generated spam. Real people. Real patterns.

Then, the Pentagon connection flashed and died. Voices shifted from debate to alarm. Analysts scrambled. Systems reset. Everyone trying to determine if it was a technical failure or something else.

"What just happened?" someone whispered.

Someone still connected started reading out the alerts, likely hitting every person's devices that were still connected to the call. "Seattle: mass grid failure. Entire metro offline."

"Detroit: under attack. Drone barrage. Multiple explosions reported downtown."

"Grand Ole Opry: blast confirmed. Civilian event ongoing. Mass casualty potential."

After a pause, the person speaking to someone else not directly connected to the call said, "This can't be right. Are you certain?"

The reply sounded drained of life, "Pentagon: internal explosion. Multiple leadership casualties. Source unknown."

Within minutes, other reports started to flood in from various agencies.

A chill ran down her spine as she pulled up secondary feeds. Static. Flicker. Then visuals. Detroit. Nashville. Seattle. And the Pentagon. Live video feeds only from Detroit and Nashville.

Sarah's hands tightened around the console edge. She felt sick. She had seen it coming. And still… it came. She thought about Sam. He had been right and freely given her the information. He was either part of it, or truly trying to help.

What followed was chaos. Hours of conflicting reports, power failures, and agency infighting. Secure lines jammed. Flights grounded. A dozen city centers went into lockdown. Governors called emergency sessions. The FAA suspended all non-military air traffic. In Seattle, New York, and Chicago, National Guard deployments began immediately; just a show of presence, to prevent mass riots or looting. It was the first time citizens had seen camo on street corners in those cities in decades.

Governors across the country declared states of emergency. In Florida, Louisiana, and Arizona, National Guard units were mobilized to support overwhelmed emergency operations. Texas began rapid deployments to protect key infrastructure. California's governor held an impromptu press conference at 9:45 PM PST, calling the situation "a test of our national resilience," and urging calm.

The Department of Homeland Security activated continuity-of-government protocols. Senior officials were relocated to secure locations. Several Cabinet members were unreachable, either in lockdown or confirmed missing.

The markets stayed closed the next morning. Despite the local, county, and National Guard presence, looting and riots started and showed no signs of slowing.

By midnight, the financial sector was bracing for the worst. Banks froze transactions in affected zones to prevent cyber bleed or further attacks, and train service was suspended along the eastern corridor.

The President was noticeably missing and social media started to light up with speculation he had been killed. Networks ran nonstop coverage, and local stations struggled to keep up. News tickers were filled with rumor and speculation, and fear blanketed the nation like fog.

Then, ten hours after the attacks, a video dropped on X.

Four side-by-side frames. Pentagon. Grand Ole Opry. Downtown Detroit. Seattle's skyline. Each scene was crisp. Silent. Until the final frame cut to black, and a single word appeared:

Coming

The video of the Pentagon was the most chilling. Due to the intensity of the blast, it was unclear who, or what, had filmed it. But the angle left no doubt: the footage came from inside the room where the explosion occurred.

At the White House, the press secretary made a brief, cautious statement just after 10 AM, finally acknowledging "an evolving situation with national implications." By then, nearly every major network openly questioned the administration's silence. Even international outlets had begun running headlines speculating on U.S. leadership paralysis.

By 11:30 AM, more than fourteen hours after the first strike, the President finally stepped behind the podium. He carried himself with presidential calm, but his eyes looked weary from the strain. The tension in his body showed in the mechanical precision of his movements. Each word landed like its own sentence—rehearsed, deliberate, and uncomfortable to hear. The delay had already defined the headlines; now, the speech must fight to reclaim the narrative.

"This was not a failure of intelligence," he said. "This was a calculated act of terrorism. Cowardly. Coordinated. We will not rest until those responsible are found and brought to justice."

Sarah didn't watch the whole speech. She was already back at her console, having gotten a few hours' sleep on base.

SEVENTEEN

In a cold room beneath the Alaskan permafrost, Sam watched the footage on a six-panel display; four panes on loop, one showing each attack site, one tracking national power infrastructure, and one displaying a rapidly updating social media trend index.

He leaned forward, elbows on his desk, jaw set. They hadn't just wanted to kill. They wanted to ignite. He could feel the tremors already beginning. Public rage. Calls for vengeance. Speculation about who to blame. The right target wouldn't matter. Only that there was one.

He tapped a single command. Reroute fallback nodes. Activate secure redundancies. Flag all underground transit prep centers for review. They had months. Maybe.

"I need new routes," he said, restrained. "New identities. More lift capacity. And cold storage; we'll need more of that, too."

He knew what was coming. Not another attack. A war. Not civil. Not clean. But internal. Brutal. Directed. And someone, somewhere, was already building the story to justify it.

Sam stood, stretching his back, and looked to the far corner where a digital board flashed a single word in red:

STANDBY

* * *

James had spent the anniversary at home. The house felt warm and inviting, at least to him. A woman might've added more color, but the rustic furnishings suited him perfectly. The worn leather sofa was still the most comfortable place he knew.

He'd decided to spend the day reading, an enjoyment he wanted to make a habit, and avoided turning on the TV or opening a browser. Anything connected to the outside world would be a hammer blow of reminders. Christina had wanted him to move on, had made him promise he would. Reminders of the first attack, now two years in the past, would only hold him back.

So, he sat in his home, tearing through The Screwtape Letters by C.S. Lewis in a single sitting. The book wasn't long, but it carried a certain intensity that made devouring it in one day a challenge. Through a series of fictional letters, Lewis painted the world of demons with vivid imagery and unsettling clarity. Not that James fully agreed with the premise of "young" and "old" demons; he believed they were simply the fallen angels mentioned in Genesis, the ones who had rebelled. Still, it was a good read. Christina had always told him he needed to read it someday. The anniversary felt like the right day.

So the next morning, it was both a surprise and not that the world had fallen into chaos. Of course, there had been another attack. Everyone knew it was coming. He woke just late enough to catch the news: the next cryptic word had dropped, completing the phrase.

Coming… Wrath is coming…

He stared at the screen and exhaled slowly. *If wrath was still coming, what had the last two years been?*

Was there an organization with that much power and that many people? One capable of orchestrating all this destruction and still implying the worst was yet to come?

James was at the hangar by 8 AM, and his copilot was already waiting. He'd called him before leaving the house and told him to be ready to fly as soon as they got clearance. The FAA had grounded everything, but as a military contractor, the company would likely get approval for aid flights into affected zones.

Three days earlier, the company, *well, Sam, let's be honest*, had already loaded the plane with emergency medical supplies, anticipating the need. It was a matter of time before they were given the green light.

Detroit was his expectation. Maybe Nashville. But from what he'd heard, Detroit was worse off.

By 9 AM, they were airborne, heading, as expected, to Detroit.

The weeks that followed blurred into a relentless rhythm of flights: a rotating crew, constant takeoffs and landings, endless drops of medical supplies, emergency shelter materials, donated goods, clothing, books, food, and water. Everything you'd expect to see sent into a war-torn country was being dropped right here, inside the United States.

Not just into the initial blast zones, but to Portland, New York, Austin, Los Angeles; cities where impatience, fear, and a growing sense of doom had sparked mass riots and fresh devastation. Fires burned. Supply chains cracked. Civil order buckled under the weight of something bigger than any one attack. With no threat to direct hostility at, the country was coming apart.

* * *

Sarah almost felt like the SCIF should have changed, like the world had, but it was the same. The air was dry, recycled, and carried the stale mix of burnt coffee and sweat. The coffee always seemed three hours old, and it tasted like ash. The carpet was still worn nearly to the concrete.

She'd spent most of the last three weeks here since returning from her too-brief time with James. This windowless room, watching social feeds and fragmented datasets tick upward; noise, people had suggested, until the attack.

Three weeks ago, she'd spotted the pattern. Sam had nudged her toward it, but she'd been the one to run the checks and push it up the chain—a twenty-five percent spike in the word *Coming*, the same signal that had preceded *wrath*. Homeland had brushed it off as "linguistic drift."

That dismissal still burned. Especially now.

In the hours after the attacks, her SCIF overflowed. Someone upstairs had routed secondary personnel. Suddenly, she was running the room, fielding orders from people who didn't even know where the new chain of command began.

Trish kept the back end alive, patching partial data from downed systems, re-establishing links with damaged nodes, and manually flagging social chatter even when the AI filters were missing.

Sarah slept in ninety-minute shifts for the first three days. She crashed on the small couch in her office, wringing every spare minute for work. She was fully focused, and when she had a conversation, it was about the attacks or intel they had located. When someone finally referenced her report, the one about *Coming*, it was just a footnote. She had been right, but people would soon find a way for her to be wrong and right at the same moment, just to cover themselves.

Her promotion came on the eighth day. Just past 0200.

A sealed side room; technically still within the SCIF. The signal scrubber was humming low.

A man waited behind the desk. Nice black suit, distinctly not military.

"Sarah Whitaker."

"Commander Whitaker," she corrected reflexively, then frowned. She wasn't a commander.

He slid a folder across the desk. "You're being promoted. Effective immediately."

"Why?"

"Because the last person in your new seat is dead."

His voice was flat and held an edge that told her he was done answering questions.

"Clearance is already upgraded. You'll transfer by week's end. Provisional Joint Task Force. Small footprint. Discreet location."

She opened the folder. A single line stared back: JTF RAVEN – NODE THREE

Location: Classified

As Sarah boarded her transport, she caught a glimpse of Trish boarding a different transport. Sarah found a seat, dropped her bag at her feet, and settled in for a long flight west. She figured everyone on board was going to the same unknown location, somewhere west of Florida.

They landed in Yuma. She'd been here once, years ago. It had been less busy. Today, it was bustling with activity as it became the host location for the new JTF Raven.

The sun beat down like an accusation. The transport stopped near a lone concrete building and a rusted chain-link fence.

A corporal met her on the strip. Staring at the clipboard in his hand the entire time.

"Commander Whitaker?"

"Yes."

"You're assigned to Node Three. Follow me."

A half-mile walk down gravel and heat to what looked like a decommissioned munitions bunker. Inside were rows of workstations, segmented data feeds, and the constant hum of officers trying to reconstruct a shattered nation.

They called it a fusion node. It felt more like a lifeboat.

Her placard was already up: CMDR S. WHITAKER

Her credentials worked. Clearance active.

By the end of her second day, she'd briefed two colonels, flagged four false positives in *Wrath* chatter, and dismissed a junior analyst who tried to hand her coffee like she was still someone's aide.

Now, most of her hours were spent elbow-deep in pattern analysis, rerouted surveillance packets, and encrypted briefings from what little remained of the NSA's east coast infrastructure. She slept in four-hour shifts. Ate whatever the mess had. And spent too much time thinking about what the long-term impact of the attacks was likely to be.

By the end of week three, the tempo had normalized, at least enough to breathe. She'd fallen into a rhythm. Command respected her. Her section ran smoothly.

It was late morning when she heard it. A cargo plane, C-130, but too smooth, like it had been perfectly tuned. She stepped outside, shielding her eyes. The sun burned white against the runway. A plane descended on its final approach.

Sleek. Civilian. Clean lines. Tail number scrubbed of identifiers. It looked like a cargo jet that had been surgically refined; military-adjacent, but too elegant. She was certain it could only be a LM-100J.

Her pulse kicked up. There were only ten in existence. It touched down like it belonged; smooth, exact, low profile. *No way*, she thought. She waited, standing just outside the entry ramp of Node Three, until the engine noise dropped to a low whir and the loading ramp lowered. A figure stepped out.

She recognized her from the day Sam walked up and introduced himself. It was only two months ago, but it felt like a lifetime. Sarah had never gotten her name; it was just a glance, the kind reserved for Secret Service or elite handlers.

But it was the same woman; the easy movement, more like watching water flow than a person walking, was unmistakable. She was wearing black slacks, a dark green utility jacket, and sunglasses, and presented herself as professional and unflinching. Her confidence said she belonged there.

Behind her, emerging from the cockpit stairwell…

A pilot. Civilian clothes. Clean-cut. Tired. Walked straight toward the officer from base logistics, who met him halfway, clipboard in hand, motioning toward temporary quarters.

The woman paused at the end of the ramp, then smiled.

"You must be Commander Whitaker. Mary Rosenfeld. Assigned to your unit. I think you'll find my background… useful."

She'd seen the file: civilian clearance, deeply embedded contractor, too many classified redactions for comfort. Now, it was her unit that Mary was being assigned to? Someone planned this.

Sam. Of course, it was Sam. His fingerprints were all over this. The aircraft, the timing, her… everything. He wanted eyes in the room. Eyes on Sarah.

"I saw your credentials. Impressive," she said flatly. "The corporal will get you situated."

As she turned back toward the plane, her eyes caught James, clearly having heard her. He stood frozen, disbelief written plainly across his face.

Sarah took a few steps toward the logistics officer and asked, "What quarters is the pilot in?"

The lieutenant turned, irritation already rising, until he registered her insignia.

"Ma'am—uh—temporary quarters, Hangar C. End unit."

"Very good," she said coolly. "I'll take care of him, Lieutenant." Placing extra emphasis on his rank.

James stepped down from the ramp and closed the distance between them in just a few strides. He pulled her into a hug. It was solid, warm, and exactly what she needed. Sarah stiffened for half a second, conscious of uniform and surroundings, but then let it happen.

When he let go, he just gave her a look. That familiar, steady calm. She had missed it.

"I didn't know if I'd see you again." He smiled. "Certainly never expected to find you landlocked at some tiny base no one's heard of. When I saw you, I figured maybe you pissed someone off and they shipped you here… but Commander? Not the case."

"I wasn't sure either." She gestured toward the path. "Come on. I'll show you around."

They walked side by side through the maze of sun-blasted concrete and low-rise security doors. His quarters were near the back: modular, basic, but clean.

"You likely could sleep somewhere on that plane of yours. Bet it has some hidden space with amazing little quarters," she said. "But at least you'll hopefully manage a little rest here. You look like you've slept about as little as I have lately."

They walked to the mess next. Like all coffee on every base in the world, it tasted terrible, but it was hot, black, and full of caffeine. They sat in the sparsely filled mess, away from everyone, so it felt like they were alone—alone in the same way the Wardroom had felt back at the Academy all those years ago.

Then she asked, "So. Why here?"

He leaned back, holding the mug in both hands like it helped him think.

"I didn't plan on it," he said. "But the plane was preloaded three days before the attack. Sam had it stocked and sealed, like he knew. Medical gear, trauma kits, food, and shelter tech. All ready. Just waiting."

Sarah raised an eyebrow. "And that didn't seem suspicious to you?"

James gave a restrained chuckle. "Oh, it did. But not wrong. Just… out in front. Everyone else waited for a memo. He acted. The attacks weren't a surprise… just their locations, the numbers, the mechanisms. Everyone in the U.S., heck, in the world, knew they were coming. The government just chose to sit on its hands and wait before acting."

He sipped, then added, "You should've seen the warehouses. Crates were stacked high enough that they had to rotate air traffic to get things moved out safely. Stuff you'd think would be impossible to source. Thermal blankets, rare meds, backup batteries; everything. And all of it was already sorted and labeled for post-disaster distribution. Sam wasn't preparing for a possibility. He expected this."

Sarah listened and watched James.

"He's not normal," James said, setting the mug down. "I don't think he sleeps much. Doesn't need thanks. Doesn't want attention. But you can tell… every move he makes, it's for someone else. To save people before it's too late."

She traced her finger along the side of her mug.

"Do you trust him?" she asked, barely audible.

James nodded.

Sarah looked up. "You do?"

"Completely."

That word hit harder than she expected. She knew James; he didn't say things like that lightly. Maybe, despite her suspicions, Sam perhaps was one of the good ones. Maybe he just did not mesh with the government machinery well, but someone who still wanted to help. Someone who couldn't operate inside the rules… but hadn't stopped trying to do good.

She let out a slow breath. "Maybe he's not insane."

"Maybe not." James tilted his head. "But even if he is… he's the kind of crazy I'd bet on."

They sat in silence again. This time, it felt different. Familiar. Like years ago, talking by the water during liberty weekends. But this time, it was more. She was in love and knew it. She feared he didn't feel the same.

It was just a few months ago, on his back porch, when he had said, "Someone who still loves you." She hadn't let herself dwell on it; she had half dismissed it. They had always loved each other. They were family. But this was different.

Had that difference been what he meant back then?

She didn't want to move. And she didn't want the moment to end. Being near him made the world feel sane, like everything had found a little footing again.

EIGHTEEN

Sam hadn't slept much since the third wave hit. But then, sleep never came easily, not in this place or in life.

The house above ground didn't creak or shift like old timber homes did. It was steel wrapped in wood, a ten-thousand-square-foot marvel tucked deep into the Alaskan range; built to impress, to misdirect—a decoy for what lay beneath. But Sam lived in it anyway, just because sometimes it helped to walk hallways that had sunlight.

He moved barefoot across the heated floor, mug in hand, hoodie loose on his frame. MIT. Faded black cotton, sleeves pushed to the elbows. A relic. He'd found it in a trunk two days after the LAX bombing. His sisters had all worn it when they visited. They always complained about how cold it was there, despite the constant geothermally controlled temperature and heated floors. He had long ago decided they were cold because they looked outside and saw the snow and ice, and their brains told them it was freezing.

The espresso machine hissed to life; an indulgence, but it kept his hands busy. The feed from below flickered silently across a recessed screen in the stone backsplash: protest vectors in Chicago, signal spikes in Charlotte, three flagged speech patterns in Denver. He didn't look at them yet.

He leaned on the counter, fingers pressing into the stone. His chest tightened, but he didn't let it settle. He turned back to the tablet on the table.

One thread sat pinned above all others:

Mom + D. + Em + Raquel

He tapped it. The last reply was a week old. Still thinking and still deciding.

His mom and dad, well, stepdad technically. Sam had always called his biological father Frank. When Gary came into the family at twenty-five, he called him Dad. It had felt right. They'd said they wanted to wait. Things weren't bad in inland Washington, and getting to the house wasn't far away. He'd scoffed at that. Yeah… not too long. Forty-five hours by car, assuming no stops and no traffic. Or a near six-hour flight.

So, he stationed a plane at their local airport, Davenport Municipal, and left a pilot on standby. The pilot had a cake job… mostly waiting. Occasionally, Sam sent him to move goods or ferry a passenger or two. But never far from the airport, never gone for more than eight hours. It was a small private jet, just a Cessna Citation II.

Raquel didn't want to leave her clinic. Animals had always been her life, and she said they needed to be protected, too. Her practice was tucked into a small storefront in Orange County, California. Her exit would be more difficult and would require Sam to reroute assets to get her safely out. Once it got worse there, it would go bad fast. He had argued with her for hours. There was no use.

Emily hadn't said a word, but she was watching. She had always been the stubborn one, a strong-willed middle child. That strong will was probably why she had managed to keep her family together and raise three kids. She had settled in Nebraska, and Sam figured her exit would be the easiest.

So far, it was just Diane.

She'd arrived the day after the third attack. It had been too much for her. She didn't like the idea of being stuck there; too remote, nothing to do. But she liked the idea of surviving.

The main house was ten thousand square feet, but the guest houses were only about two to three thousand each, depending on who he'd built them for. Diane had one closer to the two-thousand-square-foot mark. Enough to give her space, but really, it was just her. She had never married and never gotten close. Her love was God and the church; she'd found a wonderful one in eastern Ohio and thrown herself into it. She volunteered for everything and was there all the time, so much so that they finally gave her a paid position, mostly, he suspected, because they felt guilty.

Now stuck near Poorman, Alaska, she spent her days reading the Bible and poring through commentaries. She often went into the underground and tended the plants. She'd been amazed by the wide assortment of fruits, vegetables, and grains Sam had managed to collect. It gave her a way to pass the time.

They almost always ate together. And he prayed more of his family would come soon. She needed more than just him. He was aware he wasn't good company. He just never quite understood people. Some of that could have been the strange way Frank raised him. Not just the camping trips, but every activity he ever did was a test of some sort, always crafting him into the soldier he never became.

He lowered himself into the long leather chair by the glass wall; mountains beyond it, bare and brilliant in the noon sun. The heat inside was steady, but he lit the fireplace anyway. Real flame. Old wood. Some habits stayed. He stared into the fire.

He didn't want power. He didn't want recognition. He didn't want revenge. He wanted people to live. And he was running out of ways to make that happen.

Wrath had successfully covered their footsteps. No digital fingerprints anywhere. It made sense, he thought. They'd been at this decades longer than he had been.

Diane would be in soon, wanting to cook him breakfast.

So, he picked up the well-worn Bible, thumbed to where he left off, and started his day the way he always did: thirty minutes of Bible reading, fifteen to twenty in prayer. Sleep didn't matter. Chaos didn't matter. If God had put him here to save lives, what would have been the point if he had ignored God in the process?

Sam had just finished his morning time with God when Diane wandered in, chipper as always, even though he knew she needed more. "I'm dying for biscuits and gravy today. That work for you, Sam?"

"Sure." It didn't matter; everything she cooked was ten times better than anything he'd eaten before she arrived. Sam wasn't big on cooking, and sometimes he would just grab a protein bar or an MRE.

As she cooked, he traced back through the last few weeks.

Cities burned in scattered rings: Detroit, Nashville, Portland, Seattle, Los Angeles, others. But those weren't the real targets. They were distractions. The fractures were spreading wider than the flame fronts. Power vacuums. Social cracks. Chain-of-command collapses. And into those cracks flowed chaos.

Sam had watched feeds, ten or more at a time. There was no sound, just movement, eyes scanning for the patterns others missed. Movements when things happened in the background. He had evaluated crowd density, heat signatures, and signal traffic. The sound was always off: human noise and noise from panic. They only got in the way. The patterns were what mattered.

His focus narrowed to a cluster in Austin; protest lines had held for forty minutes before someone threw the first Molotov. From there, it was textbook police over-response. Firestarter disappears. Secondary agitators emerge, masks up, faces blurred, movements practiced. *Wrath.* Or, at least, *Wrath's* foot soldiers. The disposable ones.

He traced their exit path. Side alley. Black van. No plates. No trail again. Ghosts.

Then a chime. A change in a priority asset. He turned to the console.

Whitaker, Sarah J.

PROMOTED – CMD

REASSIGNED: NODE THREE / YUMA (CLASSIFIED JTF)

Sam exhaled through his nose, a muffled note of amusement. So, they were pulling her in.

He tapped a few keys: standard routing protocols, encrypted logs, and satellite flags for surveillance intake. Her new posting was high-level enough that direct contact was now off the table.

He was too watched. He needed a buffer. His eyes flicked across a different monitor. Mary's personnel shell lit up, mid-rotation, currently flagged as available.

"Not ideal," he said aloud.

Mary wasn't his best or most adaptable operator, but she was confident, competent, and unflinching. More importantly, Sarah would never trust her—not fully, not enough to get close.

Which made her perfect. No risk of association or contamination.

If Mary got burned, she'd handle it professionally. If possible, she'd use the escape plans. And if she didn't get away, he would add her to the ledger, which he never stopped carrying. If not, she'd still get Sarah the correct intel at the right time, without Sarah ever realizing who had pulled the strings. She'd believe the file. Maybe even assume Mary was Sam's data expert. That was the goal, a believable fiction. No threads leading back.

Sam opened a secure directive and keyed the transfer. Ten seconds later, Mary's assignment shifted:

NODE THREE. LIAISON, LOGISTICS CONTROL. PERM LVL RED.

He allowed himself a smile. Then clicked again. James' flight data pinged in the background. Three missions in five days. All aid runs. All high-risk zones. He'd volunteered for every flight.

Sam shook his head. "You need a break, brother."

He issued the redirect under the guise of crew rest rotation. Yuma would hold him for a few days, long enough. Sarah needed the air. James would give it to her. Maybe being near each other again would remind them why any of this still mattered.

During breakfast, Diane finally seemed to realize the truth.

"It will never be over for you, will it, Sam? No matter how many you help, how many you save... if there's even one more that can be saved, you'll keep trying. And every soul you lose, the ones who didn't make it, even the ones who gave up and ended their own lives, you're going to carry them. All the way to when you're standing before God Himself."

Sam smiled sadly.

"Yeah," he said. Then paused in thought. "God gave me this as my mission. Gave me every tool I needed to do it. From the training Frank drilled into me, to the love Mom never stopped giving. The understanding of patterns and tech that let me make the money to build all this. But he also left me with a personality people instinctively don't trust. I don't know why. I… see it in their eyes."

He looked down.

"But my heart won't let even one go. And the hurt is real. The worst part is losing the ones I assign to help. Those ones… that's on me. I made those choices. I picked them. Sent them out knowing they might die. God forbid I ever cause someone to die before the day they accept Him."

Sam spent each day, without fail, continuing the hunt, searching for anything that might lead to *Wrath*. But every lead went cold. Every thread unraveled. Still, he forwarded snippets to Mary; bits that would catch an analyst's attention. Nothing substantial, but enough to make her seem credible. Enough to make it look like she knew what to look for. Enough to keep her in the room.

NINETEEN

Sarah sat halfway down the left side of the table, shoulders squared, posture rigid. It was the kind of formality that masked exhaustion, the kind every section chief had adopted. Around her, the conference room was filled with muted shuffling; binders closing, data pads sliding, coffee cups shifting hands. New information was rare now, and so were people actually taking notes.

The room smelled like old coffee, recycled air, and the sweat of too many bodies running on fumes. Every face around the table was pale and drawn. Eyes hollow. They had gone from analysts to placeholders.

The director entered late. A nod and a sharp look that silenced the room.

"Let's begin."

One by one, they spoke.

"Nashville: No credible leads. Military-grade shaped charge. Short-range delivery. The vehicle was incinerated. No VIN, no plating, no chassis. Possibly a work truck. No surviving footage.

"Detroit: Debris consistent with modified civilian drones. Hundreds of small fragments. No serials, no commercial tags. The control signature was wiped. We're still reverse-engineering possible flight paths.

"Seattle: The cyber vector was completely anonymized, with no digital footprint lasting more than a few seconds. Local servers were physically destroyed, and the infrastructure was shredded; repair costs are still being estimated.

"Pentagon: Best guess is explosive material embedded in furniture. Legacy items. No recent replacements. If that's the vector, we're talking about infiltration years ago; maybe more."

Sarah stared at the grain of the table, counting grooves like it might keep her focused. Every word sounded like it had already been said. She felt like she was watching the meeting on a loop, the same worn script from last week and the week before that. The Task Force seemed to purposely work on nothing and hide information they found, the opposite of its intent.

The director just listened. One after another, the section leads confirmed what everyone already knew; they'd all heard fifty times before.

They had nothing.

"All right," he said finally. "We're drawing down. Too many hours. Too many dead ends. The public is calm, the media's moved on, and we need to rotate out anyone not essential."

A few heads turned.

"You're not being cut," he added. "You're the core team. But we're rebalancing the nodes. And I want every one of you to take a break. Ten days. Off-grid, off-base, whatever you need. We have a transport lifting in ninety minutes. It'll get you to Duke. From there, you're on your own. Use it. Clear your head. I need you sharp when the real work starts."

She already knew where she was going. Montana. She booked the ticket using her tablet during the ride to Duke. Then put it away, leaned back, and closed her eyes.

The drone of the engines blurred into the hollow spaces in her head. And somewhere between the last drone briefing and the smell of jet fuel on the transport, her heart had already answered. This time, she would take the chance, not let it slip past again.

She needed James. Ten days. That's what they'd given her. Ten days to feel again. Ten days to remember why any of this mattered.

James.

Sam better be watching this time, and he better make sure James is there when I land. She still had mixed feelings, but Mary had been an asset, even if her information had not been fruitful. James trusted Sam.

Sarah arrived at Duke and grabbed an Uber straight to Phoenix Sky Harbor International Airport. Still in uniform, carrying only a personal bag, she breezed through security. At a small Mexican restaurant in the terminal, she ordered lunch and took a seat. It was the first time in months she could remember having a meal that tasted like real food.

The last time might have been at James' house.

Realizing she didn't know his address, she opened her map app and filtered through saved locations until one finally felt right. As she tapped to save the pin, a waitress approached.

"The gentleman over there wanted to buy your meal," the waitress said. "He asked me to thank you for your service."

Sarah blinked, startled. For a moment, she wondered if Sam had arranged something until she glanced over and saw an elderly man, likely in his seventies, smiling and waving—probably a former military man himself.

She found the right house and noted the address as she boarded the passenger flight to Montana. The plane was crowded, and there would be a layover in Denver. The total flight time would be about five and a half hours, just enough time in Denver to grab a decent cup of coffee.

The Denver terminal was busier than she expected for a late afternoon. She moved on autopilot, getting off the plane, up the ramp, and scanning signs for her next gate.

It was close; she had time. Enough to wander past the chain restaurants and souvenir kiosks until the smell of real coffee stopped her.

Starbucks. It had been six months since she had a decent coffee. All she had on base was the powdered ration stuff or the bitter sludge from the base galley. Real espresso. She ordered something familiar and indulgent and stood off to the side, sipping slowly, letting the warmth seep into her hands.

What are you doing, Sarah?

Once again, she was about to show up unannounced. It was crazy; completely out of character. She always planned, always checked in, always kept her footing. But now? She was flying across the country without notice, like she was twenty again, reckless and unmoored.

The thought of calling crossed her mind again. She even pulled out her phone. *I just want to be there.* He would not tell her not to come, but even that 1% chance he did kept her from calling.

That was the truth of it. His house, tranquil, warm, surrounded by trees, felt more like home than anywhere else she'd been, because James was there.

That morning, she'd stood in his kitchen, the light slanting in, the smell of coffee and sawdust and memory hanging in the air… she'd felt it.

Home.

They called her group to board. She grabbed her bag and headed down the jetway, heart pounding louder than the engines.

James.

* * *

James had received the email earlier that day. The plane was scheduled for a complete systems overhaul, and the crew arrived the next morning, grounding it for at least a week, probably more.

After nearly a thousand flight hours in six months, he had expected an overhaul. The LM-100J had kept to a steady cycle of basic maintenance, but nothing pulled it offline for more than a day or two. A complete teardown like this usually happened at three or four thousand hours. Still, this was Sam.

The upgrades alone, the flight systems, the comm suite, the structural reinforcements… probably needed twice the oversight of a regular cargo hauler. And it was a massive investment. Sam never did anything halfway.

So for now, James had time. Real-time. The first proper break he'd had in months.

He spent the afternoon chopping wood, stacking enough to last through winter and still leave a backup supply once he was back in the air. That evening, he grilled a steak and curled up in his worn armchair with a good book.

Around 2100 hours, he'd stopped reading. The words had blurred. His thoughts had drifted… Sarah, the Academy, Christina's laugh, Wyatt's tiny feet pattering through the hall.

He sometimes missed the rhythm of military life—the structure, the clarity. But for the first time, he felt like he was doing really well, and sometimes even had a say in what that good was. Sam, whatever else he was, seemed to care. That mattered.

And then there was that night. Eight months ago now. Sarah had come. Unannounced. Just for a moment. Just to be there. She'd reached for his hand, and for a heartbeat, the world had made sense.

Since then, he'd only seen her once, briefly, at that Joint Task Force base in Yuma, clearly classified. Clearly off-limits.

He missed her. He wanted her here. Maybe someday the world would calm down and they'd have real time together.

The thought barely finished forming when a pair of headlights swept across the trees. No one came here by accident. Not this far out. Not down his driveway.

He stood, heart already quickening.

Even out here, in a serene Montana town, the chaos of the last few months had left its mark. Maybe it was just someone who was lost. Or maybe Sam had a habit of appearing unannounced.

Still, James stood. He crossed to the decorative shelf, shifted the small statue that released the hidden magnetic lock, and pulled out the holster. Sliding the M&P Shield free, he locked the magazine, chambered a round, and holstered it with practiced ease.

Then he walked to the front door and flipped on the exterior lights. He exited the front door just as a familiar form stepped out from the rear passenger door, small bag in hand.

Sarah.

He blinked, barely trusting his eyes.

"No way," he called, voice lifting in disbelief. "Sarah!"

He crossed the yard quickly, barely registering the car backing down the driveway. She smiled, nervous but steady, like she'd braced herself for this moment, and he wrapped her in a hug before she could speak.

"I was just thinking about you," he said into her hair. Then he stepped back to look at her. "What are you doing here?"

She glanced toward the retreating taillights. "They're rotating crews. Gave us ten days to ourselves. So… here I am." She hesitated a beat. Then said softly: "I hope that's okay."

He smiled. "You're always a welcome sight. But you know… I do have a phone. You're allowed to call."

She elbowed him lightly as they climbed the porch steps. "Yeah, well. I thought about it. Then didn't."

He nodded. "Fair." He looked at her from head to toe, memorizing every inch. "I'm glad you came."

* * *

Inside, a fire burned. The house smelled of pine and lemon oil. The warmth was nice, refreshing. A book sat on the table, clearly where he'd left off reading when she arrived. Across the room, a shelf stood open, revealing a hidden compartment lined with foam cutouts for a handgun.

"Make yourself at home," James said casually. He walked toward the shelf and pulled a 9mm from the small of his back. He placed it and the holster into the foam slots and closed the shelf.

"A little more careful than you used to be, I see," she said.

"In today's world, you can never be too careful," he replied with a smile. "No one comes up my driveway. And since I wasn't expecting anyone…" He let the sentence trail off, clearly teasing her.

146

She rolled her eyes. "Yeah, yeah, I know. Should've called."

"You want something to eat? Or maybe clean up first? I've got a real shower. Bet you haven't seen one since the last time you were here."

He was right. After nearly twelve hours of travel, a shower sounded wonderful. But unable to resist since he had started it, she said, "What, you think I look like I need to clean up?"

He just shook his head. She was sure he knew better than to say anything at all.

"Your bag looks like you packed for the day," he said, nodding toward it. "We can run into town tomorrow and grab some clothes… something besides your uniform. But I have some sweats if you have nothing comfortable to lounge in."

After a much-needed shower, she slipped into one of his sweatshirts just long enough to feel covered and sank onto the couch, clearly tired. They talked for another ten or fifteen minutes before he gently said, "Look, you're here for a while. You look like you might pass out mid-sentence. Get some sleep. We can talk tomorrow."

She just smiled, stood, and disappeared down the hall toward the guest room… guest wing, she corrected herself. Good Lord, the house was huge. Somehow, she already felt like she was home.

The next morning, after breakfast, James drove them into the city. It was a small town by most standards, but by Montana standards, the 35,000 people who lived there made it a big city.

They hit about four stores looking for enough clothes to last Sarah for the ten days. As they pulled up to the first one, James leaned over and said, "So, this is a clothing store. They sell clothes for women who aren't planning to wear a uniform everywhere they go. You might've heard of places like this… military legends and all."

They stopped for lunch at the same café where Sam had introduced himself. The day was unlike any other they'd spent together; it was as if they were a normal couple, just enjoying each other's company. They laughed, talked, and at some point, began holding hands. She wasn't sure if she had grabbed his hand first or the other way around, but it felt like the most natural thing. They walked around most of the day hand in hand.

On the way back to the house, they made one final stop at the market and picked up everything they needed for a nice dinner; James planned to grill.

Dinner was as perfect as the day had been. James knew his way around a grill; he could achieve a perfect sear and balance flavors. They ate at the kitchen table, laughing between bites, trading stories about deployments gone sideways and coworkers they swore they would never miss. Even the subdued moments felt good. Maybe this was what life could be.

Later, they moved to the living room with mugs of coffee and sat close together on the couch. The fire crackled softly. Sarah tucked her legs beside her, leaning into him as he draped an arm over her shoulders.

She let her head rest against his chest. "I don't remember the last time I felt this comfortable," she said peacefully. "This… normal. Like the world's not falling apart. Like this is my life, and I don't want it to end."

His hand traced lightly down her arm. When he finally spoke, his voice was low. "I think we needed to lose everything first," he said, "Christina, Wyatt, Will… I don't mean that we were glad to lose them. But they made us better. Stronger. They showed us what love really looked like and what commitment cost. And then they broke us."

She didn't move. Just listened.

He continued, "I used to think we missed our shot—too many almosts. Too much timing gone wrong, but maybe that wasn't it. Maybe we just weren't ready. Maybe we needed to be cracked open first, to feel the kind of grief that burns away everything else. And now, what's left is just… real."

He shifted slightly, just enough to meet her eyes.

"So let's not waste what we have now. Marry me," he said. "Tomorrow. Not someday. Not if things settle down. Just… now. While we still have this."

She took it all in.

Part of her wondered if he was chasing peace, the way he had before with Christina. That wedding had come fast, too. She remembered the photos, the way he smiled, and the way Christina had asked him. He'd said yes because it was good and it made sense.

Sarah looked at him, and in his eyes she saw home. She saw her love reflected back, steady and certain. This wasn't because Christina had once asked; this was because he loved her. She was his home as much as he was hers.

"Okay," she said.

The next morning, they drove to a small courthouse in town. The clerk asked their names and had them fill out a simple form. A judge squeezed them in between civil appointments. James wore a collared shirt and clean jeans. Sarah pulled her hair back and borrowed a white sweater from the shop they'd stopped at two days before. They exchanged rings... plain, silver, picked up that morning from a local craftsman. Traditional and solid.

It was done in ten minutes. And yet somehow, it felt like the most permanent thing she had ever done. They took the long way back to the house, enjoying the drive and being with each other. She held his hand the entire drive.

And when they turned onto the gravel road and saw the car waiting in front of the house, they both slowed. It was a sleek black town car with tinted windows. A driver stood near the rear door in a dark jacket. James parked beside it. The driver gave a slight nod, opened the rear door, and stepped away.

Inside, on the backseat, sat a single cream envelope with her name handwritten in deep blue ink.

Sarah opened it slowly:

I thought you could use some time where no one needs anything from you. The jet's waiting. You'll be back before anyone even knows you're gone. The house is yours. The staff is discreet. The beach is peaceful.

– S

She looked up at James. "Did you know about this?"

He shook his head. Smiling now. "Nope. But I'm not surprised."

They got in the car, the driver closed the door and drove to the airport.

TWENTY

She had wanted to stay. He'd walked her out to the car in the early light, the frost still clinging to the grass, their breath visible in the air between them. She kept her duffel slung over one shoulder, not ready to say it. He waited.

"You'll be okay?" she finally asked.

James smiled, "I've got fuel, food, and a job I believe in. You?"

Her eyes stung. She blinked it away. "I've got orders and a reason. The job… I just am not sure the JTF is doing its job. But I am doing mine."

They stood close for a long moment. She reached up and touched the side of his face. He kissed her once, slow, firm, steady.

"Go do your part," he said. "I'll be right here."

She nodded, turned, and when she reached the end of the driveway, looked back. He still stood there, hands in his jacket pockets, watching her go.

By the time her boots hit the tarmac at Yuma, Sarah was already back in uniform—if not the fabric, then the posture. Her shoulders were squared, her mind clear, and her emotions sealed behind the practiced mask of command.

The heat pressed down hard. It always amazed her how late in the year it lingered in Arizona. The walk from the transport to the operations wing was short, but every step was a reminder: the world was still breaking, and this was where she could do something about it.

She bypassed the main bullpen. Her credentials opened the secure hallway. The nameplate on the door was new—hers. The room felt earned by survival more than promotion. Fewer officers. Fewer analysts. Same threat, only muted now.

She dropped her bag inside, pulled the chair back, and powered up the console. The screen flickered, hummed, then settled into the blank gray of a system waiting to be told what mattered.

A soft knock broke the silence. Then the door swung open.

"Took you long enough. I've been stuck on this base for a week now, and not another person with a personality in the place," Trish said, already halfway through the threshold, iced espresso in hand.

Sarah looked up, surprised, then grateful. "You're here!"

"Obviously." Trish strolled in and dropped into the guest chair like she owned it. "New orders. Mid-cycle reassignment. Some genius decided the base could use more caffeine and common sense, so here I am."

Sarah leaned back, arms crossed loosely. "You requested it?"

"Nope. I think someone upstairs remembered I was the only one who ever got you to sleep more than four hours or eat something that wasn't a protein bar. Thought maybe you'd need that again."

Sarah smiled, small, genuine. "They weren't wrong."

Trish took a long sip of her drink. "Besides… they had to have at least one person here who isn't a drone. You and I need a night out. Blow off steam. Find a club. Flirt shamelessly. Leave a trail of smiling, confused men wondering what just happened."

Sarah looked at her old friend with something close to wonder. "I missed you, but I don't think that's happening." She raised her hand, displaying the silver ring.

Trish's eyes widened. "Oh my God! You actually did it? James, right? Oh, please tell me it's James!"

"Yes, it's James." Sarah gave a soft laugh. "During the break—a quick ceremony and a quiet trip to the beach."

"Amazing! It's about time. You should have married him the first time around." Trish grinned and stood, the last of the ice clinking in her cup. "I'll pull the latest reports from Signals and Ops. Maybe we'll get lucky."

"And if not?"

"Then we start making our own luck."

The door clicked shut behind her, and for a moment, Sarah just sat, hands still, eyes on the blank screen in front of her. Then she exhaled, rolled her shoulders, and went back to work.

The days bled together.

Reports came and went. Trish dropped by every morning with caffeine and sharp commentary. She cracked jokes in secure briefings and sorted mission files with ruthless efficiency. She kept Sarah honest… about how much sleep she wasn't getting, how much weight she'd lost, how often she stared at maps without seeing them.

Wrath had gone dormant. The Task Force shrank. Analysts reassigned. Commanders rotated out. A few vanished entirely; names were removed from logs with no explanations.

Sarah held the line. Built timelines, mapped possible vectors, and re-ran behavioral models. Everything pointed backward. Nothing pointed ahead.

"They're still moving," she said once, late in the evening.

Trish looked up from her console. "Yeah?"

"This isn't over. It's just a long fuse."

Trish didn't argue. She never did when Sarah got that look in her eyes.

Somewhere deep underground, far from the dust and silence of Yuma, a signal broke the pattern.

* * *

Sam remembered the moment the ping hit; subtle, routine, almost easy to ignore. Sarah had been granted leave. That alone wouldn't have drawn his attention, but the secondary marker came moments later: a private travel request, no destination declared. He filled in the gaps before she packed her bag.

She was going to James.

He waited until her name cleared the outbound logs. Then he flagged the LM-100J for maintenance. The aircraft didn't truly need the overhaul, not yet, but the timing was perfect. Ten days on the ground, right when James wouldn't need it. He knew from the travel request that Sarah hadn't told James she was coming. It mattered to Sam to preserve that moment for them. Not everything needed his fingerprints on it.

Two days later, another ping. A different kind of alert.

Marriage license.

He didn't smile. Not outwardly. But he sent the car anyway. No label. No instructions. A note tucked neatly in the center console: "Use it if you want. No strings."

The car was there when they arrived home that night. He hadn't checked if they used it. Hadn't cared if they stayed at James' for their honeymoon or took the jet to the island escape, where the staff had seen guests maybe three times in five years. That wasn't the point.

Now, months later, Sam sat in front of the screen again, staring at something he didn't quite trust. A signal, maybe. A pattern forming, but it felt thin. Wrong. Like it wanted to be seen. Or worse, like it wasn't anything at all.

A rabbit hole. He knew the feeling. The kind of lead that devoured time and returned nothing. But his gut said otherwise.

Wrath wasn't as big as they acted. That much he was certain of. They played loudly to cover how few pieces they had. Sam had learned to listen for silence, and this silence was wrong. Like someone pretending not to breathe.

He was certain the instigators, maybe even the perpetrators, had just been money-hungry nobodies, doing the work for a paycheck. And likely, many were already in shallow graves somewhere in a rarely traveled part of the country, silenced before they could speak when the time came.

He guessed their hacker was the typical hacker: skilled, confident, truly remarkable, able to keep them and himself completely invisible. But hackers were lazy unless they had a cause, and money wasn't a cause.

He leaned forward; fingers poised over the keys. Maybe it was nothing. But perhaps it wasn't. He glanced at the time… 5 PM. It was time.

Mom and Dad had arrived the day before, just as planned. They'd agreed to come three months ahead of the anniversary. Finally, Diane would have more than just his miserable company. He had adjusted his life for them and made it a plan. *Wrath* was dormant. He had time. He could spare the time to be with them.

He mentally ticked off the list as he walked back toward the main house.

Diane: Safe.

Mom and Dad: Safe.

Raquel: Finally agreed. Her location made extraction tricky, but she'd promised to come a month before the anniversary. She'd stay long enough to care for the animals, then leave it behind.

Emily finally reached out. Her love for the family had beaten her stubbornness. Of course, she'd come. It would be a getaway. Her, the kids, her husband. All safe. They'd come up three days before the anniversary, just enough time to settle in before it hit. After that, they'd return. Quickly.

As he stepped inside, he caught the smell of garlic and onions. Diane and his mother were in the kitchen, talking low, stirring pots. Something comforting, familiar.

"You know," his mom said from across the counter without looking up, "this place is beautiful, if you consider nothing to be beautiful."

Sam shrugged. "That's the point."

She turned toward him, wiping her hands on a towel. "Nothing is fine until it becomes a problem. Then it's a very long way to help."

"Help isn't coming," he said evenly. "That's why I built it."

His dad chuckled from the table, raising a glass of water. "And here I thought you brought us here for the fresh air."

Sam smiled. "That too."

Dinner came together slowly. Diane set the table while his mother pulled garlic bread from the oven. The conversation stayed light: old stories, gentle teasing, memories of when things were simpler.

He let himself enjoy it. He didn't do that often. But later that night, when the dishes were done and the house had gone noiseless, he found himself back at the screen.

The signal was still there. Slight. Inconsistent. Like a heartbeat out of rhythm. He followed it deeper, unsure whether he was getting closer to a pattern or just chasing a shadow.

He was on a timetable. Maybe this was a rabbit hole that went nowhere. Maybe it wasn't. Maybe it led to the pot of gold. Two months until Raquel arrived, and he would use every day of it. It was the only lead he had.

Six weeks later, he had it. He'd mapped all three attacks. Different entry points, but the rest? Identical. The same type of node shifts. The same packet trails. The same deletion protocols, executed at the same time intervals.

It wasn't just a fingerprint… it was choreography.

He didn't have their content, but he had their path. And that was enough. This time, he would mirror it, track it in real time, slip past the cleanup, and ride the signal upstream. He had six weeks to perfect the algorithm— maybe less—but for the first time in months, he had a target.

Two weeks later, Raquel arrived with the family. It was good to see them. Her husband was an amazing man, though he clearly never quite knew how to take Sam.

The house came alive again, warm with the richness of voices and clatter and shared space. He missed this. He'd given it up… this, and all other real human contact, for his mission.

It had been worth it. But having it now and the joy it brought him hit harder than expected. In three weeks, Emily would arrive.

* * *

Sarah stood in the war room again; hands on the edge of the table, eyes on a screen that had shown the same information for the past week. There had been nothing new. There weren't even dead ends; it felt like data was being scrubbed to look like there was nothing. There were always variances to expectations, so there should have been dead ends if nothing else.

Trish walked in without knocking, holding two coffees, and raised an eyebrow as she approached.

"You know," she said, setting one down beside Sarah, "if you stare at that thing any harder, your eyes are likely to just melt out of your skull."

"It's the same data. Just restructured. Still nothing." Sarah said flatly.

Trish took a long sip. "You sure? Because either you're decoding an attack or conducting a séance."

That earned her a glance.

"Well," Trish added with a shrug, "the intensity says both."

Sarah shook her head and took the coffee. "Thanks."

"Always here to keep you caffeinated and sarcastically grounded."

They stood in silence for a moment. Then Sarah spoke, softer this time. "It's been too long."

"Yeah," Trish said. "Too quiet usually means too late."

Sarah nodded, eyes fixed on the flickering map. "Something's coming. I just don't know what."

Everyone knew the anniversary was close. And *Wrath* was sure to resurface.

The next day, it hit.

The word *Wrath* had bumped again, trending upward across platforms, subtle enough to miss unless you were watching. But Sarah was always watching. Twenty-five percent. A nudge. Just like last time.

Arrogant fools, she thought. *Telegraphing again. Same signal as before.*

But then she saw it. Another bump.

God.

Same increase. Also, twenty-five percent. That wasn't how it worked. It was always one word. A single term would rise; a code, a harbinger. Not two.

She leaned closer to the screen, scrolling back through logs, pulling comparisons. It could be a coincidence. Maybe people were talking about *Wrath* again. Perhaps some were invoking God in the mess of it. But the math said otherwise.

Same rate. Same timing. Same spread. Two words this time. Something was different. Something had changed. She tagged the anomaly and pushed it to the JTF lead with a summary and timestamp markers.

The next morning, the lead stopped by her office in person.

"Interesting," he said, nodding toward her screen. "But it's two words. Doesn't follow the previous patterns, and we're earlier than before. Probably just noise."

Sarah looked over at him. "It's the same bump. Same timing. It's too perfect."

He shrugged. "Or just chance. We've seen chatter spike before without a hit. Keep looking."

Then he was gone. Sarah sat back, unsettled. It felt wrong. Too clean. Too easy to dismiss. She kept watching. For days, nothing else spiked. The word counts held steady, persistent twenty-five percent.

Each morning, the JTF lead dropped by. "Anything more?" he'd ask. And each time, Sarah shook her head.

It was mentioned in the first week's JTF coordination call, during which remote units fed in updates from across the country, and was quickly dismissed.

"Doesn't match the pattern," someone said. "We're earlier than before. And it's two words."

"More likely it's just noise," the lead added. "People talking about God and *Wrath* doesn't exactly narrow it down."

"Maybe we're just not seeing it," Sarah said softly. Her comment seemed to pass unnoticed.

Someone else chimed in, trying to lighten the room. "Could be a throwaway word again. Like 'is.' Last time was obvious. This time? Maybe it's something we'll never trace."

Heads nodded.

"They wouldn't make it traceable twice," the lead concluded. "We got lucky the first and third time. This time, they'd bury it."

And that was that. But Sarah was certain the words were correct.

The following week, just three weeks from the anniversary, the words didn't even come up. The daily briefings, the coordination calls, even the hushed hallway chats had all moved on. The team had dismissed the bump entirely.

And still, something gnawed at Sarah. Something about the timing, the symmetry... pulled at her like an invisible thread.

The next morning, Sarah stepped into the lead's office.

"I need a breath and a real coffee," she said. "Going to make a quick run off base; be back in an hour or so."

The lead nodded, barely looking up from his terminal. "No problem. Probably the last time we'll get to clear our heads before things ramp up."

Sarah gave a quick nod and turned. She walked out, headed to the gate, and ordered an Uber.

When she'd thought, *I need a real coffee*, she hadn't realized it meant a 30-minute drive, but here she was, sitting at Starbucks, breathing and enjoying the drink. The first sip scalded her tongue... real coffee, not powdered sludge. For a moment, the hum of the room faded. She needed a second point of view... someone she could trust to tell her she was right or wrong without worrying they were also trying to cover themselves or bow down to the higher-ups.

Mary sat down across from her. She smiled. "I know, let's just skip the next part. You don't trust me, I get it." She slid a flip phone across the table to her, got up, and walked away.

Two minutes later, the phone rang. She stared at it. Frustrated, she picked it up on the third ring.

Then Sam's voice: "Please, step outside. Cleaner audio. Fewer eyes."

Still wary of Sam, but trusting James' instincts, Sarah did as asked. She needed his brain anyway; someone not afraid to tell her when she was right... or insane. Honestly, she wasn't sure Sam would recognize crazy if it bit him.

"I have a lead. It's not much, but perhaps a code I can follow to track where these guys, or at least their hacker, is. They are consistent. Never change. I think this will work."

Sarah's heart sank. "I saw a bump in *Wrath* and *God*. Both at twenty-five percent. But as I've been told over and over, they're too early. And there are two words."

Silence. Then clicks on a keyboard.

"Yeah... you're right. It's exactly the same percentage bump. Maybe they're being cocky. Trying to throw you off? It's different, strange. It's certainly the same, but different. But why is it different?"

"I hoped you would know," she said.

"You can't bring this phone back on base. Toss it in the trash before you call your Uber back," Sam said, and the line went dead.

Sam's line echoed: *They're consistent. They never change.* It echoed in Sarah's mind. For the first time, she questioned herself. Maybe she was wrong. Perhaps this wasn't the pattern.

But he had also confirmed it.

But with no other leads and no other signal on the horizon, she would ride this one until it ended... or until something new finally broke through.

TWENTY-ONE

Until his conversation with Sarah, Sam had felt good. He'd dug through that tangled mess of a rabbit hole, found the threads, tied them off, and built an algorithm. He was ready—not to stop anything, but maybe to crack the surface and help steer people toward the real threat.

Then Sarah spoke. It was the same. But different. That phrase haunted him. He went to bed with it circling his thoughts like vultures over a dying squirrel. He slept restlessly; half-conscious, half-trapped in a dream where the pattern gnawed at him like maggots on a wound, eating through the rot and leaving only the living flesh behind.

When he woke, he knew.

It wouldn't be ten hours later. It would be sooner, maybe, as it happened. It wouldn't be a word; it would be a statement. Final. Definitive. Live.

Everything before had been a prelude.

This would be the moment *Wrath* defined its target and let the public do the rest—riots, rage, and reaction. They would unleash chaos and use it to reshape the nation. This was never about revenge. It was about revolution.

He had only days. He needed a message—not to stop them—he couldn't—but to cut into the signal, hijack the stream, and deliver a warning before the lie calcified.

He wouldn't win. He'd always known that. He hadn't built the network to win. He'd built it to survive. To help others survive. Winning was never the goal.

* * *

James trusted Sam, and that gave Sarah some measure of comfort. For the first time, she knew Sam wasn't part of the problem. He might not be trustworthy, but he was trying. She believed that now. Trying to stop whatever came next.

Wrath is coming.

Now: *Wrath. God.*

What was she missing?

It was different. But also the same. They were getting cocky. They believed they couldn't be stopped or traced and that no one was smart enough to piece it together.

It wasn't words anymore. It was a phrase. A statement. A name.

Wrath of God.

The word 'of', so small, so common... it slipped through every algorithm. Like 'is', it was filtered out. Invisible. They knew that. They used it.

She walked straight into the JTF lead's office.

"The words, they're both right. We're just missing it. We can't see what's not tracked. It's not a single word this time; it's a phrase. A name."

The man looked up slowly, face tired, wary.

"*Wrath of God,*" Sarah said. "They told us it was coming. This is the declaration. It's here."

The lead nodded, unconvinced. "Maybe. Maybe not. Put it together, file the report, and push it out to the members. Let's see what they think."

So, she did. She saw the comments roll in; skepticism stacked on doubt. Wrong timing, they said. Why a phrase now? Why not another keyword? Too convenient. Too vague.

"They're just words," someone wrote. "People say stuff like this all the time."

The theory was dismissed. Just chatter. Noise. They said *Wrath* three years ago? Probably a coincidence. Said *Coming* a year ago? Just speculation or worse, planted after the fact.

During the morning briefing, the JTF buzzed with life one week before the anniversary. Reports came in from every direction: status updates, tactical briefs, and political escalations.

The nation had gone quiet under curfews. The courts and Congress would adjourn tomorrow. The President was scheduled to arrive at Camp David that night.

During the morning brief, the lead brought it up.

"*Wrath* and *God*," he said. "Some suggest it might be *Wrath of God*. Or something similar; maybe *God is Wrath*, we're just not detecting. Low-signal words like 'of' or 'is' could be slipping through."

Someone else started to dismiss it.

This time, Sarah spoke up. "You're wrong. This is it. It doesn't tell us what… but it tells us when."

Someone scoffed. "Still doesn't line up. Too early."

Sarah froze. "Exactly," she whispered. "It's early. One week…"

Her eyes widened. "Oh God."

She turned to the room. "One week early. They got sloppy."

Voices stilled.

"Get the President into the secure bunker. Evacuate Congress. Clear the courts. Shut down every public space you can. It's not coming on the anniversary… It is coming now, today!"

The hush in the room and on the screens was absolute. No one moved. It was like the air itself had thickened for a second, maybe two. Fear dripped into their bones; slow, cold, penetrating. What if she was right? What if it wasn't three weeks before the anniversary… but three weeks before the attack?

A ping sounded behind Sarah.

"Ah… sir," someone said.

The lead turned. The screen switched.

An X feed went live: a black screen with only an audio pulse. Then a man's voice, clear and calm.

"We warned you. For years, for decades… for centuries."

The sound cut. The pulse continued. He was still speaking—Sarah could see the faint vibration in the audio line—but the words were gone.

A different voice broke through, higher-pitched, urgent, threaded with panic. Sarah recognized it instantly from her calls with Sam.

"Stop. The man behind that voice is lying. Whoever he names, whoever he blames… that is his target. Don't fall for it. Don't let your rage… become his weapon. Don't—"

Silence again. Only the pulse. Then the first voice returned.

"…the family, then rebuilt it as mockery: man with man. Woman with woman. Then worse… You made men into women and women into men, and dared to call it truth. You told the faithful we were wrong; we were hateful. That we were the problem. You were warned."

The voice hardened.

"We are not one. We are not many. We are everywhere. You cannot find us. You cannot stop us. But you will see us."

A pause so slight it felt intentional.

"We are in every town. Every city. Every church. Every house."

The audio line flattened.

"For too long, the world watched the corruption…" The screen switched to an image of the Supreme Court.

"The greed…" The screen's image switched again to the Capitol dome, then a split screen of both House and Senate chambers.

"The power abused…" The image switched to the White House.

"We waited. We prayed. We pleaded. But now… we strike."

The screen suddenly split into dozens of feeds—state capitols, federal buildings, landmarks across the country. One by one, each erupted in fire, smoke, and dust.

The screen faded to black. White text appeared:

Wrath of God.

Sarah was frozen. The conference room dissolved into sound and motion around her; voices rising, chairs scraping back, feet pounding toward exits.

Her ears rang. Her breath caught somewhere between her chest and her throat. The light from the screen burned the image into her retinas… fire, smoke, and the words *Wrath of God* etched in white over black.

She barely registered the voices.

"They were live. We're confirming; those feeds were live."

"The President's secure. Relocating now."

"The Supreme Court… Jesus, they were in session…"

"So was Congress. Both sides."

A hand touched her shoulder. She flinched.

"You said this," someone murmured. "You've been saying this for weeks."

More voices followed; sharp, panicked. "Why didn't we act sooner?"

"Who signed off on the dismissal?"

"I told you to flag her last report!"

Sarah staggered back until she hit the wall. Her legs folded beneath her, and she slid down, arms wrapped around her knees. The noise blurred. The screen kept flashing, looping devastation—proof.

She'd seen it. She'd known. And still… no one listened. No one cared.

It was today. The pieces had been in front of her for weeks, but she hadn't seen them. She kept looking for something different, something new. But it was just early. The same message, the same pattern… shifted by a week. That was the difference. That was the clue. And she'd missed it until it was too late.

A hand touched her shoulder again. She looked up.

"Now's not the time," Trish said softly. "Come on."

There was urgency and care in her voice. Trish crouched beside her, steadying her with a hand, anchoring her back to the moment. She helped her up. She knew what this was and all Sarah had tried to do.

She'd seen Sarah dismissed for weeks, brushed off, and ignored. She was the one who caught it, the one who named it. And now the screen said it all: Sarah had been right.

That couldn't bring back the dead. It couldn't undo the smoke or the screaming. But Trish would remember. Others would too. She had tried. That would matter.

* * *

The words still echoed when Sam replayed the feed.

His fingers flew across the console, isolating the signal, hunting for the moment his own voice slipped in.

There. A flicker. Then confirmation. Partial. Distorted. But audible.

"Stop. This is a false flag…" His voice had made it in. Not the whole message. But enough. Enough for someone to hear.

Then, just as quickly, it vanished—a burst of static. Then, the original feed resumed, overwriting everything.

A different voice, not his own, followed in Sam's ears: "That overlay wasn't accidental. They patched it. Covered it."

He'd seen it happen in real time, but now he knew. They had control. Whoever broadcast the message, *Wrath* or someone posing as them, had

165

anticipated interruption. Sam's voice was gone from the rebroadcasts. Scrubbed. Silenced.

Except for his copy. And maybe a few others. It would be heard. It had to be. He leaned back and called up new data. Satellite feeds. News reports. Infrared confirmations. Sensor pings.

The White House: leveled.

The Capitol Building: demolished.

The Supreme Court: collapsed into dust.

Monuments across the city: shattered.

Ten state capitols: rubble.

His throat tightened. Not fear. Not yet. Just the crushing weight of confirmation. This had always been the plan. All the signs. All the years. All the warnings.

And now?

Now the country was leaderless. Lawless. And *Wrath* had a name.

He stared at the blinking cursor in front of him. How many more can I save?

TWENTY-TWO

The Presidential seal filled the screen.

The background was a neutral, secure location, undisclosed but unmistakably reinforced. The room was dim, and the flag behind him lit with only a soft glow. The President looked drawn but composed, his face pale with fatigue, his jaw set with conviction.

"My fellow Americans, today, our nation has suffered a tragedy unlike any in our history. The heart of our government was attacked: our Capitol, our Court, and the very institutions that have upheld this republic for nearly 250 years. Had it not been for a last-minute warning, I would not be speaking to you now.

"Another warning, however unexpected, did not come from within the government. Even as *Wrath of God* began its broadcast, another voice cut through: clear, firm, and urgent. It came from a voice we did not authorize, but one we now believe told the truth. It told us this was a lie. That whoever *Wrath* blamed was their next target. We now know the voice was a hacker—an American acting alone. He did not name a group and did not spread fear. He gave us a choice: to think or to react.

"Let me be clear. This government will not hunt people based on belief. We do not convict by association. We do not turn suspicion into guilt.

No American of any faith will be targeted for who they are. We will find the people who did this. We will hold them accountable. But we will not become them. We will not become wrathful. In response to this coordinated act of terror, this declaration of war, I have invoked the Insurrection Act. Effective immediately, all federal forces, including the National Guard, are authorized to assist states in restoring order, protecting civilians, and enforcing federal law.

"Governors and mayors cannot do this alone. Not this time. *Wrath* struck at our foundations. And in the wake of that, too many have chosen chaos. Too many have turned on their neighbors. So, the military will assist in securing cities. It will prevent the persecution of religious groups. It will help local officials rebuild, not just structures, but trust. And to those in office, those still standing, I say this: begin the process now. Restore your elections. I do not want the authority that falls to me now, and I will not hold it longer than I must.

"This country was designed to prevent power from resting in one man's hands. So act. Let me help. Let us reinforce your cities. Let us protect your citizens. Let us hold the line.

"I ask for peace. For calm. For restraint. Remember, the people of this nation are your neighbors. Your friends. Your family. We are Americans. And we rise."

* * *

Sam stood stunned as the President's final words echoed through the room.

Then… nothing. No alerts. No pings. Just stillness.

He had just witnessed the impossible: a modern President of the United States stepping away from power.

For all of Wallace's flaws, Sam had been sure he'd seize the moment if it ever came—hold onto the reins of a fractured nation under the guise of unity. But he hadn't.

Wallace didn't want to reconstruct the nation in his own image. He truly wanted it to heal. To become better, and not just survive. And in that moment, Sam saw it: something had changed in the man. Or maybe it

168

had always been there—buried beneath the politics, waiting for the fire to burn it clear.

Sam had spent a lifetime preparing for collapse. The day the republic fell, his hidden network would be the last safety net—not to fight, not to take back power… but to save the remnant.

And now, the man at the helm had just proven he was worth saving, too. But it hadn't fallen. Not today. Not yet.

The President had heard the warning and had believed it. And instead of lashing out and grasping for control, he'd answered with truth; measured, firm, and filled with a mercy Sam hadn't dared to hope for.

A sharp breath escaped him, then a startled, breathless laugh.

He turned, already moving, feet pounding toward the stairwell.

"Mom!" he shouted. "Raquel! Diane, Emily… he listened!"

Footsteps above. Doors opening. Voices rising. His family, those he'd kept safe for so long, came rushing to meet him.

"It worked," he said again, louder now. "God help us, it worked."

The feed looped behind him, but Sam didn't look back. He pulled them into the moment, letting it break through the constant readiness. Not with bravado, but with tears on his face and a weight finally lifted.

Maybe this wasn't the end. Maybe it never had to be. He didn't return to the screens. Didn't check the feeds. Not yet.

He walked past the control hub, the silent monitors, and the neatly blinking redundancies he'd spent decades perfecting. All of it was built to survive collapse, humming in a restrained, rhythmic calm. He stopped in the center of the room and sat—no keyboard, no headset, no mission—just stillness.

And into that stillness came the truth.

He had given up so much: normalcy, companionship, and belief in the goodness of people. Not because he didn't care, but because he cared too much to take the chance.

He hadn't believed the country could survive. Hadn't believed the people in it would stand. So, he had built a refuge instead of standing with them.

And it still might fall. Maybe this wasn't over. But it wasn't falling today. Not this hour. Sam exhaled a laugh that cracked into something else. He covered his face with one hand as the tears came, unguarded and sudden.

He had been wrong. Thank God… Thank God, he had been wrong. He sank to his knees. Not out of despair. Not out of exhaustion. But because the truth was still unfolding, growing clearer with every breath.

He had spent his life preparing to be a shield, a steward, an unseen hand of mercy. And maybe, in part, he had been. But not because God needed him. Because God had wanted him. Wanted to work *through* him. Not to save the nation, but to reach him. To let him feel love. Presence. Grace. The very things he had walled off in his pursuit of readiness.

What had begun as a calling quickly became an obsession. A fortress of purpose turned idol. Built in God's name, but not always in God's presence. He knelt lower, hands to the ground, shoulders trembling. And for the first time in decades, he let go.

* * *

James stood beside the plane, one hand resting against the fuselage, the other clutching his phone. The President's speech had ended an hour ago, but he'd watched it repeatedly. He let the final words echo again in his mind, because he needed to believe them.

And somehow, he did. It came in layers, like sunlight pressing through heavy clouds — not brilliance, but permission. He hadn't felt it in years: in the uniform, in the cockpit, or even with Wyatt asleep against his chest. Those moments were love, duty, peace… but this was something else.

This was hope.

For so long, service had been the only shape his pain could take—a way to keep moving, keep flying, keep outrunning the ache. First, the Navy. Then the contractor work. Then the runs for Sam, always one more load, one more disaster to answer, one more way to feel useful.

But tonight, it was about possibility. For the first time, service felt like the right thing — something he could choose, because he had hope.

His life had always been surrounded by chaos and death. His mother, his father, his grandmother, Christina, Wyatt, the war zones he flew into, the devastated cities he flew out of, the soldiers he dropped into firestorms, some of whom never came home. Every mission, every sacrifice, every loss taught him the same thing: hold the line because no one else will.

But tonight, something shifted. Here, in the middle of what should have been the worst day in American history, in the shadow of burned cities and shattered institutions, a man stood up. To lead.

He could have declared martial law. Could have pointed to *Wrath's* enemy and turned suspicion into blood. He chose resolve. Mercy. Service.

And for James, it changed everything. He looked up at the stars, sharp and still in the mountain cold.

If they called… he would go. Because for the first time, he hoped there was a future worth flying toward.

* * *

Sarah sat motionless in her chair, the soft glow of the monitor still reflecting off her skin. The speech had ended minutes ago, but the words still echoed in her skull: *We will not become wrathful.*

Sarah nodded slowly, still processing the speech.

"If I'd figured it out even thirty seconds later," Sarah said, voice nearly flat, "he'd be dead."

Trish turned. "What?"

"The pattern. The timing. I didn't catch it until the minute before. We all braced for an attack on the anniversary… again. We'd been lulled into a false sense of security, believing *Wrath* was consistent, unchanging, even predictable. Stupid, in a way.

"But it was today.

"And I think they made a mistake. I don't think they realized, when they began the chatter and crafted that deliberate taunt, that they had started a week too early. They just set their algorithms to work three weeks before the attack, and in their arrogance, they told us the timing, and we all almost missed it. We all missed it until it was too late."

She let out a slow and shaking breath.

"They moved it up, just enough to slip past us. And our bureaucracy. Always someone covering themselves, hedging, and staying safe. Even when the mission called for something different, it called for exposure, for laying everything bare and looking at it as a whole.

"What else have we missed because someone was afraid to get steamrolled? Who else watched them tear my work apart and kept their heads down?

"That man, the President, just stuck his neck out as far as it could go. No protection. No fallback. He understands the mission now. And he's willing to do what it takes."

Trish dropped into the chair beside her and let that weight settle.

The call came twenty minutes later. Sarah was still replaying the last year, specifically the last three weeks. Now, she had a meeting notification. Department leads, Joint Task Force heads, virtual, secure.

The camera clicked on. The President was in the same room as before, with the same dim backdrop and measured voice. But this time, he was speaking to them.

"You've all persevered. Some of you for three years. Some longer. Each of you has sacrificed more than the public will ever know. And you've done it without grandstanding, without headlines. You've done it because it was right.

"This wasn't a perfect operation. There were delays. Conflicts. Doubt. But you didn't stop. You pressed forward. You took the fragments, guesses, and hunches and turned them into something actionable. And because of that, I'm standing here today. But *Wrath* is not gone. *Wrath* is out there, exposed and ready to fight.

"So we change how we fight. The Insurrection Act is in effect. The military will stabilize the states. But that's only half the battle. Intelligence must evolve. It has to be faster, leaner, and embedded—not sitting above the chaos but inside it. We need to anticipate… not react.

"And that means the mission of this Task Force is complete. You've earned the right to stand down from Raven with your heads held high. Not in defeat. In accomplishment. Your efforts saved lives; mine included. You gave the country a fighting chance. So take what you've learned, carry it back to your units, bases, and agencies, and lead from the front. Make your teams better, smarter, and help them see what you've seen. This isn't over. But we are ready. Thank you for what you've done. And for what you will do next."

The screen went black, and that was it. Raven was officially done. The people she had worked with, fought with, and learned from would scatter, returning to their branches, agencies, and roles across the system.

Sarah felt sick. Likely the rest of the room did too. The President's words had been generous, respectful even… but distant. They would probably receive commendations, maybe promotions, but their failures to stop the event or see it earlier would not bring them any respect or trust.

They had nearly stood in the way of saving his life. Whether through doubt, delay, or self-preservation, they had been slow to act. Some had hidden their information from the group. Some had dismissed the signs.

Sarah sat still, her jaw clenched. She had fought for every step, every single day. She had flagged the chatter when no one else thought it mattered. She'd followed it, chased it, and banged on every closed door in the Task Force. And when they dismissed her, she worked around them. She was always moving the ball forward.

And now, lumped in with Raven, with the collective failure… they would forget that. They'd remember a team that hesitated, not the one voice that pushed. The President was grateful for his life.

Sarah was still packing when the knock came. A man in a tailored suit stood in the doorway, credentials in hand.

"Commander Whitaker? Your transport is waiting."

She grabbed the last of her things and followed him in silence, down corridors, past checkpoints, out into the cool night air. Frustration burned beneath her composure. She didn't need an escort. She wasn't the problem.

She was why the President was walking, talking, breathing… bringing hope to a country on the edge. And now she was being whisked away, one of the first to be discreetly removed from base. If she were lucky, she'd be sent back to NAS Jacksonville. If not, somewhere worse, forgotten, irrelevant.

She stepped aboard the small C-12A. A message in itself: a shadowed dismissal dressed as a ceremony.

She sat motionless for the flight. It was short. Too short. Maybe two hours. She wasn't headed to Jax. She was being sent somewhere further out. Maybe China Lake, where they'd assign her to monitor weapons testing. Or Point Mugu, which is beautiful and pointless for intel work. Or worse… El Centro, where she'd analyze Blue Angels flight data until she finally quit.

The jet touched down. She stepped out slowly, bracing for whatever came next. But it was Peterson Space Force Base. Home of NORAD. USNORTHCOM. Space Command.

She stood still at the bottom of the steps. This was no banishment. It was something else entirely.

A junior officer, an O-3, was waiting with a polite, composed expression and a posture that said she knew who Sarah was.

"Commander Whitaker, if you'll follow me. He's expecting you."

He?

Sarah followed in silence through unfamiliar halls until she entered the room she had seen on-screen just hours ago. Generic backdrop. Controlled lighting. It could have been any base. But now she was here.

"Mr. President," she said, coming to attention and offering a crisp salute.

"At ease, Commander," he said. "I've read the files. I know what you did. I know I owe my life to you."

He stepped closer. His tone was careful. Personal.

"You pushed every minute. Never backed down. If not for that grit, that persistence, I wouldn't be here. Where Raven hesitated, you moved. You're the reason anything got through."

He glanced at a tablet on the desk.

"I saw the logs. The decision trees. The pattern breaks. You had every reason to pull back. Others did. They found excuses and wrote it off. You didn't. You dug in."

She stood silent, letting the words land.

"You didn't save my life with intel. You saved it with conviction. And we need more of that." He extended his hand. "You're being promoted. O-6. You'll lead a new Task Force. Smaller. Faster. Smarter. No red tape. No cover-your-ass politics. I have your back."

He paused, watching her carefully.

"You can be wrong. You can chase something and come up empty. Your team can fall flat. That's fine. What I won't tolerate is fear. I want your people to bring everything. Let nothing pass untouched." He let that sink in, then added, "Find them. Go deep. *Wrath* didn't come from outside. This was internal. A false flag. An insurrection. The man who hijacked their message was right."

His voice was firm but cold. "This wasn't just a tragedy. It was a breach. We need to understand how it happened… before it happens again. You'll have what you need. Whatever you need. Thank you for not giving up." He uttered the last words softly. For once, her career came full circle, full of meaning. All those sleepless nights were worth this moment. Seeing this man spared by *Wrath*.

TWENTY-THREE

James had left Helena at 1000, just minutes after receiving flight clearance. As expected, the LM-100J had already been loaded with medical supplies, bottled water, emergency blankets, and everything deemed essential in the first wave of humanitarian relief. The sky was clear, the weather smooth, and the aircraft handled as it always had: steady, responsive, unshakable.

He flew alone, with no co-pilot and no crew—just him and the hum of engines pushing east.

Below, somewhere beneath the clouds, the nation reeled. He thought of the people… those in shock, those in mourning, those rioting out of rage or fear or both. D.C. had been hit hard. Everyone knew that. But this one… this was bigger. It was beyond chaos now. This was a line in the sand. A call to action. And he could only begin to imagine the aftermath.

Flight time had been just under six hours. Long enough to think. Long enough to wonder what he'd find waiting on the ground. He'd been granted clearance to land at Andrews Air Force Base, a rare privilege for a civilian contractor, even in times like these.

As the runway came into view, a knot tightened in his chest. He brought the plane down clean, just like a thousand times before. Taxi instructions came quickly, and he followed them without question. Medical crews and ground support were already moving and ready to unload the supplies.

He powered down the engines, flipped the final switches, and unstrapped. He just sat there for a moment, hands resting on his knees. Something deep pulled at him, like the edges of his purpose were starting to shift again.

The cargo doors were open, and the first pallets started to roll out when a man approached the ramp, Air Force Major, judging by the insignia. Tension filled his stance; he was here for James.

He waited until James stepped down.

"Captain Callan?" the man asked.

James gave a short nod. "That's me."

The man handed him a sealed envelope. "You're being recalled to active duty under IRR authority. Effective immediately."

James raised an eyebrow, so rare to be recalled via IRR. He took the envelope, broke the seal, and scanned the orders inside.

Effective immediately, LT James Callan, USN (Ret.), is recalled to active duty in the United States Navy under Individual Ready Reserve mobilization authority.

Reinstated at previous rank: Lieutenant (O-3), USN

Reporting Assignment: Joint Military Relief Command (Provisional)

Temporary Operational Posting: Provisional Air Operations – National Recovery Support

Orders issued under the authority of the Secretary of the Navy, according to Executive Directive, following the invocation of the Insurrection Act.

At the bottom, a real signature.

Rear Adm. T. L. Spencer

Commander, Naval Reserve Air Operations

Joint Military Relief Command (Provisional)

"Return to Helena. Transport's being arranged. Your new assignment details will be delivered during the flight."

The major's words were clipped and procedural.

James looked back at the aircraft, still half-full, and then toward the gray, cracked skyline of D.C. In all the chaos, something had found him again. Direction.

He pulled his phone from his pocket and dialed Sarah. No answer, likely still on base with her reception blocked or locked in a room analyzing something.

The return flight to Helena was uneventful. These missions usually had him bouncing from crisis to crisis, not running back and forth. As the engines spun down and he stepped off the ramp and, as expected, found Mary waiting.

"So," he asked, half-smiling, "did Sam arrange my reactivation, or just send you to collect the plane?"

"He had nothing to do with it, I assure you." Her voice was calm. "You're our most valued pilot. If he could keep you, he would. But we don't let a $200 million aircraft become a paperweight just because the captain isn't available anymore. It'll be reassigned soon. But if you rejoin the company after your tour… it'll be waiting."

James nodded. "No, I totally get it, Mary. Keep her safe. Whoever Sam gives her to… make sure it's someone good." He paused, eyes softening. "Three years ago, I just wanted out. To fly, to disappear, to survive. But now… now I need to be where I end up. I need to help the best I can. For the first time, I really believe the military is the right choice for me."

Mary hesitated, her expression unreadable. "Captain… " she began, then caught herself, almost saluting. Her voice cracked slightly, more heart than he'd ever heard from her. "You stay safe out there. We all want you back. In one piece."

"Thank you, Mary," he said, the ghost of a smile tugging at his lips. "But it's just Lieutenant now."

He turned and headed inside. A single uniformed courier was waiting near the small operations desk; a reservist by the look of him, not even fully unzipped from his cold-weather gear.

"You Callan?" the man asked.

James nodded. Without ceremony, the courier handed over a sealed envelope. "Follow-up orders. Straight from JFHQ. I'm just the delivery guy."

James cracked it open. A single page this time. Thicker stock. Hand-signed again.

Lieutenant James Callan is hereby promoted to Lieutenant Commander (O-4), United States Navy.

Effective immediately.

Provisional command authority authorized under Joint Military Relief Command (Provisional).

Rear Adm. T. L. Rimes

James exhaled through his nose. Wartime efficiency. Still, it meant something. He'd left the Navy just shy of this rank. Now, it showed trust.

The courier raised an eyebrow. "Good news?"

James gave the faintest nod. "They want to ensure the right guy's flying the plane."

The man gave a tired smile. "Well, sir… looks like that's you."

James offered a handshake, then turned toward the back office.

Another envelope—official, thick, and final—was waiting for him. He had until 0700, enough time to sleep and pack.

Then return… and fly toward whatever came next.

* * *

Sam wasn't sleeping.

He rarely did these days, not in the way people expected. Short naps, system alerts in the background, a mind always half on. The room was dim, paper-strewn, and hazy from the blue backlight of half a dozen displays.

His fingers tapped methodically at a mechanical keyboard. The clicks echoed. He was halfway through pulling atmospheric drone imagery from over DC, tracking civilian response patterns. Violence had spiked just as expected, clusters, points radiating out from sectors. Someone had posted a rogue video claiming to be military-issued. It wasn't. Sam flagged it, re-routed it for deeper verification by a human contact in Signals—no AI filters. No auto-parsing. Just clean, manual work.

A soft chime rang from the secure uplink. A new file was a top-level priority. He opened it. Orders, not his.

James Callan: recalled.

Sam sat back. He had known it was coming, sensed the change after the President's speech—a pulse of sanity—the first clean signal in a decade of noise. And now the system wanted James back.

James barely knew Sam, but Sam would call him a friend, his best pilot. Sam had kept close tabs on him for a long time. He cared for him deeply. While he had put James in the LM-100J to ensure his safety for Sarah's sake, the truth was, James had earned that plane more than anyone.

He glanced at the edge of the screen. A folder labeled GIDEON-D4 still blinked. Unopened. Untouched since the last upgrade cycle. He clicked a tab and verified aircraft assignment parameters. Then another. Routing clearance.

Time to move the LM-100J.

It was not just any aircraft now; it was James' plane, even if no one else said it aloud. Sam pulled a secure line and made the call himself. There were no proxies, no ghost relays.

"Admiral Rimes. Yes, it's Sam Jameson. I heard about Callan. You'll be needing the aircraft. I'll have it delivered wherever he reports. No charge. Just keep the airframe intact and let him fly her."

There was a pause.

"Yes, she's still mine. My crews will maintain her, your base or mine, your choice, but my mechanics touch her, not yours." A long pause. "No, I'm not negotiating. I've got over two hundred million in her. If you want to cut me a check…"

Another pause.

"Yes. Inspection crews are fine."

Then: agreement.

Sam hung up. He didn't smile, but the corner of his mouth lifted slightly. He had always believed in the idea of America, not always in the nation. But maybe now, those two were beginning to align for the first time in a long time.

And he was not going to let them fall apart again.

* * *

Sarah stood in what passed for an office at Yuma. The space was temporary, barely organized, but the stack of personnel files on the desk was already sorted into three piles. She'd already memorized them.

She needed twenty-three people.

She wanted the ones who'd fought to keep their sector functional when leadership froze. Some had been in Raven, yes, but most hadn't. She looked for those who flagged inconsistencies in unrelated systems, who tracked anomalies across silos, who'd gotten shut down for asking the wrong questions—people who refused to stop thinking. People willing to work around the system to get the job done.

She flipped the first folder open. Signals. A corporal named Leena Hsu, Army, transferred from Fort Meade. Hsu had built her own tool for decoding packetized shortwave traffic. Nobody ever greenlit it, but it worked. Sarah scrawled *Pull* on the file.

Next: Cyber. Petty Officer Langdon Perez. Navy. Too outspoken. Twice reprimanded for circumventing protocol, but both times, he'd been right. He'd traced an incursion to a live test cell no one had officially admitted existed. *Pull.*

She continued through the stack. A junior Marine from HUMINT who ran a dual-track social profile built on their own time. An Air Force linguist who'd requested to stay after their enlistment ended... because they believed the work mattered. An Army reservist with a background in forensic data recovery who had submitted daily situational briefs even while off-duty.

Her list extended beyond the military. She flagged two civilians from the Raven contractor pool; both had been locked out of the final *Wrath* debriefs, but because they asked the wrong questions. She made a note to override their clearances herself.

Dr. Mason Reddick: FBI forensic analyst and behavioral profiler. Brilliant, caustic, and impossible to manage. He'd connected three *Wrath*-linked deaths before the agency forced him to leave. She circled his name. "Bring him in."

Sofia Naderi: CIA counterintelligence. Redacted history, two reprimands for insubordination. In truth, she'd flagged embedded threats long before anyone else did. Buried. Twice. Sarah didn't hesitate. "She's in."

Darius Cho: NSA signals analysis. Reserved, obsessive, and too fast for the agency to process. He'd flagged irregular command activity a month before Vegas. The logs were scrubbed. She still had a copy. "We need him."

Sarah worked fast and deliberately. She didn't care about the standard chain of command or branch tradition. She wanted fighters, thinkers, people who saw the fire long before others even smelled smoke.

She had twenty-three names by the time she reached the bottom of the stack. Some would need to be flown in. Some were already en route under temporary assignments. None of them had any idea they'd be reporting directly to her.

She leaned back in the chair and exhaled.

Her hand drifted to the chain around her neck, just the chain now. The cross had fallen off the morning of the first attack. It wasn't the absence that stung tonight; it was the ache of distance. She had been married six months ago and hadn't seen her husband since.

James was out there. She knew that. Flying aid missions, doing what he did best. And still, part of her wanted to see him walk through the door; grimy, exhausted, safe, just for a moment.

The door opened.

"Ma'am," said the aide. "Transport's ready. Flight to Hill is wheels up in thirty."

Sarah nodded, gathering the files.

The war had shifted. She was building her front line now, and every name in her hand was a weapon.

After the flight from Yuma, she was greeted by a corporal who led her to a squat, concrete building near the northern edge of Hill Air Force Base. The sky above Utah was pale and hard, a washed-out gray that offered no warmth despite the sun breaking through the clouds. The mountains in the distance stood jagged and frozen, lifeless sentinels to everything that had happened, and everything that was coming.

"We'll have the cleaning crew through the office this evening, ma'am," the corporal assured her.

The building was older and clearly repurposed. No signs or unit placards. Just a single security checkpoint and a reinforced steel door. Remnants of snow were on the ground.

Perfect.

Inside, the air was stale, unused. The lights hummed to life as she walked through, motion sensors detecting life for the first time in who knew how long. Rows of empty desks, dust-covered and featureless, stretched across a wide operations floor. Upstairs, a row of glass-walled offices overlooked the room. The windows were streaked, and one of the chairs was still wrapped in protective plastic.

This was it—the new home of Task Force Phoenix. Sarah moved slowly through the space, trailing her fingers across the edge of a desk. There was nothing of Raven here. Just potential. Just space. That, and silence.

She stepped into the largest office, her own, by default, and dropped her bag onto the desk. It thudded heavily, breaking the hush. She closed her eyes for a moment. They would make this work. Somehow. Even if she had to build it from dust and bone.

Two days later, her Task Force was all on base and reporting for their first day. Each had received orders, generic reassignments to Hill. No one knew why they had been reassigned.

"Good morning. The President himself requested this Task Force. I am Captain Whitaker, the Task Force's leader, but make no mistake, everyone in this room has equal weight. Your voice will be heard. You'll be free to make your case until we believe you or you believe us. We are not expected to be mistake-free. There will be no punishments for errors, only inaction.

"This is our opportunity to find *Wrath*. This Task Force's job is not to prevent an attack or follow dead-end leads. Our job isn't defense. It's understanding *Wrath* and ending them."

She looked around the room.

"Does anyone have any questions?"

A pause. No one moved. The air was thick with uncertainty and resolve.

Afterward, Sarah pulled up her emails and spotted a reassignment notification. Her whole team was present, so the alert irritated her until she saw the name: James Callan, reassigned to Hill.

Her phone buzzed. She answered, "James Callan, were you planning to let me know they called you up?"

There was a pause on the line, then his voice was half-apologetic and half-stunned. "Honestly? I'm still in shock that they did. I haven't flown military in years. And you are not exactly the easiest person to reach."

She'd only just seen it herself, but the words still felt good to say. "Well, they assigned you to my base," she said, unable to suppress the smile tugging at her lips. "So I'll see you when you land."

Another beat of silence. Then a muted laugh. "They, uh... didn't mention that."

"They better give you the night off," she said, voice low. "Because I haven't had a night with my husband in six months... I am not wasting this one." She hung up without waiting for a reply.

TWENTY-FOUR

By the end of day two, the hope Sam had been filled with had already begun to bleed out.

The President had spoken with conviction, measured, noble, even merciful, but words didn't put boots on the ground. And faith, no matter how sincere, didn't deploy troops faster.

Wallace had believed the warning. Sam knew that. He'd moved quickly, at least by government standards, likely aware that only the military could stop what was coming. But knowing wasn't doing. The motion had begun, but it wasn't enough.

That night, the world burned.

More than a hundred churches were torched before sunrise. In fifteen cities, mobs took to the streets, dragging believers from prayer meetings, smashing stained glass, and chanting. The first death tolls trickled in: over 2,500 confirmed. Most were Christians. Most had never raised a hand in defense.

Arrests crossed 50,000 by morning. They weren't rounding up terrorists. They were dragging worshippers out of pews. And it wasn't stopping.

Sam stood over his desk, fists clenched. This wasn't about waiting anymore. Not for truth. Not for justice. That had passed. Now, it was about rescue.

By the third morning, his entire network was moving. Hushed phone calls, secure messages, trusted contacts embedded in hostile zones, all reaching out to pastors, families, youth leaders, and anyone they knew to be faithful and in danger.

The goal was not war. Never retaliation. It was an exodus. Veiled. Fast. Untraceable.

That same morning, the President spoke again. Sam watched, jaw tight, as Wallace pleaded for reason, patience, and restraint. He condemned the arrests and called for documentation, due process, and facts.

The governors didn't blink. And Halstead? He struck within the hour.

"These aren't religious crackdowns," the Vice President claimed. "They're targeted actions against known extremists. Every one of these individuals is facing serious charges: aggravated homicide, conspiracy, arson, treason. This is law enforcement doing its job."

Sam had seen the same data. Maybe one in ten names were accounted for. The rest? Ghosts. Sam's original estimates had been built on logic… not hope. He hadn't let himself hope.

He'd layered it all: political leanings, church saturation, local law enforcement temperament, media hostility, proximity to friendlier borders. Every model had assumed some level of resistance, but also some delay; some window of hesitation before panic turned to persecution.

He hadn't accounted for this. The speed. The ferocity. The sheer cruelty of it. Even in states he had flagged as "moderate," the margin for error had collapsed. In some regions, the only path to safety was through a single, fragile corridor: one stretch of highway, one state line, one compromised checkpoint.

And yet… in that narrowing, there was clarity. The corridors gave his teams focus. Each bottleneck was a gate they could guard. Movement could be organized, patterned, or disguised. The chaos became, paradoxically, structure.

But the numbers didn't lie. At full throttle, every hand working, every route active, every forged ID accepted without pause… his network could move fifteen hundred people daily.

Fifteen hundred. And right now? Fifty thousand were already behind bars. Thousands more were being hunted. Millions were watching the walls close in.

Sam turned from the wall of monitors, chest tight. The room hummed, lights blinking in rhythm, systems ready… but it wasn't enough. He had spent twenty years preparing to save lives. Now he was watching them disappear by the hour.

Fifteen hundred. He whispered it aloud. Not a prayer. Not a curse. Just a number. As the tears rolled down his face, not from fear or frustration, but from grief and guilt, his network was not good enough to save them all. A number too small to matter. It wasn't a complete failure, but a failure all the same.

The crackdowns weren't organized; they were unhinged. Rash, sloppy, rage disguised as order. *Wrath* had pivoted from surgical strikes to brute violence. Their goals were unraveling, but instead of recalibrating, they were flailing, lighting matches in every dry place they could find. They were trying to collapse the country through madness. They would drown the war in noise and fire if they couldn't win the war clean.

Sam saw it. He saw the reach. He saw the panic. He saw how close they had come to succeeding, and how far they were willing to go now that they'd failed. Their plan had failed. But they weren't retreating. They were escalating.

Every political, racial, religious, and regional fault line was being split wide open. They were counting on governors to panic. On mobs to riot. On fear to finish what the bombs had only started.

And fear was winning. Sam's jaw locked. His breath caught in his chest.

Halstead… The Vice President's absence during the Capitol bombing had been suspicious. Just enough to raise questions. Just enough to make Sam pause. But it was everything after that turned suspicion into certainty.

He hadn't hesitated, mourned, or even flinched. He'd applauded the arrests and defended the fires. Painted tyranny in the colors of safety. It wasn't just silence. It wasn't just complicity. It was designed. Orchestration.

Halstead hadn't merely survived *Wrath's* attack; he had profited from it and stepped into the vacuum. Filled it with calm, practiced control. And now, he was publicly validating the exact nightmare *Wrath* needed to legitimize itself.

He was the inside man. Maybe the most visible one.

Sam didn't speak. He just pressed both hands to the desk, arms trembling with the weight of restraint.

Extractions weren't enough. Not anymore. He needed surveillance. Coverage. Leverage. He needed eyes on Halstead. Everywhere.

Sam stared at the screen, blinking against the blur of numbers. Another extraction confirmed: family of four, out of Pennsylvania. Five more queued in Ohio. Eight stalled in upstate New York. One dead. No details yet.

His fingers hovered over the keyboard, useless.

1,500 a day. That was the ceiling. A number that once felt enormous. Now, it was a rounding error—a bucket in a wildfire.

He had built the network to save the remnant. To be Noah's ark when the flood came. But Wallace's first address had changed something in him. It wasn't just the mercy… it was the possibility. Maybe the flood could be stopped. That maybe, just maybe, his ark would never need to launch at all.

And now the water was rising. Faster than he could bail. Faster than anyone could. He felt it in his chest, that old, bitter certainty that he wasn't enough. That no matter how much he built, planned, sacrificed… it wouldn't save them all.

He could keep the machine running. Keep extracting those he could. But it wasn't the answer. Not anymore.

The answer was truth.

Whatever *Wrath* had buried, whatever lie they were using to pit the country against itself, Sarah needed to find it. If she could crack it open, if she could expose the infection at the root, maybe the bleeding would stop.

Sam leaned back in his chair, eyes unfocused, breath shallow.

"Let it run," he said aloud to no one.

The network would move without him. It was built that way.

But Sarah needed more than silence. She needed a second mind, a second set of eyes. Someone not bogged down by official channels or fear of the truth.

He tapped the encrypted terminal and began drafting the message that would change everything.

* * *

Sarah was already in the office the next morning, poring over a wall of reports from her newly assigned team. Coffee sat untouched. The overhead lights buzzed faintly. She had barely slept. One night together after six months apart hadn't been enough, and now he was gone again.

One lead she was determined to pursue was Raven… the sidelined Task Force no one talked about anymore. She'd picked up several of its former members during her team assembly, and the moment they arrived, she gave them a straightforward assignment: go back. Dig into everything Raven had collected that never passed a section lead.

They had spent most of the night tearing through old files: coded traffic, background dossiers, fragmented intel drops, and redacted witness reports. The volume was overwhelming, and the quality was inconsistent.

Still, a few pieces stood out. Patterns emerged. Dead ends that felt too abrupt. Messages flagged as low priority… until now. There was no clean line. But Sarah could feel something just beneath the surface, waiting.

By 0800, her team had gathered around the central display in the Task Force briefing room; there was no formal seating chart, and no ranks were emphasized. Uniforms, civilians, analysts, linguists, cyber specialists… Sarah made clear from day one that titles and ranks stayed at the door.

She tapped a few keys, bringing up key snippets from the Raven archive. Each was annotated, color-coded, and cross-referenced with current incidents.

"These are the fragments I want to focus on," she said, voice even. "They were buried, never escalated or dropped due to lack of corroboration."

The room leaned in.

A reference to a shortwave relay in Maine flagged by a field agent but dismissed due to the source's age. A data dump from an overseas server cluster registered to a shell company with ties to several now-defunct NGO contractors. Once flagged for erratic behavior, a background check on a minor contractor in Arizona had resurfaced in several patterns tied to *Wrath's* targeting methods.

One by one, she walked them through the signals. The floor was open. People spoke readily.

One of the Raven veterans spoke first, pointing out that the relay report had been paired with an earlier tip from a private-sector whistleblower. Still, the match had been logged under a different project and never reconciled.

Another noted inconsistencies in the contractor's travel records: locations that, in hindsight, aligned uncomfortably well with Wrath activity.

It was more forward motion than Raven had seen in its final six months. And this time, no one was going to bury it.

"I've been sitting on something for a while," said Carl DeWitt, the explosive ordnance forensic specialist from the ATF. He leaned forward, arms resting on the table. "It's bothered me ever since I saw the first images from the attacks."

He tapped a few times on the folder in front of him.

"The first *Wrath* attack, Flight 2247, was a bombing—a massive one. Most of the cargo hold was filled with high explosives. We always said it was stable, military-grade: C-4 or Semtex most likely. The blast pattern, the video feed… it all lined up. And they pulled it off without detection—fast placement. Clean detonation. Remote trigger. That takes planning and access."

A few heads nodded around the table.

"But then, nothing. For two years. Only one confirmed use of explosives in any of the attacks. People said they were cycling through tactics, targets of opportunity. But what if that wasn't it? What if they weren't improvising?"

He let the silence hang for a beat.

"What if they were sending a message?"

Sarah tilted her head. "What kind of message?"

"Breadth of reach. Psychological dominance. They wanted the world to believe they were new, unpredictable, chaotic, flexible, and massive. That way, no one would think to look deeper. But this wasn't improvisation. It was misdirection."

He glanced around the table, eyes hard.

"They've been here all along. Concealed. Embedded. Patient. And now… every attack this time is explosive-based. But not from the outside. Every blast site we've reviewed, D.C., the state capitals, originated inside the structure. Deep inside."

He opened a binder and slid it toward the center of the table, revealing internal blast diagrams.

"We're not talking pipe bombs in closets. These are high-yield charges, likely rigged into structural cores. The kind of charges that collapse buildings." He looked up. "To level the Capitol, the Court, and the White House like that… we're talking tons of explosives. That's not just infiltration. That's embedded access."

Someone across the table exhaled sharply.

"So," Sarah said slowly, "you're saying they were placed… years ago."

"Or during major renovations. Or even original construction in some cases. But yes. These weren't planted last week. They've been waiting."

Sarah leaned forward, her tone steady but sharper now.

"So that would mean we're not looking at a group working from the outside: sneaking in and planting charges. We're looking at people with access. Clearance. Possibly for decades."

She stood, eyes scanning the room.

"We need to stop limiting ourselves to the last five years. Start pulling records from the last twenty-five, thirty, if they exist. When were the last renovations done on these buildings? Who got the contracts? Which companies were involved, and who signed off? We need names. Crews. Subcontractors. And I want federal access logs: anyone with long-term clearance to those sites."

She paused just long enough for the gravity to land. "And not just the buildings that were hit. I want the same data on every state capital that didn't go up in flames. Where do the patterns break? Who's missing? Who overlaps?" Her gaze swept the table. "We just got a flood of direction. Start chasing it."

She began assigning tasks, quickly and without ceremony.

DeWitt got site data and blast point comparisons. Two Raven analysts were pulled into combing through renovation histories. Others were split between clearance logs and contractor databases. One team would focus exclusively on the unhit capitals, building a profile of what didn't happen.

Following the meeting, she returned to her office and saw an urgent encrypted internal communication. It was titled 'Proposal':

Sarah,

I need to be able to do more, and you need the best people you can trust in each field. You know full well that advanced pattern recognition and signals intelligence are areas few, if any, can best me in.

I want to join your team.

I can get clearance. As a defense contractor, it will be easy and fast. But the real question is, can you trust me to help you? Can you let me save more people than I ever could with my network?

—Sam

TWENTY-FIVE

James pulled off the base road and turned toward the hangars, his knuckles pale on the wheel. The sun crested the mountains, its pale light throwing long shadows across the tarmac. It should have felt familiar—returning to uniform, structure, and the routine he had once worn like a second skin. His mind drifted to Sarah, finally getting to hold her last night. He pushed it aside just as quickly—distractions were not an option in his role.

But today felt different. He was back in the C-130J. And he hated it.

The C-130 was a workhorse, proven, reliable, tough as nails. But after nearly two years in the LM-100J, it felt like climbing into a time capsule. Heavy. Slow to respond. Dumb, by comparison.

The LM had spoiled him. Sleek, overbuilt, modified beyond anything the public spec sheets would ever admit. Sam had turned it into something else entirely. He'd come to love its responsiveness, adaptability, and the way the onboard systems learned from him. The AI copilot alone had saved his ass more than once.

But this… this was the military's domain again.

And with it came armor plating, missile countermeasures, and defensive jammers, things the LM lacked, but he no longer missed. There was comfort in stepping back into something built to take a hit while the world burned. But the transition tightened something in his chest like he was leaving behind the last peaceful piece of himself.

James exhaled through his nose and pulled into the hangar lot, where a line of Humvees idled along the far fence. A few other pilots were already walking toward the ready room. He killed the engine and followed them in.

The briefing room was functional but cramped. It had old metal chairs, fluorescent lights buzzing overhead, and a stale pot of coffee steaming in the corner.

"Good morning," the mission coordinator said without looking up. "You're in Hangar 4. Your bird's prepped, but it's been upgraded; full countermeasures suite installed over the weekend. You'll be running into Albany today. Supplies inbound, evac on the turnaround. You're wheels-up in ninety."

Great. Just great. He wasn't flying a C-130J. He was likely flying some KC-130 retrofitted for cargo instead of mid-air refueling... or worse, a C-27J Spartan rigged with slapdash upgrades because, with the recall, there just weren't enough planes. Both were good planes, but he was a C-130J pilot. The Spartan was slower, smaller, and carried half the load with half the range. The KC, while effectively a 130, was a mid-air refueling plane.

James blinked. "Albany?"

"New York. We have a federal presence embedded. The capital was hit hard, and infrastructure, communications, and the transport grid were lost. Situation's fluid. Some civilians are being pulled today. You're support and exfil."

"And the evac?" he asked.

"Mixed load. Some soldiers, mostly civilians. You'll be briefed on-site." The coordinator handed him a folder. "Keep your head on a swivel."

James accepted the file, then made his way toward Hangar 4.

The moment he stepped inside, he knew. It wasn't a C-130J or a C-27J waiting for him.

It was the LM.

James froze. For a second, the hangar seemed to go still with him. Every instinct said this shouldn't be here. And yet… There it was. Fresh matte paint. New call sign. And a defense package.

He approached slowly, eyes sweeping across the modifications. Infrared countermeasure blisters mounted under the tail. Active radar pods lined the forward fuselage. Twin flare dispensers nested just below the belly. Heat shielding along the cockpit glass.

This wasn't just Sam's version of the plane anymore… it was the world's now. Hardened. Claimed by the moment.

But the turnaround time for the upgrades screamed Sam. He had to have had the gear sitting in storage, waiting for the green light. James would bet the whole system had already been pre-wired, waiting for the right day to bolt it on.

The next-gen avionics package blinked to life as he climbed the ramp. Everything looked military-grade now. The interior had been refitted with reinforced struts, double-hardened floor panels, and a new modular seating system that could convert in mid-flight.

James placed a hand on the bulkhead.

"You weren't supposed to end up like this," he whispered.

And yet… it made sense. The world was no longer one where good intentions could fly unguarded. He climbed the ramp and found the crew aboard, running pre-flight checks.

The copilot stood quickly; young, maybe late twenties, one hand nervously adjusting his cuff. "Sir. Lieutenant Mason Kearney. I'll be your right seat today."

"James Callan," he said, shaking the offered hand. "Good to have you, Kearney."

"I, uh… gotta say; this isn't the bird I expected when I saw the manifest."

James offered a faint smile. "Wasn't what I expected either."

Near the cargo rigging, the crew chief gave a curt nod. Grizzled. Worn boots, worn eyes. Probably logged more hours than anyone on the flight. James glanced at the name stitched on his chest: Ortega.

"Ortega," James said with a nod.

"Callan."

Then James spotted the last crew member, crouched by the avionics bay, tapping through diagnostics with practiced ease.

He tilted his head. The engineer was one of Sam's, Dean Raskin. Dean had been with the LM as long as James had been. "Didn't think I'd see you on this run."

The flight engineer looked up with a faint grin. "Didn't think you'd be back in uniform, Captain… err, I mean… Lieutenant Commander?"

James let out a low breath through his nose. "Still getting used to that, Dean."

"Yeah," Dean Raskin said, standing. "Me too."

James gave Dean a final nod, then turned to address the others.

"Alright. I know most of you haven't flown this bird before. It's civilian… was civilian," he added, glancing at the reinforced panels. "It's a lighter, more agile cousin of the C-130J. Controls and behavior should feel familiar. Everything you need will work the way it should."

He paced once down the center aisle.

"Flight systems are military-grade, updated over the weekend. You'll see some non-standard layouts in the diagnostics, but if you've flown anything in the past decade, they'll feel familiar."

"We're keeping this first run simple. In and out. Supplies off, evac on. The auto-loader system should speed up our turnaround. We'll get final headcounts en route, but we'll adapt seating as needed once we're inbound."

His eyes landed on the four soldiers near the bulkhead, gear already strapped tight.

"When we land, Security moves first. First out, last in. Assume the zone is hot. If someone looks off… intervene. But remember: these are American civilians. Scared. Disoriented. Possibly injured. Don't go hands-on unless you have to. No unnecessary injuries. No accidents. Your job is to protect the plane and everyone on board. Period."

He paused, letting the weight of it settle. "Questions?"

Ortega shook his head. "We'll make it tight, Commander. Count on it."

Kearney gave a tight grin. "Noted, sir. And if something does go off, I'd really prefer it be outside the hull."

Nods and silent acknowledgments. They all knew what was expected.

Luis Ortega, the crew chief, gave the nearest cargo latch a final check and thumbed upward. "This auto-loader," he muttered as he passed James on the way to his seat, "I could get used to this kind of luxury."

Mason Kearney was already strapping in at the front, flipping through the startup checklist with quick, efficient motions. "Sir, uh, Lieutenant Commander… I've flown modified C-130s before, but nothing like this. How long've you had her?"

James slid into the left seat and settled his headset. "A little over two years. She's seen more than her share in that time." He flicked a few switches and glanced at the monitors as Dean confirmed all systems green.

Mason nodded slowly, eyes scanning the panel. "It's just… everything's so smooth. Like it's reading ahead."

James gave a faint smile. "She's built for that."

Dean's voice came through the intercom. "Tower's cleared us for taxi. No delay on departure."

James keyed his mic. "Roger. Everyone strapped in?"

"Locked and loaded," Ortega replied from the back.

"Security's tight," one of the Army team confirmed. "We're good to go."

James eased the LM-100J out of the hangar. The plane moved like it remembered him; responsive, agile, even with a full payload. As they accelerated toward the runway, the weight in his chest began to shift. Maybe, just maybe, this descent into chaos would be offset by the advantages of the LM.

"Hill Tower," he radioed, "this is Ghostbird One, requesting takeoff clearance."

The call sign was new—no tail numbers. Just a name, likely chosen from on high.

"Ghostbird One, you are cleared runway two-one. Wind calm. Godspeed."

The wheels lifted before he expected. She was eager, ready. And so was he. They banked east, climbing toward the horizon where the light was catching up with the world. Behind them, mountains. Ahead, Albany. And somewhere below, a country trying to decide what it would become.

The descent into Albany was smooth; too smooth, James thought. The stillness was unnatural, like the city held its breath.

"Albany Tower, this is Ghostbird One inbound with humanitarian cargo and evac request," Mason said into the headset, voice steady but a touch tight. "Requesting final approach vector."

The reply came back clipped and dry. "Ghostbird One, cleared for landing runway one-niner. Taxi to military apron, Gate Three. MP escort will meet you."

James leaned forward. From this altitude, the damage was still hard to see—no rising smoke, no craters. But the outline of the Capitol building, charred and roofless, was unmistakable even from the air.

Below them, Albany International had been transformed. Civilian traffic was gone—no jetliners, rolling luggage, or passengers milling around the windows. The tarmac now hosted rows of Army transport trucks and canvas tents. A Black Hawk squatted off to one side, its rotors still. Humvees crawled the perimeter like beetles on guard duty.

James lowered the flaps and brought the LM in clean. The plane settled with a soft thud on the runway, and the taxi lights picked up streaks of dirt, dried coolant, and tire marks that didn't belong to anything commercial.

As they rolled toward the designated gate, a pair of military police vehicles pulled alongside, guiding them in. James spotted more troops ahead; likely Army MPs with a few Air Guard mixed in. Fast, efficient people who'd already seen too much in too little time.

"Welcome to paradise," Ortega muttered from the crew station.

James shut down the engines and unbuckled, nodding to the others. "Stay sharp. We'll know what we're loading soon."

James descended the ramp slowly, boots hitting the cracked tarmac with a low thud. The cold bit sharper here than back at Hill, wind cutting across the airfield with a bitterness that matched the landscape. Albany had always felt tucked away, but now it looked hollowed out, like someone had scraped the life out of it and left the shell behind.

The civilian terminal was dark, long since commandeered. Military vehicles lined the far end, and a temporary command post had been set up using modular prefab structures. A flag whipped above one, half-torn, faded, but still flying.

He found the officer in charge near a stack of supply crates, barking orders at a private with a clipboard. When she saw James approach, she turned; face pale, eyes sunken, voice firm.

"You Callan?"

"Yes, ma'am."

"Colonel DeSantis." She gave a tight nod. "It's chaos. We're moving fast. You're not here for long. We've got sixty-three civilians cleared for evac. Families, the elderly, and a few with medical needs. Also, eight of our own. Injuries and reassignment."

"Manifest?"

She handed him a tablet. "Grouped by household. Most are pre-screened, but no promises."

He scanned it quickly. "Load order?"

"Security escort first, then medical. You'll have a mobile med unit to help with that. Civilians next, soldiers last. We don't want to scare the passengers."

James nodded. "Understood."

She hesitated, lowering her voice. "You'll see some uniformed civilians; state agency types. They're scared out of their minds. One of them swears they saw a drone tail their car here. Could be nothing. Could be *Wrath*. Or it could be locals with a grudge. Either way, you leave fast. You don't stay on the ground more than thirty minutes."

He glanced toward the horizon... dull grey, broken by smoke and a skyline still fractured from the blast that took the Capitol. "Copy."

By the time James returned to the plane, the tarmac had shifted. A line of buses pulled close, escorted by two Humvees. He could hear crying, arguing, and children asking if this was another drill.

He met Ortega at the top of the ramp. "Sixty-three civilians. Eight soldiers."

Ortega didn't blink. "We got room?"

James gave a faint smile. "We'll make it."

They deployed the modular seating as the med team brought up stretchers. Raskin handled internal weight distribution, walking the aisle with a laser measurer and balancing cargo on a tablet display that updated in real-time. Kearney helped two elderly women to their seats, awkward but sincere. The soldiers boarded silently, grim-faced.

The process was not as smooth or fast as James wanted, but eventually everyone had boarded. The ramp hissed shut. And just before takeoff, as the last security sweep completed, James caught sight of a man near the back. No ID tag. Clothes: clean but mismatched. Low-profile. Observing everything.

Raskin followed his gaze. "Something wrong?"

"Not sure," James said.

But in the silence of the cockpit, as the engines wound up and the runway cleared, James let himself believe, just for a second, that this was working. That some of these people might make it.

He suspected Sam had routed them here through his connections. It felt like his fingerprints were there—a whisper of order in the middle of the storm.

The LM-100J touched down at Wright-Patterson AFB just after 2000 local, tires kissing the runway with a satisfying grip. The flight from Albany had been uneventful in terms of airspace, but heavy with the weight of what they'd carried: dozens of civilians, eight soldiers, a few stretchers. The hangar doors slid open as James taxied toward the assigned bay. The sky was dark now with the final band of daylight gone.

As the plane rolled to a stop, ground crews surged into motion, offloading remaining cargo and guiding evacuees to waiting shuttles. A new security detail approached the ramp, gear fresh, eyes alert. James dropped the flaps and leaned back in his seat as the whine of the engines wound down. His body ached, but with recent years and non-stop flying at times, he had become used to the ache.

A base operations officer climbed the ramp briskly, clipboard in hand. "Commander Callan?"

James stood. "That's me."

"We've got another outbound flight request. Albany again. Civilians only, no military. Departure in seventy. We can fast-track refuel and reload."

James took the clipboard and glanced at the manifest. Another thirty-two passengers were flagged for emergency relocation. The airfield was running like a triage center, with everyone moving as fast as the system would allow.

"I'll check with my crew," he said.

He stepped into the bay where Ortega and Raskin were overseeing the offload. "Ortega—another run to Albany. You good?"

The crew chief gave a short nod. "Still breathing. The plane's solid. I'll check the hydraulics, and we're good to turn."

James turned to the flight engineer. "Raskin?"

"Better than sitting in a tent waiting for orders. Let's do it."

Back at the front, Mason Kearney met his eyes. "Sir… you good?"

James cracked his neck with a low pop. "Back in the early days, I was running relief in shifts. Slept on the plane while the other crew flew. Did it for almost a week. We've got better systems now."

Mason gave a slow nod, then glanced toward the ramp where a fresh four-man Army team was climbing aboard. "New security's loading in. They're briefed."

James exhaled through his nose. "Then we're good."

He headed down the ramp for a final inspection before takeoff.

The landing at Albany was smooth, but the situation on the ground had shifted.

The manifest had grown from thirty-two to sixty-eight. Most of the new additions were civilians, reserved and withdrawn, clustered near the edge of the runway under a makeshift canopy.

As James approached, he caught the details that no one else seemed to notice. Crosses. Bibles clutched in hands. Rosaries twisted tightly around trembling fingers. It wasn't just one or two. It was most of them. Same as the last flight. A pattern, clear as day, if you were looking. A whisper of order in the middle of the storm. He figured only Sam could pull the strings for the emergency evac of healthy civilians using military resources.

Back at Wright-Patterson, the LM touched down just after 0200. The runway lights shimmered off the damp tarmac, and the air held that peculiar stillness only found in the dead of night. James powered her down smoothly, the engines' hum fading like breath exhaling after too many hours awake.

He was running on instinct, barely, but still sharp enough to notice the details that mattered.

As he stepped off the ramp, jaw tight from the day's strain, he spotted the incoming maintenance team. They were all contractors. They were all wearing identical dark-gray jumpsuits, the same minimalist logo stitched over their chest pockets, Sam's company.

Toolkits open. Scanning gear was already active. No wasted motion. This was a full diagnostic crew. James stood momentarily, the exhaustion giving way to a flicker of reassurance. Sam was still overseeing the LM's care. And if Sam were watching, the bird would be flight-ready by morning.

The following two days blurred into a rhythm of takeoffs, landings, and exhausted in-between hours. Supply flights out, evac flights back. Hill to Albany. Wright-Patterson to Manchester. Stewart to Syracuse. Then back again.

The northeast was reeling… worse than most had realized. Major roads were impassable. Airfields were half-manned, some still burning at the edges. And yet the military presence was growing. Each stop brought more boots on the ground, triage tents, and flags.

But what struck James most was the passengers. Every return flight was full, overloaded, really. Strapped-in and shoulder-to-shoulder, seated on rations crates, rigged benches, anywhere they could fit.

And nearly every evacuee carried a sign. Crosses. Bibles. Prayer cards clutched in tired hands. Children with matching scripture shirts. Families grouped by instinct and desperation. Neighbors. Congregations torn from some shadowed corner of New Hampshire or upstate New York.

James knew. These were the people Sam had built his network for—the remnant.

It was the first return trip on the fourth day of flying when everything went sideways.

They were just minutes off the tarmac, climbing steadily. Passengers were strapped in, and clearance was confirmed. Albany was fading behind them. The cabin was muted, calm even. James glanced down at the nav panel when the warning tone hit.

A sharp, grating chirp. Then a red blink appeared on the threat screen—missile lock.

Kearney's voice cracked through the headset, high and tight. "Missile lock, missile inbound!"

James reacted instantly. "Deploy countermeasures. Now."

The cockpit flared with light as the flares launched, trailing hot magnesium against the cold sky. Chaff followed a heartbeat later, clouding their radar profile in an instant.

James dropped the nose hard, banking them into a sharp dive and throwing the throttles forward. The LM groaned but held. Passengers screamed behind them.

Through the haze of sensor noise, the threat display pulsed again; trajectory still inbound.

Then… detonation.

The sky behind them flashed white, followed by a jarring thud that rolled through the fuselage. Close. Too close.

The display flashed:

MISSILE NEUTRALIZED — PROBABLE FIM-92 STINGER (IR-GUIDED)

Smoke streaked past the tail. Warning lights blinked, then cleared. Systems held.

James steadied the plane, leveling it out once the lock dropped. The headset was silent except for the soft hiss of the cabin mic.

Then Kearney let out a breath. "That was… that was close."

"Yeah," James muttered. "Too close."

He glanced back over his shoulder. No fire. No damage alerts. The LM had taken the near-miss like a champ. But something sat heavier than the explosion. He'd been shot at before; downrange, years ago. Middle East. Hot zones with hot tempers. But never here. Never inside the borders of his own country.

He knew things were bad. Knew the Northeast was unraveling. But this… this was a line he hadn't expected to cross. Being a target in American airspace. He tightened his grip on the yoke. They weren't just flying into chaos anymore. They were flying through it.

TWENTY-SIX

Sarah had met him on the tarmac. When she'd accepted Sam's offer to help, she'd half expected him simply to appear—step through a hidden door in her office or slip in unannounced like a ghost. But even Sam, it turned out, had to go through military red tape.

Things moved fast, though. Two days later, he arrived: boots hitting the concrete as the biting Utah cold sliced through everything.

She walked up with a smile and extended her hand. "Hey, Sam. It's good to see you again. Let me show you where we work and your quarters."

He took her hand and shook it once. "Glad to be here. It'll be good to focus on something other than the loss of life for a while. Be somewhere I can make a difference… Mary can run the network for now."

She knew the reports. Over ten thousand dead from riots and raids on churches. A hundred and fifty thousand arrested—mainly believers, almost all from the Great Lakes, Northeast, and Atlantic seaboard states. From the hollow look in Sam's eyes, she wondered if he carried the weight of each of them.

"We're trying to figure out what happened," she said softly. "But even if we do, I'm unsure how that helps you. Not really."

Sam gave a tired, sad smile. "Once the truth is out… once people know… maybe they'll believe it. And maybe these killings, this tearing apart of a country I love, might finally stop."

When Sarah introduced Sam to the team, the NSA signals analyst, Cho, narrowed his eyes. "I know your name," he said evenly. "The NSA lists you as brilliant… and highly unstable."

It was close enough to an accusation to leave the room a little hollow.

Sam was steady. He offered a faint smile and replied, "And what do you suppose they'd list you as if you left the NSA?"

The man blinked, paused, then gave a reluctant nod. "Fair enough."

The morning briefing unfolded with its usual rhythm, more frustration than progress, but a few solid threads. They had direction. Leads. Pieces that might eventually form a picture.

ATF's explosive ordnance forensic specialist, DeWitt, gray at the temples, wiry and direct, voiced a concern he'd raised before. "I need to get on-site," he said. "At one of the locations, ideally more. Without firsthand data, I'm working blind. The video and photos just aren't detailed enough. The blast patterns were strange, and I need to understand them better. Without boots on the ground, I won't get what I need to truly help."

Sarah shook her head. "Still too hot. D.C.'s seeing near-daily exchanges: three wounded yesterday, two the day before. Until it calms, command won't authorize entry."

Sam said little and watched. He was calm and focused. Sarah found the way he listened almost eerie, as if he were recording not just words but tone, breath, and subtext.

Just as she was preparing to wrap up, he finally spoke. "It seems all ideas are welcome, so here goes." He leaned forward slightly. "I'm assuming you've already considered that *Wrath* didn't want the President to survive. That he wasn't supposed to. And if he hadn't… well, there would've been no one left above the Vice President. No challenge. No oversight. A clear path."

A few heads turned.

"But instead, he lived. And then someone, probably someone in this room, hijacked their broadcast. That wasn't part of their script. That screwed everything up."

He paused just long enough for the weight to land.

"Yes, they pulled off mass destruction. But they failed at the core objective. The regime change didn't stick. And what do you do when your masterstroke falls short?"

Silence.

"You adapt… or you collapse. But *Wrath* hasn't pivoted. They've gone dark. Dormant. That's not a strategy. That's a limitation. I don't think they can pivot."

Sarah folded her arms, watching him closely now.

"I think this was it," Sam continued. "The big show. The one shot they'd built toward for years. And now… they're stuck. Because they never planned for failure. Because they expected to have a friend in power. And instead…"

"They got Wallace," someone muttered.

Sam nodded. "A President who, for all his flaws, doesn't seem interested in revenge or power consolidation. He's grounded. Measured. That wasn't the plan."

He leaned back. "That's why this one can be traced. They got sloppy. Desperate. And desperate people leave footprints."

The silence lingered for a beat. Sarah collected her thoughts and took a breath, assuming the conversation had ended.

"Okay, let's—"

"I'm sorry, Captain Whitaker," Sam interrupted, calm but direct. "One more thing."

She paused. So did everyone else.

"I can break away two hundred fifty contractors, highly trained operators, and supply the vehicles to match. If Command is still holding back because of site instability, maybe they'd reconsider letting Mr.

DeWitt"—he turned slightly toward DeWitt—"on-site at the White House and Capitol if he had that level of protection with him?"

DeWitt was silent, but Sarah could see the spark in his eyes.

She nodded. "Yeah. That just might work. They'll push back on the cost-to-value ratio, but I'll fight for it. How much is that going to cost, Sam?"

He waved a hand dismissively. "No cost to them. I'll foot everything: personnel, transport, insurance, all of it. That should speed things up. Command always likes extra boots when they're free."

A few around the table exchanged surprised glances.

"They can dictate the best path forward," Sam continued, "but I can handle air travel, ground transportation, even helicopters to the site—if they're willing to open a staging base for us to coordinate from."

Sarah blinked. She'd known Sam ran a defense firm; small, but capable. Still, this? Two hundred fifty elite operators, full transport, insurance, and logistics? That had to be twenty million… maybe more. And he'd just offered it like spare change. She wasn't sure whether to be grateful or alarmed. What kind of man had that kind of power and offered it so casually? The man had come in under a cloud of suspicion, and five minutes later, he was offering more tactical and logistical support than the entire Task Force had received in two weeks.

Cho, still not convinced Sam belonged in the room, asked, "Why would you give away twenty million dollars of revenue for this?"

Sam said calmly, with a distant thread of genuine emotion in his voice, "My defense contractor company is just a small part of my portfolio. Every dollar of profit goes straight into humanitarian operations. I don't take a cent. This…" he gestured slightly, "this is just another mission. And I can't think of a more urgent humanitarian cause than stopping *Wrath* and telling the truth about them, before the public tears this country apart."

Sarah caught a few nods around the table; surprising, even encouraging. Cho even gave Sam a slight head tilt, marking it as the first sign that he might be warming to him.

The request went through faster than she expected. Two days later, DeWitt was on-site, walking the cratered Capitol grounds under contractor protection. He'd planned for three days; methodical, thorough, by the book. But things didn't hold up that long.

The after-action briefings painted the picture: a coordinated assault. Sam's contractors and the military barely held the line. Seventy-five dead. Several of their own were lost. She hadn't seen it happen, but DeWitt's hollow stare told her enough.

The mission was cut short.

Still, at least as it stood for the White House, DeWitt had gotten what he needed. Even three days would be light for a full inspection, but it was enough to pinpoint the explosive detonation points. Enough to start. Enough to work. Enough to run. But Sarah doubted any of them would forget what it had cost.

Sarah called a meeting the following day when DeWitt was back on base. He was visibly shaken; unsurprisingly, given he hadn't seen live combat before, but he spoke clearly and slowly.

"I was only able to investigate the White House," he began. "The explosive appears to be military-grade plastic: possibly C-4, maybe something close. We'll need lab tests to confirm the exact compound. But that's not what got me." He swallowed, glanced at the table. "It wasn't one massive blast. That's what we assumed, right? But I counted at least 120 separate detonation points. One hundred and twenty. This was coordinated… layered. Each charge was buried and placed with purpose. This wasn't just destructive; it was surgical. Whoever did this knew the building inside and out."

He paused again. Everyone waited for his next words.

"And that's just the ones I could find. There could be hundreds more. For all we know, some of them were in place for years. Maybe decades. This wasn't a last-minute attack. It was a long-term operation; carefully embedded, carefully triggered."

He shook his head slightly.

"I had just arrived at the Capitol when the assault started. I didn't get time to investigate properly, but from the initial signs, it's the same. Dozens, maybe hundreds, of individual charges. This wasn't suicide bombers. This wasn't a flash-mob event. This was years in the making."

He let out a long breath.

"I'll put together a full structural diagram for the White House. It won't be perfect... but it'll be something."

Sam stepped forward from the edge of the room. "That lines up with what I expected," he said, voice restrained, thoughtful. "I've never had hard evidence, not really... but for years, I've tracked... patterns. Operations that made no sense. Agency moves that seemed more designed to erode trust than defend it. At the time, I couldn't prove anything. Still can't. But they left footprints. Not just in what happened, but in what should've happened but didn't."

He met Sarah's eyes. "It's why I left the NSA. I was part of some of those ops. Missions that felt off... counterproductive to national security. I waited for someone to explain the bigger picture, but no one ever did. Eventually, I realized there probably wasn't one. Just decay. Shadow plays. Strategic fractures that always seemed to benefit national collapse." He looked back at the table, his expression tight.

She'd seen him intense before, but this was focused grief.

"This feels like the endgame of that thread. Not a conspiracy, just a current. Something real, pulling under the surface for decades. And now it's breaking through."

Sam let the silence linger before continuing.

"This feels like their last-ditch effort. The target didn't matter, not really. Just that it would destabilize the country, tear it apart at the core. And it's not just today, or last year, or twenty years ago."

He looked around the room. "People fixate on who killed JFK. But the better question is why. And even that's not the real trap. The trap is that we've been taught to ask who, to chase shadows, rather than ask who benefited."

He shifted his stance. "The Rodney King riots. What happened was brutal. But the response? They burned their own neighborhoods. Destroyed their own economic base. Why? Who gains from that?" He didn't wait for an answer. "Millions crossed the border under Biden, sure. But that wasn't always a Democratic platform. Obama deported more than any President before him. Even César Chávez, California's labor hero, opposed illegal labor because it crushed domestic workers. So why rewrite him? Why honor him for the opposite of what he stood for?"

Sam exhaled, slower this time. "That's the pattern. A thousand veiled edits. Things just off enough to be missed. Narratives reshaped so slowly you don't realize what's been lost."

Sarah caught herself leaning forward, her pen forgotten against her notepad. She could feel the weight of the room—eyes fixed, breaths held. Even those who had bristled at Sam earlier were listening now, caught in the pull of his logic.

"It's not a conspiracy theory… it's erosion. Strategic, generational, and deliberate in its indirection." He looked at Sarah. "It's the same story across politics. There was a time when Democrats and Republicans wanted the same end; they just disagreed on how to get there. But now? Now they believe the other side wants to burn the whole system down. They can't see it even when they're fighting for the same thing. Because the narrative's been twisted just far enough that cooperation looks like betrayal."

Sarah's chest tightened. She'd lived the numbers, analyzed the demographics, but never seen them tied into a single thread like this. It unsettled her, the way his words made familiar data feel like evidence of design.

"And why, when history is so damn clear, does the government keep designing programs that disincentivize traditional family structures? Rome collapsed when its citizens stopped forming families. The Weimar Republic glamorized self-interest right up until the fascists took hold. The early Soviet Union tried to erase the family, only reversing course when it realized an army without fathers couldn't win a war."

Sarah continued to listen, but something in her chest tightened. She'd never heard it laid out that plainly. She'd lived the numbers, analyzed the demographics, watched the rise in childless couples, but she'd never seen the pattern for what it was: disincentive by design.

"We've seen it. Over and over. Yet we built a system that penalizes marriage, dual incomes shoved into higher tax brackets. Welfare programs that offer more to single mothers than to married households. We subsidize daycare but offer nothing to the parent who stays home."

A flicker of unease stirred—personal this time. She'd always assumed she was the exception, the outlier. But maybe she wasn't. Twice married. No children. No home that ever felt permanent. The system had fit her. That realization unsettled her more than she wanted to admit.

"In cities, 'affordable housing' means a box for one: zoning laws that choke out multi-bedroom units because families aren't part of the plan.

And if a couple somehow beats those odds, they send their kids to schools that don't answer to them. Schools that don't ask permission to parent their children."

Sam's voice didn't rise, but its weight deepened. "It's not just neglect. It's design. We didn't forget the family… we replaced it. And we wonder why the country's ripping apart."

She swallowed. The room was still. He was right.

He folded his arms. "Look back. The wealth and innovation of the 1920s led to the Great Depression… but why? How does the richest era in American history collapse overnight? Then the seventies: an oil crisis in a country with more oil than almost anyone? In the eighties, interest rates shot to twenty percent. It crushed small businesses. Unemployment hit nearly eleven percent. Who benefits from that?"

The room felt tighter. "Then came the dot-com bubble—ordinary people found a way to build wealth fast, and it vanished like steam. The housing collapse of 2008; millions of lives ruined, trillions poured into banks and corporations. And every time, the result's the same: the public retreats inward. They blame each other, and they blame the government and how it functions. They stop watching the horizon." He paused. "These weren't random outcomes. These were accelerants. Each one pulled faith, stability, and ownership away from the individual and handed it to systems too complex to question. That's the pattern, too."

He let out a small breath, then rubbed the back of his neck. "Sorry," he said, a flicker of sheepishness breaking through. "I don't get around people much. And the ones I do see would think I'm crazy for thinking this much about patterns. Maybe I am."

He glanced around the room again, more gently this time. "But for the first time, maybe ever, I'm sitting with a group that might actually listen. And it might help. It might help us find *Wrath*, because I don't think that assault on DeWitt's team was random. I think they knew he was close. I think he was about to find something that could lead us straight to them."

The silence held for a beat too long. Cho exhaled, then looked at Sam with a glint of dry humor. "Well, that proves it. The NSA was right. You are unstable." He held the beat, then added more sincerely, "In the best possible way… but definitely unstable."

That got a round of faint chuckles and a few nods around the room—an easing of tension, even if no one was quite sure whether to agree or be afraid he might be right.

Sarah was stunned. She'd seen analysts pull together fragments before, seen gifted minds trace enemy movements through chaos… but this was different. Sam didn't just see the signals others missed. He saw what should have been there. He tracked absence like a scent, logic like a map. And somehow, impossibly, it made sense.

They'd all heard theories before. Half the analysts in D.C. had a pet hypothesis about erosion or controlled chaos. But Sam hadn't pitched a theory; he'd laid out a map. And at that moment, she wasn't sure if she was more impressed… or afraid he might be right.

Sarah glanced around the table. The silence lingered, but the air felt different, charged. They might finally have a path.

"All right," she said, her voice steady. "Let's figure out what they didn't want DeWitt to find." She paused, then added, "And let's take another look at who stood to benefit if the President had died and that message had gone out unchallenged. If *Wrath's* narrative had landed clean—no survivors, no counter-broadcast—who would have gained the most power? What should have happened, and what changed when it didn't? That might bring us closer to who *Wrath* really is."

TWENTY-SEVEN

It had only been two weeks since the attack, but the country was already unrecognizable.

President Wallace was still fighting, desperately trying to hold together a nation determined to tear itself apart.

Sam watched the broadcast in silence. Wallace stood behind the podium, eyes sunken, voice flat from exhaustion. He looked like a man trying to do the right thing while the world came apart around him.

Then the President spoke: "It is with the deepest regret that I address you tonight. Just moments ago, twenty states declared themselves a separate nation. They have named Vice President Halstead as their leader.

"They claim to speak for the people. They claim authority over the District of Columbia, our nation's capital. But let me be clear: D.C. remains part of the United States. It remains under our control.

"The Constitution still lives. It is not gone. It is not ignored. And under its authority, we will act. We will stop the mass executions of the religious. We will end the unjust detentions of the faithful. These states, whether by neglect or design, have allowed and even orchestrated the deaths of more than fifteen thousand Christians. And those are just the numbers we can confirm.

"We have verified nearly half a million illegal detentions. We have seen the real, unfiltered footage of citizens executed for daring to question their new state authorities.

No more. We will not plead. We will not persuade. We will restore order. The military has been authorized to take all necessary actions to bring these states back into the fold."

Sam leaned forward, eyes still fixed on the screen.

For the first time in years, someone in power had spoken the truth—and not a version of the truth, not filtered, not politically palatable, just… truth. But Sam knew that truth, by itself, was never enough. Now he knew, neither was hope. Hope without action was waiting to drown.

He had spent the last four days buried in data with DeWitt, trying to reverse-engineer the blast that had torn the White House apart. Every day since DeWitt's return had blurred into the next; hours of silence broken only by keystrokes and the soft hum of processing cores.

The White House was one of the most photographed structures on Earth. That morning, two weeks ago, it had been surrounded by tourists, news crews, cyclists, and drones. The volume of video footage was overwhelming. But for once, overwhelming was useful.

Using that footage, DeWitt had mapped 120 confirmed blast points. It should have explained the detonation. It didn't.

The damage pattern was wrong; too symmetrical, too complete. It wasn't just the rotunda. It was the understructure. The support columns. The north face. Even the curvature of the debris told a different story. They fed it all into a layered 3D model, testing detonation sequences against visual collapse. Even with perfect timing on all 120 charges, the simulation didn't match.

So, they began adding more—carefully, reluctantly, trying not to chase ghosts. It wasn't until the model reached 204 synchronized blasts that the collapse sequence aligned.

"Acceptable margin of error," DeWitt had said, adjusting the screen.

For Sam, that phrase would usually mean failure. Acceptable wasn't good enough. Not when the structure in question was America itself. But he let it stand this time because the model was just one thread.

The real work, the kind Sam lived for, was beneath the surface. He had written custom search tools to crawl every recorded work order, purchase requisition, subcontractor delivery, and building log associated with the White House, the Capitol, and the Supreme Court. Nothing in public record, and even less in government logs, was ever truly clean, but patterns could be found.

While he hunted blueprints and paper trails, the others chased people: names, backgrounds, connections. Anyone with access to sensitive areas, anyone whose clearance had outlasted their job, anyone who had been there too long or moved on too discreetly.

The question wasn't who planted the explosives. Not anymore. The question was: How long had they been there?

Sam's systems weren't AI… not technically. He hated the term. Hated the assumptions that came with it. His programs didn't think. They didn't guess. They didn't learn. They remembered. That was the difference.

He had spent decades designing them to crawl government systems, not scrape the surface, but dig deep. His search algorithms didn't just pull metadata or flag keywords. They traced the chain, followed the context, and immersed themselves in the bureaucracy.

To the untrained eye, the outputs looked like AI; webs of connected actions, decisions, and outcomes tied together across thousands of pages. But it wasn't intelligence. It was brute-force logic, stacked with contingencies and redundancies so vast they bordered on intuition.

Nowhere were his tools more effective than in government systems. He'd lived in their architecture, knew how procurement forms changed format depending on the department, how delivery records updated two hours after clearance logs, how internal chat systems bled into archived email chains no one ever really deleted.

He didn't write programs to find answers. He wrote them to follow stories. And somewhere, buried in the stories, was a war.

This time was different. For the first time in his life, Sam wasn't working around the system; he was working within it. He didn't have to break through a firewall, spoof a badge ID, or wait for a buried backdoor to slip open. He had access—full access.

Every clearance level. Every buried archive. Every system was partitioned or mislabeled by bureaucrats who'd long since forgotten where anything lived. No one was watching him. No one was blocking him. No one even knew he was there, because this time, he belonged.

His programs had never moved faster. Without the friction of intrusion, without constantly masking activity or rerouting queries, they could breathe. They could pivot and adjust in real time, making them more agile and dynamic than ever before.

Sam had always believed in building tools for when, not if, the system failed. But now, standing inside it, inside the wreckage of what used to be the most powerful government on Earth, he realized something else. This is what they were really for. Not to escape. Not to hide. But to map the ruins and maybe find the source of the fire.

Sam had gone down all the obvious paths.

Material contracts, supply chains, personnel logs, renovation schedules—his systems had already churned through millions of data points, and there were a hundred—no, a thousand times more—waiting in the queue.

He wasn't expecting a breakthrough. Not yet. But then his heart kicked. Just a flicker. Not confirmation, intuition. A tight cluster of actions and messages flagged by one of his deeper logic loops. Not for content, but for pattern.

It was over thirty-five years old. It was just a short email chain. A mid-level facilities clearance employee had messaged a supervisor questioning a recent order. Something new had been approved for installation, but the employee didn't understand the need.

Why was the product ordered? What was it meant to do? Was it secure?

The supervisor's reply was curt: *Authorized for maintenance performance improvement. Sign for delivery.*

That was it—routine on the surface, buried among tens of thousands of similar threads. However, the employee was terminated two days later. There was no write-up, no citation, no exit interview, just a change in status and the stealthy closing of an account.

Sam sat back in his chair. His eyes stayed fixed on the screen, but his focus shifted inward. It wasn't proof. It wasn't even a clue, not by usual standards. But Sam didn't follow normal standards. He followed the current. And this… this felt like an undertow.

Sam didn't announce his presence; he just stepped into the side room where Dr. Mason Reddick had set up shop, surrounded by printed case files and digital overlays. The FBI profiler had a methodical calm that seemed unshaken by chaos. Sam respected that.

"Tell me about Randall Simmons," Sam said, voice low but direct.

Reddick didn't look up right away. He finished a note, clicked something closed, then turned his chair slightly. "Who?"

"He worked at the White House in the late '90s. Admin-level. I've got records showing brief supervisory authority and was fired without cause. No follow-up investigation. No reason given."

Reddick narrowed his eyes, processing. "You think he's connected?"

"I don't know. But he questioned a shipment, one line in one email, over thirty-five years ago. Then he vanished. It's a thin thread. But it's the only one I've found that pulls even a little."

Reddick leaned back. "Alright. It's not exactly the level or timing I've been focused on; he doesn't fall into the 'had access' group, and he's well outside the twenty-year window I've been digging through. But give me a couple of hours. I'll see what I can find."

He contacted Mary on a secure line for an update. He needed the numbers… not for a report, but for his own sanity. As long as his network was extracting more people each day than the regime was killing, it felt like the scale might still tip, maybe not toward victory, but toward meaning.

Mary's report came quickly, quietly. The network had taken hits; fractures in the usual paths, checkpoints that weren't supposed to exist, but they'd adapted. The unexpected help had made a difference. People inside the breakaway states who didn't buy the narrative reached out. They disagreed with their governors. Some didn't even know who Halstead was. But they'd seen the videos. Not the broadcast; the warning. And something in it rang true.

Mary had found them, vetted them, and folded them into the extraction routes. Right now, the network was moving an average of 3,500 people a day out of the breakaway states into safer, Wallace-aligned territory. It wasn't enough, but it was something.

Sam hadn't realized he'd dozed off. Maybe it was the relief, knowing people were still getting out. Perhaps it was just exhaustion finally catching up. Either way, his eyes snapped open at the sound of a voice.

"I'm honestly shocked you haven't come to bug me three times by now."

Dr. Reddick stood in the doorway, holding a tablet, half-smiling.

Sam blinked, sat up, rubbing his face. "So, I do sleep now and then. Who knew?"

Reddick chuckled. "Sorry to wake you, but I finished looking into Simmons."

Sam pushed himself upright, stretching the stiffness out of his back. "I'll take anything you've got. Just need to know if the thread's worth following, we don't have time to chase ghosts."

Reddick shook his head slightly. "Then I'm sorry. There's not much here."

He stepped in and set the tablet down on the table. "Randall Simmons. Age 25. Hired under the Clinton administration, part of an initiative to diversify federal staffing. Worked at the White House for exactly eighty-nine days. Terminated without cause, no notes on the file. Background's clean. Lower-middle-class kid from Jacksonville, Florida. No college, probably couldn't afford it. High school grad with decent scores. Before the White House, he worked mostly manual labor, construction gigs."

Sam nodded, a flicker of something sharp and electric moving under his skin. "And after?"

"Two weeks later, he was killed. Gas station robbery gone bad. Clerk survived; Simmons didn't."

Reddick's voice was steady, clinical… but the silence that followed wasn't. Too clean. Too convenient. But too old to chase directly. Sam stared at the file, jaw tight. It might have been nothing. But it didn't feel like nothing. No. This was the thread. He could feel it deep in his chest; silent, steady, certain.

This was the right one.

"Perfect," Sam said, his voice laced with genuine excitement.

Reddick blinked. "Really? I thought this was the dead end. The kid doesn't connect to anything. No background. No motive. He's not even around anymore."

"Exactly," Sam said, eyes bright now. "It's not about the kid. It's about what he saw."

He leaned forward, the urgency returning. "He knew construction. And whatever that shipment was bothered him. Something didn't add up. He flagged it."

Reddick frowned, catching on. "You think the supervisor?"

Sam shook his head. "Probably clean. Just passing along orders. But those orders came from somewhere… and that's the thread. That's what I need."

TWENTY-EIGHT

James heard it; the whole world probably heard it. The President's voice crackled over the secure military band, calm but final.

War. Declared. Twenty states.

The same twenty James had been flying into for the past two weeks, hauling supplies in, pulling civilians out. One of them was where they'd taken fire. Where a shoulder-fired missile missed by seconds.

Now it was open war. He glanced left. Kearney had gone pale, hands stiff on the yoke. James hoped the kid was ready. Hoped he was, too.

He thumbed the comm. "Raskin, bring the full suite online. Everything we've got. Just in case."

The AI suite blinked to life, washing the cockpit displays in layered data. Secondary and tertiary flight routes lit up; some rerouted, some flashing yellow. Hot zones pulsed amber across the map, growing wider with every hour.

Military emplacements populated in real time, tagged by branch, strength estimate, and last confirmed activity. More troubling were the red circles:

SAM sites with disputed or unknown allegiance. Formerly federal, now… maybe not.

Raskin's voice came through calm but clipped. "Suite's up. We've got live telemetry out of Wright-Patt, Hill, and Fort Drum. Eastern corridor's tightening. A lot of radar noise, but I'm filtering it."

James adjusted the HUD overlay, narrowing his focus to their corridor.

"Mark everything. No assumptions," he said. "If it blinks, we fly like it'll shoot."

Kearney let out a low whistle. "I've… never seen anything like this," he said, eyes wide as the display updated again. "This isn't airlift work. This is a war map."

James kept his eyes on the map. "It is now."

From behind them, Ortega muttered, "Looks about right. Never thought I'd live to see the U.S. go red on a friendly ops grid."

Thirty minutes later, the LM touched down hard—too fast, too heavy on the left side, but within the margin. At Wright-Patterson AFB, James held the flare until the rear wheels bit, then let the nose settle with a tired groan. The landing strip was secure—military-controlled and Wallace-aligned—but the tension stayed high until the engines powered down and the main hatch was released.

Dust swirled across the tarmac as ground crews moved in.

James slid the headset off, running a hand over his face. Two weeks ago, this was a civilian cargo plane with a few tricks under the hood. Now, it was warfighting logistics—deployed in every hot zone they could thread.

Kearney stepped off ahead of him, pale. Raskin hung back to secure the systems. Ortega double-checked their supply offload before heading toward the makeshift barracks.

A uniformed captain approached, tablet in hand. "Commander Callan?" the man asked.

James gave a nod. He was still getting used to being in uniform again, but it was happening, and Commander in front of his name had stopped surprising him.

The captain didn't smile. "Sir, you're to report to Tactical immediately. Hangar three. We've got your ten-hour rotation already slotted."

Fifteen minutes later, James entered the dim room, half-lit by screen glow and dotted with officers rotating through seats. A large map dominated the far wall, with color-coded territories shifting in real time. Dotted red arcs marked conflict points. Overlaid icons showed known anti-air emplacements, including mobile SAMs and unverified National Guard posts. None of it looked stable.

A colonel stood at the front, clearing his throat. "As of 0600 this morning, presidential authority confirmed active hostilities against twenty breakaway states. That includes all border zones. Do not assume any National Guard forces are friendly unless verified by signal or escort."

James sat still, arms crossed, reading the board.

"You'll fly twelve-hour shifts," the colonel continued. "Twelve on, twelve off. Primary assignments: supply runs into besieged strongholds, evac of civilians or compromised units, and transport of surgical teams. You'll also rotate in night ops; deep run exfiltration."

He looked around the room.

"You all know your planes. I don't care what patch you wore before. This is war now. You're lifelines."

The room was silent. Then James raised a hand.

"What's the tactical state of the corridor south of Harrisburg?" he asked. "That's where we took a lock three days ago."

"Escalated. Two full Guard battalions defected yesterday. Artillery dug in. We don't fly there unless we have cover."

James gave a short nod. "Understood."

After the briefing ended, James headed for his temporary barracks. He dropped his pack next to the cot. The room was small and shared with three others, two of whom were already asleep, boots still on. The air smelled like sweat, dust, and reheated rations. He pulled off his boots and sat down slowly. His hands were still steady. That surprised him. Nine hours to rest. Then back in the air. The rhythm of war had started.

James' sleep was restless, filled with fragments that were somewhere between memories and dreams.

Christina and Wyatt are sitting on Flight 2247. Laughter. Christina's voice was soft and hopeful.

"Your daddy's here to meet us, sweetheart. I bet you can't wait to see him."

Then the plane jolted. She unbuckled her seatbelt—orange flame.

Gone.

His voice, screaming: "No!"

A sound that lived behind his ribs now, etched into his bones. And then, Sarah. An anchor. An angel. The only one who could reach him in that darkness.

James woke with a slow breath. He knew this day. This was the day the war started for him. Not the President's speech, not the battlefield. LAX. That fire. That loss. That was the day his world changed.

Today, in some strange way, he was… okay. He had Sarah. A wife he didn't deserve. A woman he loved fiercely, even if there was never enough time with her.

He still missed Christina. Still missed Wyatt. Some days, the ache threatened to tear him open. But now, with war declared, he saw it for what it had been: An inevitable march from that fire at LAX to this moment. James put the thoughts away and refocused on the now.

The first flight of James' twelve-hour rotation took him from Wright-Patterson to a lightly held airstrip in Maine. The state's National Guard barely controlled the field. Estimates said maybe 40% of them had sided with the President. It was enough to hold the runway, but little else.

Multiple aircraft had been routed in, packed with reinforcements. Supplies. Soldiers. These were the elite, the ones who pushed past the front lines to control the area.

SEALs, Force Recon, Green Berets—men and women trained for chaos. They carried the latest gear, the confident swagger of experience, and an unmistakable edge. Sometimes, James wondered if they actually felt fear, or if whatever made most people hesitate had long since been burned out of them.

The flight from Wright-Patterson AFB to Bangor Air National Guard Base was 870 miles, two hours, and fifteen minutes direct. But James wouldn't take risks, not with his plane or the people on board.

He plotted a course that avoided major cities and National Guard-controlled sites, steering clear of likely surface-to-air missile zones. The detour stretched the flight to nearly 1,100 miles and added close to an hour of flight time, but the safety was worth it.

Back in the Middle East, the serious pilots, the ones who came home, had drilled it into him: you don't fly these birds to fight. You fly to furnish fighters with what they need—supplies, troops, medevacs, fuel.

That meant avoiding the conflict, taking the longer, safer path. Because *it didn't matter how fast you were if you didn't arrive. Better to be late than dead.*

While the flight path was long, James arrived without incident, just as planned. He landed fast and soft, cargo hold dropping open before the wheels stopped turning. By the time the aircraft slowed to ten miles per hour, soldiers were already spilling out.

Ortega was moving fast, offloading supplies the troops hadn't taken with them. On the far end of the strip, medics and security escorts began loading the injured and a small group of civilians.

James watched the whole thing unfold with rising impatience. The area was still hot, very hot, and it could flare at any moment. They needed to get off the ground. He and his plane made the perfect target for the worst shot on earth. Even if they couldn't hit the broad side of a barn… they could still hit him.

James said a silent prayer as the tension spiked. Too long. In a place like this, they should've been off the ground in five minutes, tops. He leaned out of the cockpit and started shouting…

"Let's go! Move! Get on, now!"

Then, a look at Ortega; sharp, loaded. We're in trouble. Get them in.

Ortega got the message. He'd been around long enough to read that look.

He started hustling the last civilians and medics up the ramp.

"Strap in wherever you can; just get inside!"

The moment the final pair crossed the edge of the ramp, Ortega slammed the close button.

James didn't wait.

He began pivoting the plane even before the ramp was fully sealed.

Then… Crack.

A bullet punched through the unarmored fuselage.

Then another. A dozen more. The LM-100J could take hits to the skin, but the tires? A single shot to the gear could cripple them. He throttled up. The engines roared, and the plane began to roll. Outside, the soldiers who'd ridden in with them laid down suppressive fire… returning heat toward the source with disciplined fury.

Thank God for them. They'll take it personally. Someone's shooting at their ride. James pulled the plane into the air. The instant they had lifted, he keyed the comm.

"Ortega, everything okay back there? Anyone hit?"

There was a pause… then Ortega's voice came through, tight and shaken.

"Yeah, Commander. We'll be okay… mostly. Medics are with the civilians; some caught shrapnel."

A pause.

"But… Raskin got hit. It's bad. But he knows. He knows his time's up."

The next hop was short, only fifty miles to NAS Brunswick.

Before the third *Wrath* attack, it had been a ghost base. But after the assault on the Pentagon, the Navy moved back in—fast, recommissioned, and fortified.

James was on the ground in under twenty minutes. But it was still too long. Raskin had died within five minutes of the wheels leaving the ground at Bangor.

After landing, James learned that fifteen flights had touched down at Bangor, delivering nearly 1,100 soldiers. The airstrip was now considered firmly under U.S. control, and ground forces were already deploying from NAS Brunswick to establish a secure corridor between the two locations.

His crew stepped off the LM while it was refueled and inspected. The damage was minor: several hull punctures, nothing structural. Light repairs were completed in under an hour, giving everyone enough time to shake off the adrenaline.

Kearney threw up about five minutes after stepping off the ramp. Ortega didn't miss a beat. The grizzled crew chief clapped the younger officer on the back, his voice dry as ever.

"Don't worry, Lieutenant. Give it a few more days, I'm sure you won't puke every time we take fire."

To the kid's credit, Kearney took the comment in stride. From James' experience, that had been about as hot a zone as you ever saw outside a full-blown battlefield. If the lieutenant could hold it together there, vomit or not… it'd be easier from here on out.

Over the next few days, the LM took fire once more: just a burst from a light weapon, likely a pistol, fired as they climbed out from a forward zone. It gave them a scare, but nothing punched through the skin. Just noise. Still, it was a reminder; even the small stuff could kill you if it got lucky.

On the sixth straight day, James turned to Kearney in the cockpit.

"Look, this next run sounds easy. We don't even touch down. Ortega's got the hardest job; at least that's probably what you're thinking. But make no mistake… this is an airdrop because the zone's too hot to risk a landing. That's it. That's the reason."

He paused just long enough to make sure the kid was listening.

"We're not relaxing because it's simple; we're staying airborne because it's dangerous. So stay alert. Watch everything. If you see something out of place, you call it out. No second-guessing. Clear?"

Kearney managed only a barely audible, "Roger," his face a shade paler as he turned back to the instruments.

James didn't want the lieutenant scared. But he had to know this was anything but routine. Of all the missions they'd flown so far, this one had the highest potential to go sideways. If they were lucky, it was just a drop into the fire and a fast way out.

They weren't as lucky as James had hoped. He'd prayed on the way in, asked for a safe drop, a clean run. But God didn't answer this one the way James had hoped.

Ortega had just released the first package when the crack of small-arms fire rang through the hull. They were high enough and reinforced enough that the rounds didn't punch through. But later, they'd find the indents. Deep ones.

Kearney squinted through the forward glass as the final package cleared the ramp, and the door began to close.

"Why is that guy just standing there?" he asked, pointing about 1,500 yards out toward the ground.

James looked. Froze. Then shouted.

"Strap in, Ortega! Now! Things just got wild."

James banked hard, scanning for the cleanest escape vector as the infrared warning pinged in his headset.

"Flares… now," he barked.

He dropped the throttle and pushed the yoke. "Move, baby. Move."

"Missile inbound!" Kearney shouted, eyes wide.

"Countermeasures active," the AI reported, flat and emotionless.

A second later, a flash of light… Detonation registered. The explosion was heard, not felt. James kept the bird in an evasive climb, zig-zagging, trading altitude for safety.

Kearney exhaled, wiping sweat from his brow. "Man, that was close."

"Not yet," James said, voice tight.

The second IR lock pinged. Higher tone. Closer range. A new inbound.

"Oh God," Kearney breathed.

"Missile two incoming," the AI confirmed.

"Countermeasures, now!" James dove this time, hard, pressing their stomachs into their spines.

The second missile took the bait… but as it exploded, a jagged piece of shrapnel sliced through the wing and clipped Engine Two.

A groan. A sputter. Engine Two coughed, then caught… barely. James gritted his teeth and pushed the remaining three engines to the limit, climbing again, desperate for altitude in case Number Two quit entirely.

James was just over 130 miles from Joint Base McGuire–Dix–Lakehurst.

Initially, he'd been scheduled to set down at an Air National Guard base in West Virginia, friendly territory, but ill-equipped. The fighting in New Jersey was lighter than in Pennsylvania; Pennsylvania had become the focal point of the war.

Wallace's commanders executed a clear strategy: divide the Halstead states into three isolated sectors, cut off their supply lines, fragment their coordination, and collapse the rebellion from the inside.

It was working.

Halstead threw what little he had at defending Pennsylvania, but it was a losing battle. Everyone could see that, except maybe Halstead himself.

Estimates put his total force under 300,000, cobbled together from loyal Guard units and militias. Wallace's forces numbered over 1.7 million, and they had better gear, better logistics, and complete control of federal weapons systems. Halstead had only what he could pull from Guard armories and sympathetic civilian caches; most of it was ten to fifteen years out of date. But he was putting up the fight he could, using civilians as shields and cities as barriers.

James knew the Guard base in West Virginia wouldn't be able to handle repairs on his bird. Not with the damage Engine Two had taken.

New Jersey was the only viable option. He keyed the radio, called in his course change, and banked south. It was only 130 miles as the crow flies. But to avoid hot zones, he'd fly closer to 200 miles.

Safer. Slower. Worth it.

James turned to Kearney.

"Well, Lieutenant… I can promise you that's the closest you ever want to come to losing a plane. If you go down in a zone like that, even if you survive the crash by some miracle… you're not surviving the welcome."

Kearney just nodded, still pale, still processing. Once they were on the ground at McGuire, a captain approached the crew, tablet in hand.

"Looks like you're grounded for a while," he said, eyeing the side of the aircraft. "I'd bet that's a new engine."

He scrolled through James' rotation log and gave a low whistle.

"Judging by your flight record, you and your crew are overdue for some R&R anyway."

He looked back up. "Expect at least seventy-two hours before you're airborne again. We can arrange transport to Hill if you'd prefer, or you're welcome to stay here... assuming nothing's calling you away."

James immediately thought of Sarah. He had three days, and he'd spend every second with her.

"I'll take a ride," he said. "I'll fly if you need me to."

The captain shook his head. "No need. We've got regular transports running to Hill."

He scrolled through his tablet. "In fact... I can get you on one in sixty minutes."

He glanced at the rest of the crew. "Any of you heading to Hill?"

Ortega grunted. "Any rack's good for me. I'll hang with the bird."

Kearney and Williams both shook their heads, choosing to stay behind. An hour later, James was in the back of a smaller C-27J Spartan, the drone of the twin turboprops humming through his boots.

Heading west. Heading home... if only for a little while.

TWENTY-NINE

Sarah sat at her desk, her shoulders tight, her eyes bleary from too many hours in front of too many screens. Sam sat across from her, still, tempered, unreadable.

"DeWitt says drones are a no-go. He has to be on-site," Sam said.

She rubbed at her temple, more from frustration than pain.

"We don't know what we'll find there, but maybe… maybe enough to link it to Simmons. Whatever arrived at that site, it mattered. But the logistics supervisor looks clean. They process too many requests… there's no way to track which item Simmons flagged. I've chased every angle. Every rabbit hole. Nothing."

She pushed back from the desk. "I know we need to get back to the Capitol. But D.C.'s the second-hottest zone in the country."

She turned back to Sam. "We go in, we need more than instinct. We need confirmation. Otherwise, I'm sending people into hell without a damn map."

Sam's voice was low, ragged with exhaustion, something rare in him. "I don't think Halstead wants DC because it's symbolic. I think he wants it because he knows something's there. And if we get to it first… his end comes even faster."

She stared at Sam, frustration crackling beneath the surface.

"Then you need to get me something more," she said. "A plan. A sellable reason. A…" Her voice caught. Trailed off mid-sentence. Her eyes had shifted, locked on the far side of the ops center. "…James."

He stood just inside the doorway, dust still on his boots, one arm stiff from the strain of the flight, the other dropping slowly from a half-salute.

For a second, no one moved.

Then Sarah rushed around the desk like she was being pulled by gravity. Behind her, she heard Sam, his voice lifting just slightly, the closest he ever got to outward warmth.

"James!"

She crossed the room and wrapped her arms around him. He caught her in a full embrace, strong and grounding. They kissed, long and unhurried. A minute, maybe more. As if the world had vanished and they were the only two left.

Then, gently, she heard Sam again.

"I'll work on something," he said, the smile audible in his voice. "But for now… I don't think I'm needed here."

A pause.

"Maybe the two of you should take a day. Not here."

The exhaustion hit her all at once as he held her. The tension in her shoulders, the constant forward motion, finally cracked. It had been at least eighteen hours since she had slept and more than three weeks since she had a day off.

No, she corrected herself. *I worked the three weeks before that, too*—a solid month and a half, nonstop.

She pulled back just enough to meet his eyes and managed a tired smile.

"Let's get out of here," she said softly. Then, almost afraid to ask… "How long are you here for?"

"A couple of days," James said gently. "Let's get you back to our quarters. You need sleep."

They left the ops center together, walking quietly through the corridors, the weight of the war momentarily softened by each other's presence.

Sleep wasn't the first thing on either of their minds, despite how tired they were. They spent some time together, just the gentle closeness of being whole again, if only for a while. Eventually, exhaustion caught up with them. They drifted off in each other's arms, the room still and noiseless, the world outside held at bay.

The smell of bacon pulled her from sleep. Sarah blinked, stretched, and glanced at the clock. 0800. She slept later than she had in years. She rolled out of bed and padded into the kitchen, where she found James at the stove, just finishing up breakfast.

She smiled, crossed the room, and kissed him softly. "So," she murmured, still waking. "Why are you here?"

James gave her a sideways grin. "Well," he said, "unlike you desk-job people, the military apparently doesn't like its pilots and crew pulling too many twelve-hour shifts without a seventy-two-hour break." He plated the bacon and added, "Also... I needed a new engine."

They spent the morning catching up.

Over eggs and coffee, James walked her through everything that had happened since the war began; missions flown, fire taken, lives lost, and saved. He kept his tone even, but Sarah could hear the weight behind his words.

In return, she told him about the investigation. About Simmons. About the possible lead they had, one that, on paper, looked solid. But without hard evidence, it wasn't enough.

"It dates back to 1997," she said, pushing her plate away. "And no one in the brass wants to greenlight a high-risk op based on an over three-decade-old logistics thread and a gut feeling. Especially not a return to the Capitol."

She could see James mulling it over in his mind.

She looked down. "I've already lost people there."

Later, after they had finished breakfast, Sarah sipped her coffee, legs curled beneath her on the couch. "Do you think," she asked softly, "if it had been you… Christina would have moved on?"

James thoughtfully stared at the mug in his hands.

"We talked about it once," he said finally. "Early on, before we were married, she just sort of blurted it out. She made me promise if anything happened to her, I wouldn't waste my life staying broken." He looked over at Sarah. "I want that for you, too. If… something ever happens."

Sarah reached for his hand. Held it tight. James only had a little over forty-eight hours. He'd need time to travel back, prep his aircraft, and at the very least, get a nap before his next shift.

Sarah realized it might be a while before they saw each other again. And with the investigation stalled, leads going cold, and morale stretched thin, she made a decision.

She was taking the day off. In fact, she'd take the whole forty-eight hours he had. She'd tell her team to do the same; just a short reset — maybe a little distance would shake something loose. Sometimes, breakthroughs came when no one was looking for them.

She knew Sam wouldn't rest. If she were lucky, he'd take eight hours instead of four. But there was zero chance he'd take more.

The city around Hill had grown peaceful, almost normal again. Most states outside the twenty Halstead-aligned and their bordering regions had begun returning to something like normalcy.

About twenty states had already announced plans for special elections. These things didn't happen overnight, but they were moving as fast as possible. The funny thing was that once those elections were held, the winners would be seated immediately as official members of the current Congress. And that meant the sooner a state held its elections, the sooner its officials gained seniority. Days might not seem like much, but in Washington? Days still counted.

They spent the day outside the base, just the two of them. They revisited old memories, made new ones, and reminded each other what it felt like to be seen, to be held, to be loved. For a while, they almost forgot the war existed. In each other's eyes, there was peace, real peace.

She knew, deep down, that God had meant for them to be together. Did it take the struggles, the near misses, the losses to make them right for each other? Maybe, but she was certain of this: with James, her world was finally right.

They could've left the base and found a hotel in Layton or Clearfield. But none of them were more than passable; comfort without soul. She wanted peace, calm, and him. Not comfort rebranded as luxury.

So they stayed close. An undisturbed walk outside the wire. A shared meal in the back corner of a half-forgotten commissary lounge. And for now, that was enough.

They spent the night tangled together, the kind of sleep that only came with complete trust and shared exhaustion.

When the sun rose, they enjoyed the slowness of waking. They walked side by side to the small coffee shop on base, comfortable peace between them.

The day stretched slowly and simply. Just another day lost in each other.

When morning came, reality returned.

James had to report back, and Sarah had to reopen the investigation with clearer eyes and a rested mind.

They walked together to the tarmac silently, hands brushing, fingers laced. At the transport, they paused. Sarah leaned in for a final kiss, holding it a moment longer than she meant to. A single tear traced her cheek as they pulled apart.

"Don't worry," James said softly. "This will all be over soon. We'll be together again."

She nodded, her voice catching as she whispered, "I love you so much."

James smiled and stepped backward toward the stairs.

Sarah wiped her cheek and called after him, firm and steady. "You stay safe. I'm holding you to that *together again* part."

THIRTY

Sarah had told them all to take 48 hours off… back at 0800 two days later. Everyone needed a break. They'd been hard-charging for weeks.

Sam had been hard-charging for decades.

The idea of taking 48 hours off felt like a betrayal of the people who would die while he failed to solve the mystery. He understood the science—people needed breaks, needed rest. In every company he ran, he enforced mandatory vacation. People worked better when they had time to recharge.

But he was wired differently.

He had never understood why until he read the 2009 study on the DEC2 gene mutation. A tiny fraction of people who didn't sleep long, not because they wouldn't, but because they didn't need to. Their bodies skipped the long drift through light sleep, dropping directly into REM and deep sleep. Four to five hours was enough.

He wasn't broken. Just… rare. Tonight, he would allow himself to sleep. He closed his eyes.

The dark turned fluid, threads of color weaving into sound. It was a dream, not sleep, but it came too fast for him to question. He was still aware, still present, just far enough gone to watch his thoughts turn into images. He could wake if he wanted, but he knew this dream. And he knew it needed to come.

It was the late 1990s. He was in the field with Rogers. Rogers was a good man, ambitious, while Sam was reserved but loyal—loyal to the Agency and the country. They were walking a gray corridor in the building, heading to a briefing.

Sam looked at him with a solemn respect. Rogers didn't treat him like an oddity. He saw Sam as he was: understated and brilliant.

"Did you notice that line in the Wrathenburger video?" Rogers asked. "He kept saying 'doorway,' but the way he described it, it's not a doorway. I think it's a panel. Something hidden."

"Hidden panels in the Capitol?" Sam gave a dry look. "Yeah, that'll go over well."

Rogers chuckled. "I know. I wasn't gonna bring it up in the brief. Just struck me weird. Why would anyone add panels now? If it were fifty years ago, sure. But the place has cameras everywhere now."

He paused. "But Wrathenburger doesn't seem crazy. And he never said he added them. Just asked about them. It's probably nothing. I'll let it go."

But at the briefing, after another brutal round of bureaucratic nothing, Rogers finally cracked.

"There is one odd comment. Likely nothing," he said. "But something about panels being installed at the Capitol."

The Director didn't even blink. "Yeah, I saw that. Everyone saw that. It's meaningless. What... do you think they're secretly rebuilding the Capitol with hidden passages?"

Afterward, Rogers gave a sheepish shrug. "I couldn't take it anymore. Had to give him something. Went over just like we thought, but at least it ended the damn meeting."

Sam hadn't blamed him. It was a scrap. Something to show they'd done their job.

The next morning, Rogers didn't show up.

At 10 AM, Roberts walked in. His face was pale.

"Rogers was killed last night," he said. "Liquor store robbery. Looks like he tried to stop it. Took a bullet. Died on scene."

Sam woke up.

Five hours, he noted—a long sleep for him, at least.

He got up and checked the reports from Mary. Another luxury. One he hadn't allowed himself in days. But Sarah had told them to take time off.

The reports were as expected. The network was still functioning, but the formal war had reduced its reach. Where they'd once funneled nearly 4,000 people in a single day, the number had dropped.

Now it was 1,800 a day and falling. Not by much. A few here, a few there. But Sam saw the slope. Saw the inevitability in the curve. If the pattern held, it would stabilize at 1,298 daily within a week.

He returned to the office. Just the low hum of the fluorescent lights, outdated fixtures the military should've replaced with LEDs a decade ago. The power savings alone would have justified the switch. But Sam knew the real cost wasn't energy. It was the slow drain of productivity, the way the flat, unnatural flicker of fluorescents hollowed out a person's focus.

LEDs weren't just cheaper. They felt like daylight. Like the kind of decision someone who actually cared about human performance would have made.

Simmons.

He had asked about the same doors, or panels, or whatever they were… like Rogers.

Sam was certain. He couldn't prove it. If only he knew what they were. If he could confirm the suspicion, maybe he could find the trail and trace it back to where it started. To explain why they were there. If they were there.

However, the Capitol and the White House were among the most photographed buildings on the planet. How could a door be hidden? Even a panel? He had chased down every mention, every offhand comment the supervisor ever made about doors and panels. They had to be something else. Something like a door. Or like a panel. But what?

A window?

What if it wasn't a door, or even a panel? What if it were a window? Or something referred to as one? Or something attached to one?

Windows, even in the Capitol. Even in the White House, still had to be replaced. Upgraded for ballistic resistance. Blast shielding. They were accessed. Routinely. Discreetly.

He sat up straighter and started the search, pulling every conversation, note, and fragment the supervisor had ever logged regarding windows. For the next twelve hours, he read about them. Debates on window clarity, reports on the levels of ballistic and blast shielding each type could provide, timelines on procurement orders, arguments over misfit specs and the wrong sizes delivered, and installation delays.

Everything no sane person would ever want to know about windows… he read. And as he read, he couldn't help but admire the government's uncanny ability to take some of the most minor, irrelevant details imaginable and spin them into a year's worth of work for forty-five people, ultimately achieving less than what a decent window salesman could've wrapped up in an hour.

Sarah's insistence that they all take a break wandered through his brain. He stopped. Logged into his private interface. And opened the reports he'd been avoiding—the ones from Mary.

Estimates: at least 1.5 million arrested. At least 250,000 dead. Mostly Christians. And the ones who tried to help them.

He read the number. Then again. But he didn't see a number. He saw the faces. A retired logistics officer who ran extractions through abandoned rail lines. A teenage coder in Des Moines who rerouted drones with scripts Sam had written. A grandmother in Georgia who ran her farmhouse like a field hospital.

Seventy-five of them. Gone. Not just dead but found out. Executed, or bombed, or caught in the collapse they tried to outrun. The Christians they had helped, gone too.

Sam leaned back, closed his eyes, and prayed the kind of prayer that didn't ask for anything specific, because the loss was already done.

"God, hold them. All of them. Give them peace. Give their families strength. And if there's still a way back for this country, show me. Show someone."

A pause. A breath.

"And God… if Halstead can still hear You—make him listen."

The silence that followed didn't feel empty. It felt like a weight.

Then the Defense Department's casualty update: 45,000 killed or injured, mostly on Halstead's side. The blood was spreading.

Pennsylvania and D.C. were still war zones; chaotic, violent, hopeless. Other hotspots flickered just enough to block a full military reclaim. South Carolina, the southern edge of Halstead's reach, was fraying. Its support was fractured. Its defenses were thin. While all eyes stayed on Pennsylvania, Sam saw the truth: South Carolina would fall first.

He spent the next day much the same way. He read the reports. Took a moment to pray for their souls, for the ones already lost, and for those still out there, running out of time.

Then he went back to the windows.

Fourteen hours; buried in supply logs, installation notes, spec sheets, internal debates about glass clarity and frame integrity.

He slept for five hours.

The following morning, he didn't open the casualty reports. The forty-eight hours were over. And now, he needed to be focused and not distracted by the dead.

He was at his computer by 0600. Pulled up the last entry he'd read: frame integrity, an even less interesting topic than the window itself.

But something stuck. Frame integrity. It was everywhere. It was not just a passing phrase but a point of focus. Whole paragraphs debated it. Long threads from engineering teams, contractors, and inspectors, all obsessing over frame integrity like it was a national security concern.

And not just in isolation. It was threaded through conversations that had nothing to do with windows. People who shouldn't have been in those chains were replying. Forwarding. Flagging. Sam sat back, eyes narrowing. Maybe it wasn't a door. Perhaps it wasn't a panel. Or maybe it was both. But it wasn't in the wall. It was part of the window frame. A door or panel built into a window frame.

This was enough to justify sending DeWitt back to the Capitol. Enough to justify Sam going with him. DeWitt could read blast patterns, trace heat vectors, and overpressure zones better than anyone. But Sam knew how to find what wasn't meant to be found.

And this wasn't a one-man job. It would take a team. Not the whole Task Force; too visible, too slow. But two, maybe four people. Stealthy. Focused.

Sarah would hate it. It was the kind of lead she'd been praying for, and the type of decision that made command feel like a curse. Sam needed everything—every scrap of data, every trace. He had to pull it all, a decades-long trail of conversations, contracts, and schematics—anything that touched the topic of window frames and their integrity.

If Sarah had any prayer of getting this mission approved… A high-risk op, on U.S. soil, near the Capitol… She'd need more than a gut feeling and a hunch from him. She'd need evidence. Enough that no one could look the other way.

$$* * *$$

Sarah stepped into the ops center at 0800 sharp.

Coffee in hand, uniform crisp, expression calm. She was rested for once. And more than that… she still carried the joy of being with James. Just two days. Just enough. The ache of missing him had already settled in, but it wasn't sharp. Not yet. It was something softer—a longing wrapped in peace.

Around her, the Task Force was trickling in with fresh uniforms, light chatter, and a brief flash of normal. Reddick had brought donuts. Hsu was already checking satellite tasking logs. Naderi looked like she hadn't slept but was smiling anyway. Sarah paused momentarily at the edge of the room, letting herself feel it. The team she'd built. The mission that mattered.

Then Sam swept into the room. Urgent. Focused. Like a cat who'd finally cornered the mouse.

"Good. Everyone's here," he said, speaking quickly. "I have it. It's the windows. More precisely, the window frames. It's not a door. Not a panel. It was never in the walls. It's the frames."

He turned to Dr. Reddick before Sarah could even process the shift.

"You said Simmons worked in construction before the White House. Was he a window installer?"

Sam was talking so fast that Sarah felt like she needed to take a breath for him. He looked like he hadn't slept in days, wired not from caffeine but adrenaline.

"Sam, take a breath. Please. Before you cause all of us to pass out."

Sarah turned to Dr. Reddick.

"I'm not entirely sure I follow the question, or the rant, but was Simmons a window installer?"

Reddick tapped his tablet, brows furrowed, a few quick swipes later... "Yeah, he was... How did you..." The question trailed off. Sarah couldn't tell if it were because Reddick had already answered himself... or because he was afraid Sam would.

"Okay," Sarah said, calm and measured. "Sam, take a breath, and walk us through what's happening in your head right now."

"Okay," Sam said, drawing a quick breath.

"So, Simmons. Experienced window installer. Ends up receiving at the White House. On paper, it makes sense. The right background to inspect and manage construction deliveries. Except... I think he noticed something he wasn't supposed to."

Sam glanced sideways at Cho, not accusatory, more like an apology.

"Back when I was at NSA, my partner and I reviewed a video. Standard stuff. Nothing alarming. But the guy in the video kept talking about doors; only the way he described them, it sounded more like panels. Subtle, but my partner caught it. That's what sent me down the door-and-panel rabbit hole... The next day, my partner was dead. Liquor store robbery, wrong place, wrong time. Just like Simmons."

He paused, just long enough for that weight to settle.

"I chased doors. Panels. Nothing. Dead end. So I pivoted. Tried windows. Let me tell you, people will talk your ear off about windows. I picked up where I left off this morning, 'frame integrity.' Boring. Until I realized that term was used everywhere. And not just as an engineering note. It's threaded into conversations between departments, contractors, supply records… too many places for it to be random.

"I think there's a structure, maybe a door, maybe a panel, inside the window frames. Hidden in plain sight. And Simmons, being who he was, probably noticed." Sam looked around the room. "Then he died."

Sam turned to DeWitt. "If you were going to plant explosives for use in the future, no set date, maybe years, maybe decades, you'd pick something like C-4, right? Stable. Long shelf life."

DeWitt gave a slow nod. "Ten, maybe fifteen years if stored properly," he said.

"Right," Sam said. "But if you knew it might be decades… you'd need a way to access it. To replace it. Discreetly. Without triggering alarms. Which means… you'd hide it somewhere no one questions routine access."

He let that hang.

"Like window frames."

DeWitt shook his head slowly. "Sorry, Sam. It doesn't line up. Yeah, the White House has a lot of windows. But the blast patterns, especially on the west wing and residence, they don't track cleanly to window placements."

"And even if they did… I doubt there are 204 usable windows, let alone ones that could all be modified to hold charges."

"Okay," Sam said, recalibrating. "Not charges in the frames. But maybe… access panels hidden by the frames. Ways to reach the charges without being noticed."

Sarah turned to DeWitt, catching the flicker of hesitation in his eyes; the gears turning behind them. "Talk to me," she said.

DeWitt exhaled slowly. "Maybe. It wouldn't be simple. You'd need more than just a modified frame; you'd need structural concealment, allowing maintenance access without setting off any alert."

"But if the frame masked an entry point? Something precise, built into the original renovation…" He looked at her again, almost disbelieving his own words. "Then yeah. It's possible."

"It'd be the craziest damn thing anyone's ever pulled off inside U.S. government walls, and that is saying something. But it might be possible."

Sarah looked at Sam. He was just standing there, wide-eyed, like a nuclear reaction had gone off behind his eyes.

"Maintenance," she said softly.

His eyes flicked to hers.

"You said 'maintenance,'" she repeated. "That's what the supervisor told Simmons. *Authorized for maintenance—performance improvement.*" She didn't need to say anything else. The room was already quiet. The phrase had been nothing at the time, just bureaucratic filler. But now…

"Okay, Sam," Sarah said. "I can buy it. And I think I can sell it. Get me everything you have, and I'll work on getting your trip to D.C. approved." Looking back at DeWitt, she raised her eyebrows. "Be ready."

"I need to be there," Sam said. Dry. Calm. Absolute.

"DeWitt is probably the best in the world at blast patterns and pressure impacts. But I see things people miss. Things that were designed to be missed. If it's not obvious, I need to be there."

She hated how certain he sounded. Certainty meant risk. Certainty meant he'd already decided what he was willing to trade. Sarah nodded. "Okay. You get ready too."

THIRTY-ONE

The approval came just past midnight.

It was not a phone call or a briefing. It was just a secure push to his system: three short documents, each signed and stamped, with language carefully measured to say what no one wanted to say aloud.

They were letting him go.

The Capitol had been downgraded from contested to semi-permissive; a bureaucratic distinction, but enough to unlock options. Sarah had sold it well. They framed it as a limited-scope recon with extraordinary oversight, backed by private resources, and led by the man who had, for all intents and purposes, built half the network they now relied on.

Admiral Rimes had pushed hardest. Sam made a note of that.

Rimes had emphasized the correct details: the aircraft was privately owned, the crew was civilian contractors, and the backup pilot was on Sam's payroll. DeWitt had no commission, and Sam was just another military contractor. Only James was on active duty, and only James created a liability for command.

Two non-combatants. No more. Sarah had tried for more, likely Langdon or Perez. But the second uniformed names appeared, the brakes locked.

He understood. The Capitol was listed as semi-permissive. Not secure. Not held. But not in immediate danger of collapse. A temporary foothold, strong enough to stand on if no one looked too hard.

Sam studied the authorization again. *Limited-duration site access granted for forensic intelligence review under special mission parameters.*

They would have a convoy, clearance, and a window in twenty hours for just six hours on site. He and DeWitt would be on site. There would be no one else, no support, and no fallback. If something went wrong, they would vanish, written off as a failed operation inside a war zone.

But that wasn't what haunted him. It was what would happen if nothing went wrong and they found nothing. If this theory collapsed under scrutiny, if the Capitol yielded no secrets, mechanisms, or doors tucked behind frames, then it was over.

There would be no second attempt. No more leads. And this war, already spiraling, already splintering, would calcify. Lines were hardening. Territories were already choosing sides. Stories already chosen and believed. It wouldn't matter if he found proof a week from now. It wouldn't matter if Halstead himself had signed the orders, which Sam was sure he hadn't. The nation would have moved on and broken into the versions of truth it needed to survive. And survival would come at a cost. Not three or four hundred thousand. Millions.

If this failed, it wouldn't just prolong the conflict. It would end the United States as it had been known, not all at once, but city by city, state by state. Truth would come too slow to save what remained.

He leaned back from the terminal, eyes burning. This wasn't about the mission anymore. It was about the last chance to stop the freefall. And he was almost out of time. Wallace was sure to win this war, but the devastation would end any chance the country had to regain its life.

Sam and DeWitt had twelve hours to assemble their gear and reach the transport headed for Brunswick AFB.

It wasn't enough time, not really, but they moved fast, each aware of what was at stake. By early evening, they touched down, stepping onto the tarmac under a pale sky fading toward dusk.

James was already there.

He walked toward them with a half-smile and a shake of his head, boots crunching over the concrete. He didn't look angry. Just tired. Curious. Braced for whatever insanity Sam had dragged him into this time.

He extended a hand. Sam took it without pause, one firm shake, brief and familiar.

"What have you gotten me into now, Sam?" James said, voice low, almost amused. "You know we're looking at a sub-three-thousand-foot runway. Even for the LM, that's short. And who's my second seat? Tell me she at least knows which end of the plane is forward."

"I think you'll find her more than satisfactory," Sam said. "Israeli-trained. One of the only LM-qualified pilots left who's not on contract or in a cage. The only pilot I trust more is you."

James gave him a look, half skeptical, half conceding.

Sam added, "But bringing you is a bigger risk than bringing her. You're military. She's mine. And I still have to work with Sarah after this."

That got a faint chuckle from James, the tension bleeding off his shoulders just enough to signal he was in. "Fair enough," he said. "Let's see how tight your plan really is."

Two hours later, Sam was seated in a cramped forward conference room, the hum of base activity pressing faintly through the walls. Around the table sat James, DeWitt, the Israeli pilot, Tamar Sivan, and a half-dozen others. The Marine Corps captain assigned to the Capitol sector chaired the meeting, flanked by communications staff, a logistics officer, and a grim-faced analyst from CENTCOM who looked like he hadn't slept in a week.

A Navy commander, lean and sharp-eyed, tapped the edge of the map overlay. "Let's get one thing straight before we get too deep into logistics. You've got a six-hour ground window. Tops."

James raised an eyebrow. "That's tight."

The commander nodded. "Tight's all you're getting. Brunswick wheels up at 1930. Arrival in D.C. around 2100 if there's no hold. You land, you move. Ground op starts at 2130 latest."

He looked straight at Sam. "You need to be back in the air by 0430. We're assuming civil twilight hits around 0515. After that, you're a slow, easy target on a runway with no cover and no second chances."

An Air Force major muttered, "Not to mention the sub-3,000-foot landing pad in the dark with little more than flares to mark the path."

James rubbed his jaw. "No problem. Just pull off an urban recon op, locate thirty-year-old anomalies in the dark, and take off from a cracked parking lot before sunrise. Easy."

Sam didn't smile. "You've done harder."

Sivan sat straight-backed, eyes sharp, not wasting energy on posturing. Sam had chosen her precisely for that. There were no theatrics, no ego, just precision and nerve, wrapped in an icy calm that made her look ten degrees cooler than the room.

The captain began, voice clipped and professional.

"As of 0800 this morning, the Capitol zone is classified semi-permissive. That means controlled, but not secure. We've got full perimeter coverage for seventy-five blocks, limited drone overwatch, and a platoon embedded in the area. No known Halstead forces within a three-mile radius."

He tapped a screen. An aerial map appeared, marked in red and blue overlays.

"You'll land here: west grounds, temporary strip cleared between Constitution and Independence. Not ideal, but the LM can handle it. Once wheels down, we'll deploy convoy transports and move you to the building in under five minutes."

Sam nodded, eyes following the route as the captain walked through fallback procedures, extraction windows, and comms protocol. Most of it matched what Sam had reviewed earlier. But the reality of being here, seeing the people who would have to keep them alive on the ground, gave it weight.

DeWitt leaned in. "Any expected civilian interference?"

"None," the captain replied. "D.C.'s been under evacuation protocols for ten days. The only ones still in the zone are embedded militia or ours."

Sam glanced at James, then Sivan. Both gave small nods. They were ready—the rest of the room… not so much. Several officers exchanged glances as the captain continued. There was skepticism, unspoken but thick. No one said it aloud, but the message was clear: Don't expect a parade if you get killed chasing phantoms.

Sam folded his arms, listening. Let them think it was a long shot. Let them think he was paranoid. That was usually when he found what no one else could.

The captain finished outlining the perimeter units and nodded to the airfield liaison, a Navy commander with a blunt jaw and skeptical eyes.

"You realize," the commander said, folding his arms, "you might be able to land that beast, but takeoff's going to be worse."

All heads turned toward him.

"It's not like we can drop in a portable aircraft launcher and slingshot you off the deck. You're looking at sub-three-thousand feet, irregular terrain, and probable debris. You miss your rotation point by fifty feet, and you're scrap metal on the Hill."

James didn't flinch. "Noted."

Sivan's voice followed a beat later; calm, accented, ice-edged. "If the wind shifts, I'll take the stick. If it's stable, he will."

The commander stared at her for a long moment. Then, simply said, "Your funeral."

Sam didn't blink. This was the point everyone else started questioning, when doubt crept in under the weight of logistics and risk profiles. But not them. He leaned back slightly, letting the silence settle before speaking.

"We know the risk. But if what's in that building is what I think it is, then one rough departure is the least of our problems."

No one had anything to add to that.

* * *

As the room emptied, James stayed back, eyes on the aerial map still glowing on the wall. He felt her presence before she spoke.

"You're James Callan."

He turned. Tamar Sivan stood at his two o'clock; precise, unblinking, her accent clipped and restrained. Israeli, like Sam had said. She was short for a pilot, but she commanded the space she was in. James gave a slight nod.

"And you're the one Sam trusts more than me," he said, offering his hand.

She took it immediately. "Only on paper. I prefer to fly left seat, but I've flown backup more than enough. If it's your aircraft, I won't get in the way."

James studied her for half a second longer than was polite, then nodded. "Not worried about that. Just want to make sure we're aligned."

She tilted her head slightly, as if inviting the test.

"Plan is standard," James continued. "I take us in unless the wind shifts or I'm compromised. You call out diagnostics and nav corrections. If things go sideways on the ground, I expect you to have preflight reset by the time we're back at the ramp."

"I'll be strapped in and ready," she replied. "We get two passes on takeoff. After that, it's firewood."

James allowed the smallest smile. "I like you already."

She just turned and motioned with her head. "Preflight?"

He nodded. "Let's go."

They stepped into the corridor, the base alive with low voices, the occasional bark of orders, and the distant churn of jet engines. Tamar kept pace beside him, silent, precise in the way she moved. Keyed in, like a pilot watching wind speed before a difficult landing.

"You've flown LMs?" he asked, tone light but purposeful.

"Currently piloting one," she said. "Less modified. Nothing like yours."

So, she'd noticed. He nodded once. "Any concerns?"

"No," she replied. "But I want to know what I'm stepping into. Yours has upgrades I've only seen in test units. I want to be sure it behaves if something goes sideways."

Fair. They stepped through the hangar access door. His LM-100J sat waiting under the lights, matte black and brutal-looking, a predator dressed as a cargo hauler. Its lines were sleek, and the hard angles were softened by Sam's custom work. Most people didn't know what they were looking at. He could tell Tamar did.

"You'll like the way she flies," he said. "She's faster, heavier in crosswinds, but rock steady."

Inside the bird, someone shouted from up the ramp.

"'Bout time," called the flight engineer, one of Sam's contractors, Williams, the same one who'd stepped in after Raskin died. "AI's twitchy again. Probably just that heat drift in the forward sensor stack. I'll clear it."

He was already elbow-deep in a diagnostics panel. James moved onto the cockpit. The guy knew his systems cold; James trusted him to sort it.

Tamar slid into the right seat, eyes sweeping the panels. James took the left, instinct and repetition guiding his hands as he began his part of the checklist.

The AI came online immediately.

"Welcome, Commander Callan. All systems are nominal. The preflight checklist is thirty-seven percent complete. Mission status: Red priority."

He glanced over. Tamar's face was unreadable, but he caught the way she paused slightly at the voice.

"Yeah," he said. "It talks. But it doesn't act without us. Sam made sure of that."

She gave a single nod and returned to scanning the secondary systems. There were clean, practiced movements. He liked that.

"This bird's got enhanced thrust, upgraded gear, noise suppression, anti-jam redundancies…the works," he said, ticking items off more for protocol than conversation. "Even low-profile terrain mapping and encrypted comms. You won't find anything in here off-the-shelf."

Tamar just kept working. That was fine. He knew she heard him and knew she was more than competent. He could see it.

"Fuel topped. Payload secure. System check rolling," the engineer called from below.

James gave a quick thumbs-up and turned his attention back to the readouts. Everything was running hot but stable, with no red flags.

He adjusted his headset. "If I go down, you take the stick?"

She looked at him directly. "Yes."

He turned back to his panel, one hand resting on the throttle. The LM was ready. The team was nearly there. And as insane as this mission was, it finally felt like something might break their way.

Two hours later, the engines thundered as the LM powered down Brunswick's makeshift strip. James kept his eyes on the markers, hands firm, Tamar calling out airspeed in clipped, even tones beside him.

"Rotate."

He pulled back. They were airborne with five hundred feet to spare. The climb out was smooth. Once clear of Brunswick airspace, the flight settled into silence: steady, efficient, mechanical. Tamar ran system checks without being asked. The engineer confirmed everything was green. The AI handled minor course corrections.

James stared out into the dark, city glow far off to the west.

Ninety minutes later, D.C. rose like a jagged scar across the landscape. Roads were empty, and buildings were dark. A ring of soft blue lights traced a line across the Capitol's west lawn, the temporary strip, barely 2,800 feet long and uneven at best.

He dropped the flaps and felt the aircraft respond, heavier than usual, but stable.

"Winds calm," Tamar said.

"I've got it."

He brought the LM down low, gear down, full reverse primed. The AI called out the remaining distance like a calm co-pilot.

"Five hundred... four... three..."

The touchdown came hard, with tires screaming and the fuselage vibrating. He fought the bounce and kept her centered. Brakes howled. Engines reversed. They came to a stop with less than a hundred feet of margin. James exhaled once, slowly.

"Welcome to the Capitol."

Tamar unstrapped, already on her feet. The rear bay opened to floodlights, and soldiers rushed forward with transport trucks. Sam appeared at the base of the ramp, coat on, bag slung, eyes sharp.

James met him at the bottom. "We're in," he said.

Sam nodded. "Let's make it count."

James caught Sam by the arm before he could step off. "Stay safe. Stay alert. You don't know what's out there."

Sam gave a faint nod.

James tightened his grip just slightly. "We'll be here. Engines hot the second you're back."

That got a flicker of acknowledgment. Maybe even appreciation. Then Sam turned, DeWitt falling into step beside him as they climbed into the waiting transport; four Humvees in staggered formation, one already idling behind a mounted .50.

James stood at the edge of the ramp until the convoy pulled away, taillights vanishing between broken streetlights and barricades. He exhaled and turned back inside. They'd made it in.

Now came the hard part.

Whatever Sam found in there had better be worth the cost.

THIRTY-TWO

Sam exited the plane with DeWitt close behind, both moving quickly toward the waiting Humvees. The drive was short, five minutes at most, then came to an abrupt stop.

A soldier turned in his seat. "We're here. You've got about six hours. Be careful in there."

He gestured toward the half-demolished building just ahead.

"Nothing's been cleared or inspected. Structural integrity's a guess at best. Things can come down with little or no warning, so try not to disturb too much."

Sam and DeWitt grabbed their gear. DeWitt deployed a compact drone, its lights flickering to life as it rose, scanning the space ahead and feeding back a live video. They both clicked on their helmet-mounted lamps, casting narrow beams into the ruin that had once been the U.S. Capitol.

Silence met them.

Wind whispered through shattered halls. Debris was scattered everywhere, crunching beneath their boots with every step. The vast emptiness felt wrong. Haunted.

"We've got six hours," Sam said calmly. "Start mapping as much as you can. I'll scout around, but let's stay close. If anything comes down, better we're together."

As DeWitt made his way toward the House floor, an area they knew had suffered heavy damage, Sam followed close behind, never straying far. He moved slowly, scanning the walls and shattered windows for anything unusual. At several frames, he paused, running his fingers along the edges, searching for signs of tampering or remnants of installation. Nothing.

The first bodies had stopped them cold. They hadn't fully grasped it, not until now, that D.C. had been a war zone from day one. Retrieval had been impossible. The corpses were left where they fell, scattered through the halls of power.

DeWitt had almost died here in the fighting just after the bombings. Only two, maybe three weeks ago, Sam thought. He remembered it clearly. The day he joined Sarah's team, he had offered most of his contractors to support a three-day mission; one that barely lasted a day once the firefight erupted.

Sixteen of Sam's men died. He scrolled through their names in his mind, one after another. So much death. He had to find the answer in these halls.

As they stepped into the House chamber, the air grew still. Remains were everywhere. The once-beautiful hall, so stately on C-SPAN, so full of ceremony, was now reduced to dust, dirt, splintered wood, and death.

This was their first stop.

DeWitt would likely spend half their remaining time in this single room and still need another hundred and fifty hours to truly understand what had happened here.

Sam circled the perimeter, eyes scanning the shattered walls, stepping over debris. He dug through broken fragments; splinters of desks, bits of marble, charred remnants of history, searching. He wasn't even sure what for. But he trusted he'd know it when he saw it.

Three hours passed in what felt like a minute.

DeWitt's watch chirped. "Sam, I want to get some good video of the Senate floor too, if we can get there."

Sam nodded, grabbed his gear, and moved with DeWitt. Through collapsed corridors, shattered passageways, and the burned-out husks of desks, they finally stepped onto the Senate floor.

Like the rest of the Capitol, the room was wrecked, walls were torn open, furniture was reduced to rubble, and ash was coating everything. But it was still there. The Capitol wasn't like the White House. It was demolished, yes, likely unsalvageable, but not erased.

The White House had been obliterated. Nothing left. Not one stone on another.

"How many explosives, if you had to guess?" Sam asked softly. "What are we looking at?"

DeWitt exhaled. "A lot. Probably more than the White House, once we get a full accounting. But this place is bigger. It—"

A thunderous crack. A three-foot chunk of ceiling crashed to the floor between them, sending up a cloud of dust and debris. DeWitt froze. Swallowed hard. Then exhaled slowly.

Sam stared at the spot where it had fallen. Then looked up. Why now? Had the vibrations of their voices… just barely… shifted something loose?

Shakily, DeWitt continued. "It would've taken a tremendous number of charges to do what was done, if these were anything close to the same size as the ones used at the White House."

As Sam picked his way carefully around the edge of the room and DeWitt kept filming and measuring, something caught Sam's eye.

An intact door. One of the first he'd seen in the entire building.

"Sam, we need to start heading out soon," DeWitt called.

"There's an intact door here," Sam said, already moving toward it. "I need to see what's on the other side. Get over here, we'll want the high-res video."

DeWitt's watch chirped again.

"Sam, we're at five and a half hours. We need to make this quick. It could take us thirty minutes or more just to find our way out of this maze."

On the other side of the door stood something even rarer, a completely intact window. The first Sam had seen. DeWitt caught up, breathing hard.

"Get video of this," Sam said. "Everything. Every detail."

DeWitt raised the camera. Sam stepped toward the window, but a sharp crack echoed behind them. There was no explosion—just the deep, groaning shift of something heavy overhead. Nothing fell, but something had moved.

They exchanged a quick glance. Sam stepped forward and placed his hand on the window, running his fingers slowly along every inch of the frame. Nothing. He drew a knife from the sheath on his leg and carefully traced the blade tip along the edges.

Then, about two inches below the right side of the frame, the tip dropped into a shallow groove. Sam paused and looked back at DeWitt. DeWitt focused the camera on the spot.

Sam applied gentle pressure with the knife, prying just enough. With a soft pop, the side of the frame swung open. Sam raised his flashlight and shone it into the gap. Inside was a narrow cavity built into the wall, just deep enough to hide something. Closed, the frame formed a "U" shape, leaving an opening behind what would normally be covered by structural framing.

Playing a hunch, Sam moved to the opposite side of the window. He pressed the tip of his knife along the corresponding edge. There was no notch. Still, he pushed in gently and pried. With a faint click, the second side opened, too. It was too dark to see much inside the cavity—just shadows and silence.

Sam slung his bag off his shoulder.

"We're late, Sam," DeWitt said, glancing at his watch. "No way we're making it out in six hours. You proved your theory. Let's go."

Sam pulled a small inspection probe from his pack. It was a slender device similar to what a plumber might use to inspect a drain pipe.

"No," he said thoughtfully. "The theory's fine, but it only gets us so far."

He clicked on the probe's light and fed it slowly into the opening.

"I need to see what's inside. There has to be a detail, something I can capture. Something to guide us."

DeWitt set the drone to hover on auto, locking it in place to keep capturing whatever it was pointed at. Sam eased the probe deeper into the wall, eyes locked on the feed. Behind him, DeWitt rummaged through his gear and pulled out a compact device. It was nothing flashy, but knowing DeWitt, it was effective.

DeWitt moved to the opposite side of the wall and scanned. Starting two feet below the window frame, he swept the tool upward, back and forth in slow passes across five vertical feet of wall.

Sam barely noticed. He was too focused on the camera screen, watching shadows resolve into something more. He didn't know precisely what DeWitt was doing. But he was certain it would be helpful.

Sam froze.

"DeWitt," he said, his voice low. "Look at this."

He turned the camera feed toward him.

DeWitt leaned in, eyes narrowing. "Yeah," he said slowly. "That's exactly what you think it is."

He pointed at the screen. "See those frayed wires? Probably a mouse or a rat decided they made a good snack. They like the coating for some reason. God only knows why."

Sam didn't respond. He was staring at an undetonated block of C-4. The rat, or mouse, whatever it had been, had chewed straight through the wiring to the blasting cap. That one gnawed connection had killed the circuit and had stopped the detonation. One slip of nature, and the chamber still stood.

"Okay, Sam, we have to go. We're not getting anything more this time."

DeWitt's voice was tight with strain. "If we need to come back, we know where. But we're already late."

The tension in his tone said it all; he was leaving, with or without Sam. Sam nodded. He carefully withdrew the probe, closed both panels, and stuffed the device into his bag. Then, without another word, he followed DeWitt out.

They climbed their way out, careful but quick, each step echoing through the fractured corridors. As they reached the hallway they'd entered hours ago, a faint wash of light greeted them. Dawn…

First light was already there, stretching through broken windows and dusty air. The soldiers were waiting, clearly irritated. Without a word, they rushed Sam and DeWitt into the Humvees and started the drive back to the landing zone.

Two minutes into the drive, maybe two minutes from the landing zone, a brilliant flash lit up a side street. A projectile tore through the early light, streaking past the lead Humvee and slamming into a building across the street.

BOOM.

"RPG! RPG!" a soldier shouted.

The explosion rocked the convoy. Sam was thrown backward as their vehicle lurched, tires squealing. Momentum surged. The convoy accelerated hard, racing for the LZ. Light-arms fire erupted from both sides of the street—sharp, erratic, relentless.

Then came the thud-thud-thud of the .50-caliber guns mounted on the Humvees, their thunder pounding into the void, answering back with overwhelming force. Shell casings clattered. Muzzle flashes lit the rubble-strewn streets.

The convoy kept moving, engines roaring through the hailstorm of gunfire.

* * *

James paced beside the LM, hands clenched, eyes scanning the horizon. The aircraft was ready, and the engines were warm. Tamar sat steady in the co-pilot seat, eyes forward, calm as ever.

"Where are you, Sam?" James muttered to no one. "We have to go. You're already thirty minutes late."

The comms crackled. "We have them. Heading back to the LZ now."

James swore under his breath. This was bad. Daylight was already breaking, and his beautiful black beast, sleek in the dark, was about to become a slow, exposed target in full light.

He climbed into the cockpit.

"Fire up the engines. Get them hot," he said. "We roll the second they're on board. Prepare for a rough ascent. Countermeasures on."

Tamar nodded without looking at him, hands moving quickly over her console.

James tapped a pair of switches. The AI's voice responded, calm and precise. "Countermeasures armed and ready. Available on command."

The comms crackled again. "RPG! RPG!"

Then came the sound of gunfire; distant, but far too close.

James froze.

He whispered a silent prayer that it was one of theirs. If the attackers had a .50, it wouldn't take long. His plane had no armor, one solid burst, and the fuselage would rip like paper.

For the first time, James noticed it; just the slightest tension at the corner of Tamar's eyes.

She didn't look at him. Didn't raise her voice. She just said, flatly, "We should go. The forces here can protect them until they can be extracted. We're a high-value target with no real defenses."

"No," James said. There was no give in his voice. No room for argument.

"We're here to extract them. If they found something, if that's why they're late, it could end this war."

Before Tamar could respond, the lead Humvee tore around the corner, skidding into a flanking position near the street. Hundreds of soldiers had already converged, flooding into the reinforcement line from whatever sector they'd been pulled from. The second Humvee barreled straight toward the plane, brakes squealing as it turned hard, sliding sideways until the passenger doors faced the cargo ramp.

James spotted DeWitt first. Then Sam. At the speed they jumped out, James expected them to be up the ramp in seconds. But seconds dragged. Each one stretched like a lifetime.

James unbuckled his harness. "Get us off the ground the second that ramp starts to close," he ordered.

Then he sprinted toward the rear of the plane. As James neared the ramp, DeWitt collapsed onto it. He'd been hit.

A quick glance told James it wasn't fatal, painful, yes, but likely superficial. Still, for a man who'd never seen combat, the shock alone could take him down hard.

James waved the medics over. "Get him inside!"

Then he shouted into the chaos, voice cutting through the roar of engines at full throttle.

"Where's Sam?"

DeWitt reached up, hand trembling, and grabbed a fistful of James' uniform, smearing blood across the fabric. "He was hit," he gasped. "I don't think he can walk."

His eyes locked onto James, frantic. "We need him. And his gear." He swallowed hard. "He has the answer."

James leapt off the ramp and barreled toward the line without a thought. The Marines had moved Sam, or Sam had dragged himself to partial cover. But a good 150 feet still separated them. Not a long distance. Unless someone's shooting at you.

James slid to the ground beside him, breath tight. A stray round had sliced clean through Sam's calf. Not fatal, thank God, but there was no way he was getting back on that plane alone.

James tapped the leg of a nearby soldier. "Help me get him up. We need to move, now."

Without hesitation, the soldier slung his rifle and stepped in. The rest of the line shifted, clearing a path like it had been choreographed by a Broadway director. With the soldier's help, James and Sam pushed forward toward the plane.

James stumbled once, hard, and hit the ground. Somewhere along the way, he'd been hit. He wasn't sure where yet, but his legs were not going to get him there.

"Get him on that plane and hit the ramp close button, soldier," James barked. Looking down, he saw it was bad. James pulled himself into cover, shielding from the fire and the blast wash he knew was coming when Tamar hit the throttle.

He looked up, seeing Sam and the soldier crossing the final fifty feet to the ramp.

James ripped open the pocket on his pants, pulled the tourniquet free, and started wrapping his leg. He glanced up as they reached the ramp, Sam looked at him, as if his world had just collapsed. James could see two medics grabbing Sam. Good. He was safe. James began to tighten the tourniquet. The soldier hammered the close button on the ramp. DeWitt's face appeared concerned and confused, but it was too late for him to do anything. Tamar had the wheels turning as soon as the ramp had started to move.

James watched as Tamar threaded the needle, the wheels lifted, and the plane roared into the sky. For a brief moment, the attackers turned their fire on the plane, but it was useless, too late to take it down with small arms.

James pulled his sidearm, spun over to his knees, pain rippling through every nerve as he did. The round had likely clipped his artery by the amount of blood he had already lost.

Then he saw it. A second wave of attackers was moving up. The line was already breaking. The pain and loss of blood played with his mind, the edges of his vision failed, grayed, then black. An attacker moved into his line of sight, James fired three rounds, and the shockwaves from the 9mm hammered his skull. And everything went black.

THIRTY-THREE

Sam arrived five hours later.

The medics had stitched him up and given him meds. Not military medics, not officially. But his medics—the finest doctors he could put on a plane.

He feared injuries, planned for them, knew the risks, and accounted for nearly everything. But not for James—the man who chose to sacrifice himself for Sam.

Now, Sam sat across from Sarah. She hadn't said much. He could see it in her eyes, though—he was sure of that. Still, she sat, steady, waiting.

"I'm sorry, Sarah," Sam said quietly. "James was shot. He was saving me."

He swallowed. "He left the cockpit to get me. I couldn't walk. There were rounds everywhere. He took a hit on the way back. He told the soldier to get me inside and close the door. Tamar knew to take off once it shut. James knew she would."

A single tear slid down Sarah's face, but her expression didn't break. "They were overrun. Reinforcements are inbound, but still two hours out. We'd better have something," she said, her voice cracking.

"He was the best man I've ever known, Sam." She paused, steadying herself. "It better have meant something. I need it to have meant something."

"It did, Sarah," Sam said softly. "I promise you—it did. He's too valuable to waste. He's a pilot, lightly armed, and injured. They'll capture him. And I will get him back for you."

He rose, turned, and walked out.

Down the hall, he found DeWitt's office. The man was seated at his desk, one arm in a sling, eyes dull with fatigue. DeWitt had taken fire, too. Like Sam, it wasn't serious. A few stitches. A little blood. He'd heal.

Sam stepped inside. "So what exactly were you doing in there?" he asked.

DeWitt looked up, hollow. "I've never seen a man take a hit like that before," he said whisper-soft. "Not in front of me."

Sam's expression tightened. His voice edged sharper. "That tool you were waving around on the wall while I was focused on the C-4, what was it?"

DeWitt blinked, then nodded slowly. "Oh. Yeah. It's a sounding device. Basic setup. Emits a sonic pulse, builds a feedback diagram."

He pulled up the tablet. "Here, renders a visual of what's inside the wall."

Sam stepped closer. His eyes narrowed as they scanned the image. "I've seen this before," he murmured. He set the tablet down and walked out.

Sam was sure now. He had what he needed. He walked into his office and closed the door behind him. No hesitation. No ceremony. Just action.

He started searching.

He combed through the architectural diagrams he'd reviewed days earlier, part of the metadata pulled during his window-related scans. At the time, he hadn't thought much of them. The diagram seemed irrelevant; it was just a structural note tied to the passing mention of a window.

He'd dismissed it. But now? Now, that diagram might be the key. By 2 AM, he'd finally found it. The lines were clear. The framing, the structure, the anomaly, it was all there. The day's pain still pulled at him. The wound. The weight of James' absence. But something deeper had taken hold. Resolve.

He leaned back, exhausted, and stared at the screen. He'd trace it down in the morning.

Sam woke just after 8 AM. He'd slept nearly six hours, a near record. Likely a combination of the drugs and the day before.

Sarah's JTF had never operated on shifts or "hours". They just worked—all of them—too many hours to count—because they cared, because they wanted to find a solution, to really figure out who *Wrath* was.

Sam rolled out of bed, cleaned up, grabbed a quick breakfast, and headed into the office.

He arrived a little after 9 AM. Sarah wasn't in yet. He closed his door and got to work.

He reopened the email, the one that seemed irrelevant before. Every word, every nuance. Everything unsaid. He ran his parsing tools to crawl for diagrams that matched keywords, then expanded the search as hits began trickling in.

Soon, the JTF disappeared from his world. It was just him and the data. He found a new thread and pulled. The diagram was clearly part of a designed system, an embedded access path built into the framing. It was not just hidden but engineered to be invisible. A person who knew what to look for, how to access it, and had the proper tools could reach hidden cavities, compartments, and devices.

Bombs.

It hadn't just been installed. It had been maintained. Refreshed. The components were shipped as parts: tubes, rods, and straps. Simple. Elegant. Not over-engineered. Just precise. And ordinary. That was the brilliance: they used common materials. Easier to source. Easier to receive.

In one file, he found a note. *"Must have a trained and loyal receiver for windows. Integrity critical."*

It was dated one day after Simmons died.

He found names. People who had ordered the components. Each time, citing a reference: Diagram J47F.

The windows had been custom-designed. The biggest challenge was ensuring the structural integrity of the frames. Finding materials that fit without raising suspicion took years of trial and error.

They'd tested. They'd failed. They'd perfected it.

And all the while, it had been right there, hidden inside the walls built to protect the nation. Even Sam had never stopped to consider the sheer scale of it, just how many civilians worked for the federal government.

Even when Simmons was hired in 1997, there were over 1.8 million non-military employees, and the number had only grown since then.

Sam's programs scraped and crawled through the data, connecting bits and bytes across decades. He reviewed everything. Line by line. Thread by thread. For days, he worked. Barely sleeping and barely speaking.

Then the day came. The day everything changed. Halstead had been recruited on October 6th, six years before the first *Wrath* attack. At the time, he'd been just a junior congressman. Nothing remarkable. No one would have looked twice. But the notes pieced it together. Concealed meetings. Untraceable contributions. Changes in voting patterns. Staff appointments.

Sam stared at the screen. He had been right. He stood, walked down the hall, and went into Sarah's office. She looked up as he entered. She'd returned the morning after James went missing, 10 AM sharp. Or, as she would say, ten hundred hours.

She'd looked hollowed out that day. Still did. But behind her eyes was something else… determination. She wasn't going to let this die. Not until she had answers. Not until it meant something. He stepped forward and placed a USB drive on her desk.

"Over fifteen thousand people," he said solemnly. "Most of them are dead; war, age, natural attrition. But Halstead's on there."

He met her eyes.

"It's everything we need. Proof that this wasn't just infiltration or manipulation. This was rot from the inside. This was a long-term plan," he continued. "Designed to dismantle the government from within and rebuild it in Halstead's image."

266

He let that hang in the air for a moment. "With him as dictator."

Sam shook his head slightly. "Halstead wouldn't have run anything. That much is clear now. He was a convenient face; charismatic, ambitious, easy to steer when the time came."

He paused. "But he was never the one. Just the puppet. It's going to take time," Sam said. "A lot of time, if we ever want to track down where and when this started. But I know this much, it was well before 1997."

He looked at the drive. "That's just the point I was able to start from. You and your team can trace the rest from what I found."

Sarah picked it up, turned it over in her fingers, then looked back at him and smiled—small, but real. "Thank you, Sam."

She would find meaning in it. His work with the military was finished. "If you ever need anything else," he said, "you'll let me know, right?"

Sarah's smile lingered, faint but knowing. "I doubt I'll need to. You'll probably know before I do."

She hesitated. "So this is goodbye? Your resignation's on the drive, too?"

He shook his head. "No. Nothing formal." He held her gaze. "You don't need me anymore. But James does. And so do my network and family." He stepped back toward the door. "This won't end the war. I was too late for that. But it'll crack their resolve."

Sarah rose. "Not so fast."

She crossed the room and wrapped her arms around him—a brief, steady hug. "Thank you," she whispered. "For making it meaningful, Sam."

"Don't lose faith, Sarah. I will find him."

That afternoon, Sam left on a private Learjet, direct to Alaska. Home.

His family greeted him at the door with hugs, questions, and concerns. They all wanted to know. He said little, just held them.

As they sat down to dinner that night, Sam reached for the remote and clicked on the television.

The screen lit up, GNN coming through the sound system:

"Good evening. Tonight, we are finally seeing the edges, just the edges, of the truth.

"President Wallace today confirmed what many have feared and few dared to say out loud: that the so-called *Wrath of God* attacks were not simply terrorism. They were the product of a long-term internal corruption campaign. Not foreign. Domestic. Not rogue. Institutional."

"Over fifteen thousand names, government appointees, contractors, civilian employees, advisers, and elected officials, connected through procurement trails, communication anomalies, and structural access permissions dating back decades.

"Among them: Vice President, Halstead.

"Not the mastermind. Not the brain. Just the face. The figurehead. The lever they needed to flip the switch. Wallace didn't say it in those words, but the data speaks for itself.

"South Carolina has rejoined the Union under federal stabilization efforts. Pennsylvania appears to be in its final hours of open defiance. The war is not over, but the illusion is.

"And now we must ask: what did we ignore? What did we allow to fester? And who, who... built this system behind the curtain of our democracy?

"We'll be joined later by whistleblowers and security experts to discuss what this means for the structure of federal oversight, and whether it's too late to reform from within."

Sam turned off the TV. His family sat in silence for a moment.

Then his mother smiled, a warm and proud expression. "You never were one for words, son," she said.

Later that night, in the windowless shed beneath the Alaskan sky, Sam paused mid-report. He pulled up a fresh screen and began writing new code—search protocols to crawl every network, every video, every email he could touch. One intent guided it: find anything on James, any trace of a captured pilot.

He accessed the DoD database and combed the reports. Washington held control again. No survivors were listed in the aftermath. But James' body wasn't listed either. He was still marked *MIA*.

Sam bowed his head. "Father, help me find him. You gave the world a man who loved without limit and bore a life few could endure. Let me bring him home to Sarah."

Epilogue

Three Months Later:

Sam pored through the reports. His network was still pulling people out of states with active military conflicts. Pennsylvania was still holding on, but open war had mostly ceased; now the US military was working through cities and securing them. Nearly six months of open conflict had finally concluded with the need to secure the state. Guerrilla-style attacks were common. The remaining military units were frequently quartered in civilian homes, usually against the residents' will. It led to many standoffs and negotiations. It also led to many Halstead-aligned military units killing the civilians as a show of conviction.

South Carolina, New Hampshire, Maine, Minnesota, Wisconsin, and Ohio had all laid down arms within a week of the news of *Wrath's* actual roots being announced. Halstead-aligned states with active conflicts were now limited to Michigan, Illinois, Indiana, as one front, and Pennsylvania, New York, with portions of neighboring states.

Sam checked his tracker, custom-built to track information on one person, and only one person. James. It had become routine. He checked its progress every thirty minutes, fourteen hours a day. Only one flag in three months. It was a mention that a wounded pilot had been seen; it was a passing conversation picked up on a bank camera feed. It was hope, but contained no actionable information.

Twenty states had held special elections, and Congress was beginning to hold sessions. It had been determined that the separatist states did not qualify for representation until their war came to a conclusion. Their first action had been to ratify the war officially. This ended up passing unanimously, and the vote occurred the day after the US military uncovered a mass grave estimated to have over ten thousand bodies of Christians and Christian supporters outside of Salem, Massachusetts.

A ping sounded, Sam flipped to the screen, an alert from the tracker for James. Hospital records from a Baltimore area hospital had just come online. Sam opened the file. John Doe, age mid-thirties. Height, weight, and hair color all matched. Gunshot wound to the legs. Critical on arrival. O Negative blood transfusions. The records were poor. It was unclear if John Doe lived. Record of a surgical room, but not the procedure. Record of six pints of blood.

Sam exhaled. *Should I call Sarah?*

Sam picked up his phone and dialed.

"Hi Sam," Sarah's exhausted voice came through the phone after the first ring.

"Hi, Sarah." Sam paused, uncertain what to say, "I have a lead. It could be nothing, but I am going to track down more information. I wanted you to know that I have a lead."

"Sam, I love you for this, but he is gone. I feel it in my bones, Sam." Sarah's voice cracked as she said it.

"I don't believe that, Sarah. I won't believe it until I have confirmation. There was no reason for them to take James if he was dead. He is out there, and I am going to find him."

"Sam, it is okay. You don't have to do this. Thank you, but you are wrong, and we both need to accept that."

Sam breathed in a deep breath.

"Not until I know for certain, Sarah. I will let you know when I have something more solid, but please. Don't lose hope."

"Sorry, Sam. You do what you have to. When you find him, just let me know he did not suffer." Sam could hear the tears in her voice.

"I will talk to you later, Sarah. I will be praying for you."

He ended the call, then turned back to the monitors. Fingers flew across the keys, rerouting his network, forcing every thread to focus on Baltimore. Someone knew more than what was in the file. He would find him.

As his fingers punched the keys, he whispered, "Lord, give me the eyes to see what others miss."

About the Author

Stephen McCaskill is a Certified Public Accountant and seasoned finance executive whose lifelong interest in storytelling found its voice in And Still We Stood, his debut novel. Blending his analytical mindset with a deep curiosity about faith, resilience, and human nature, he crafts character-driven fiction that is grounded in realism and conviction.

Stephen lives in Florida with his family. This book is the beginning of a multi-part saga exploring the near-collapse—and potential redemption—of a fractured America.

Learn more at:

stephenmccaskill.com

linkedin.com/in/stephenmccaskill